Uncharted *Stars*

A sweet sci-fi romance
by Lea Carter

ISBN 978-1-951248-22-2

Chapter 1

Ava sat apart from the others, where she could watch the stars flashing past the porthole or just relax and soak in the color and sounds of the various cultures crowded onto the shuttle with her. Montgomery Galactic had concerns in every nook and cranny of the galaxy, and today it seemed like representatives from half of them were present.

A group of five or six employees, seated nearest Ava, were good-naturedly arguing about music. A little further away, three women in garishly colored clothing giggled and preened under the attentions of one of the men. On the far side of the cabin, a woman with close-cropped hair and built loosely along the lines of a compact dozer sat staring stoically out the porthole, yet Ava had the feeling she was aware of everything going on in the cabin; security officers usually did.

The lure of the sleeping compartments, located further along toward the cockpit, tugged at her, but she was determined to resist. Like most waystations, the *Beyond* borrowed its reckoning of time from the nearest planetary system, which meant it was still 'daytime' aboard. She could sleep later. Assuming she lived that long.

Ava folded her arms across her chest. Not to be comfortable, or even to warn the others off from joining her, but because if she didn't, she was going to rip off her uniform tunic and shove it in the reclaimer to be broken down to its component molecules for later repurposing.

After a full of week of traveling incognito in the drab, nearly shapeless costume common to the obsessively pragmatic Derli System, she'd expected to enjoy changing into a Montgomery Galactic uniform before boarding the final shuttle to her destination. The company shuttle was certainly an improvement on some of the transports she'd chosen to help her slip further and further into anonymity.

Unfortunately, to further reinforce her assumed identity, she'd chosen to have her uniform made from bastfiber, which was highly popular in the Derli System. Now that she was actually encased in it, however, Ava thought she knew why the fabulously long-lasting material hadn't caught on with the rest of the galaxy. It didn't give. It barely breathed. In short, it was like wearing a suit of armor that chafed every millimeter of exposed skin. Only the underlayers, made of the equally durable—yet immensely more *comfortable* plyfiber— were keeping her sane.

"Hey." The man who'd been entertaining the women across the way now smiled as he took the chair beside her. "You look thirsty." And with no more preamble than that, he offered her a glass of lavender liquid. Surprisingly light blue eyes smiled mischievously at her from beneath thick brown hair.

"No, thanks." Ava glanced at him briefly, taking in the very non-regulation orchid purple undershirt that peeked out at her from beneath his partially unbuttoned tunic.

Others onboard had chosen to wear off-duty clothes, including the trio of women that he'd been talking with before coming over. That he'd chosen to dress in the uniform but on his own terms, coupled with the handful of short braids that sprouted at random from the rest of his bushy hair, told her he was probably from one of the Nakaxian moons. While Nakaxia was considered a free system, it traded freely with its neighbor, Ua—with the notable exception of Ua's human trafficking.

"You're sure?" At her nod, he shrugged and drained both glasses. Perhaps if he could have seen how ridiculous he looked to her, with his head tilted back and mouth open while he waited for the last drops, he wouldn't have been grinning smugly when he tossed the empty containers into the reclaimer between their chairs. "Brian Steinberg."

She studied the hand he extended. Even without the blue stripes down the sides of his uniform to give his occupation away, she would've known from his short nails, the grease embedded in the pores of his fingertips, and the cocky sparkle in his eyes that he was an engineer by trade. She found it interesting, however, that his nails were carefully trimmed and smoothed instead of being left broken, unlike most engineers.

"Terina Massuk." Ava offered her assumed name and gave his hand a firm shake. As always, the new name felt a little odd at first. A strand of long, mostly black, hair slipped down off her shoulder, prompting her to flick it back out of the way.

In some ways, the hairstyle would take more getting used to than the name. Accustomed to jaw-length blond hair, she hardly knew herself when she looked in the mirror these days: six inches of red hair descended from the crown of her head, but the rest of the length was pitch black, evidence that she was in mourning.

In the Derli System, entire families and even close friends colored their hair black when someone died. Each person chose how long to continue coloring their hair, but not until their natural color was fully grown back in was the mourning period considered concluded.

Six months had passed since her own father's death, and she could still hear the lawyer's voice reading his will aloud in a room crowded with beneficiaries. Her father had been generous, to the point of provoking a startled exclamation or two from some of the recipients. Though still aching with the sense of her loss, she'd been more than glad to assure all of his beneficiaries that she heartily approved of each bequest.

Where so many cringed away from the thought of a will, her father had considered it his bounden duty as the owner of Montgomery Galactic. He'd taught Ava to feel the same way, to the point that they'd discussed their wills and any updates at least once year.

If he understood the significance of her multi-colored hair, Steinberg gave no indication. "Nice to meet you, Teri. First time out from the backwater?" He gave her a lazy once-over.

Barely suppressing a groan at the forced friendliness of the instant diminutive, Ava pasted on a smile. "First time I've ever come out this far." Oddly, despite all of the traveling she did for work, that was perfectly true. How many times had she been scheduled to join her father on the *Beyond*, only to have an 'emergency' come up? More than she could count on both hands.

Believing they still had decades ahead of them, she'd apologized to her father and raced off to 'put out this fire' or 'plug that hole.' Now an orphan at thirty-three, she thought she was finally beginning to understand why he'd been so drawn to this station. Granted, the *Beyond* was a new concept, a strange hybrid of port of call, fuel refinery, resort, observatory, and cosmic market. But most importantly, he'd somehow known it was his final project.

"First time for a lot of folks." Steinberg crashed into her reminiscing with a grin that threatened to split his face. "This station opened up a whole new quadrant for exploration! That's why I requested this assignment."

"Oh? Hoping to get assigned to a Montgomery science convoy as an engineer?" She guessed half-heartedly.

"Who, me?" He pointed at himself with both thumbs, then opened his hands and bent his wrists up and down as if his hands were laughing at the idea. "Get myself stuck with the same hundred people for the duration while they go…count stars because nobody else has done it yet? Not a chance. I *like* people. And the *Beyond* has plenty of them, new ones all the time. Convoy comes in, convoy goes out. Supply shuttle comes in, supply shuttle goes out. It's perfect!"

Ava nodded her understanding and had to squelch a niggling suspicion as to why anyone would need new people all the time. A healthy amount of skepticism was part and parcel of her life as Sigrid Ava Montgomery, heir apparent to Montgomery Galactic and arguably the most powerful woman in the galaxy. As Terina Massuk, however, she could afford to take people at face value. Steinberg was simply a flirt.

She stiffened when the sounds around her changed, grew quieter. Though the shuttle engines didn't make much noise while they were working, the absence of that noise was positively deafening. Perhaps if it didn't dredge up memories of another shuttle gone silent…

Looking out the window, the sight of the outer edge of the asteroid field allowed her to relax. Its ever-moving fuel-rich rocks stretched out and around the station, as if they were waiting to be plucked out of the sky, crushed, and processed into the fuel that powered the ships coming through the station daily.

She leaned forward as the station itself hove into view. A sphere rode on one end of a long cylinder. The sphere, she knew, housed the residential and commercial levels. The cylinder was part dock, part fuel-processing plant. The ships could offload their passengers or goods, refuel, and be on their way in a matter of hours.

Steinberg whistled, as if impressed. "We made good time. I didn't think we'd start our approach for another hour."

Ava stared at him, vaguely surprised. She'd forgotten he was there.

"I'll say this for Montgomery." Steinberg leaned back in his chair, the picture of ease, and continued without seeming to notice her distraction. "They really go for the cutting edge in equipment. That's the one thing I'm gonna miss when I transfer departments."

"Transfer departments?" Feeling the beginnings of a shift as the station's drones took over propulsion and steering for the shuttle, Ava found it hard to concentrate on the conversation. What were they talking about? Oh, yes. "That's pretty unusual." At least, for a man of his age and rank. A lot of time and effort had gone into his career at this point, both on his part and on the company's.

Steinberg launched into a lengthy explanation of how he'd planned and prepared for his new job in hospitality, of all things. "But in the end, it's not what you know." He winked overtly. "It's *who* you know."

"And you know important people." She was suddenly interested again. Favors had their place in her world, though she tried to keep them separate from her business interests. Would it be worth asking her assistant to review the transfer? Nothing deep, just a check on his qualifications.

"You bet I do!" He smoothed his hair absentmindedly. "Anybody who works on the corporate fleet and doesn't make a few friends deserves all the skinned knuckles and lousy schedules they get."

The disgust in his voice rang in Ava's ears, tipping her further toward starting an unofficial investigation. There was also the nagging question of Steinberg's 'friend' and whether or not the favors they granted were in the company's best interest.

"Attention please." A pleasant voice emanated from the hidden speakers. "We will complete the docking procedure in approximately two minutes. Please begin gathering your belongings for departure. Thank you, and we hope you had a pleasant trip."

Ava picked up her travel case, a hard-sided cylinder no longer than her arm and barely larger than a ripe tufimelon, and set it in her lap. Out of habit, her fingers sought a small scar on one side, where she'd used it to block the burst of a 'pop'-gun, the favorite weapon of the criminal mastermind who'd kidnapped her briefly, leading to her rescue some seven hundred days ago. She'd lost track of the hours spent buffing down the melted ridges until the damage was easily mistaken for the result of careless baggage handling.

"Sheesh, you travel light." Steinberg eyed the case with interest.

Ava shrugged. "Thanks to synthesizers, there's not much to pack. A few mementos, a keepsake or two…" And a few hundred thousand dups worth of prototypes she was expected to test and report on.

Steinberg snorted. "Where'd you say you were from?"

"I didn't." She was glad to hear the click of the doors locking open and the accompanying hiss of equalizing atmospheres. With any luck, Steinberg would glom onto someone else and forget all about her.

"Yeah, well." His eyebrows rose with him as he got to his feet. "You're not there anymore. There are some good shops here. Drop the bast-fiber and treat yourself to some nice, tailored clothes. You'll never synth your clothes again." After dispensing that bit of wisdom, he waved at the group of women he'd been talking with earlier and hurried to rejoin them.

Ava rolled her eyes and kept her seat, waiting for the crush at the door to dwindle a bit. While Steinberg was easy on the eyes, spending time with him was about as satisfying as a bite of tergian soup, the kind that they made with Gorak spice and made her tastebuds curl in on themselves.

Getting up at last, she joined the tag-end of the group as it made its way out through the short corridor and onto the station itself.

Taking a deep breath, Ava couldn't help noticing the difference between the air here and that aboard the shuttle. Severely recycled air, such as was necessary for health reasons on board a station with thousands of occupants, quickly grew flat, devoid of flavor. While she'd grown accustomed to it after logging countless hours in space, it always disappointed her when she noticed it.

The station air, though, seemed tantalizingly alive, offering a peek into the *Beyond*'s personality with a whiff of food here, the tang of soap there, and a few oddly damp scents she couldn't identify.

Ava frowned when she saw the man that stood partially blocking the corridor. She could only see the back of his head just then, yet there was something strikingly familiar about his squared shoulders and the way he wore his uniform, almost as if he'd been born to it. The red of his tunic was so dark as to be nearly brown, a striking accent to his jet-black hair and space-pale skin.

Her heart bottomed out when he turned to face them. *Jean Antoni Kearns.* J.A.K., for short. The man she'd never been able to forget. And, apparently, the first officer aboard the *Beyond*. She leaned closer to hear him better as he began to speak.

"Gather up." Jean glanced over the group, mentally ticking off the approximate numbers of engineers, security officers, and other departments represented. They'd lost some excellent officers to this rotation. The records claimed the new faces were a fair exchange, but only time would tell. One of the women, her hair dyed mourning-black with only a small cap of vivid red on top, caught his eye. Odd, he wasn't the type to be distracted by a pretty face. Of course, it was hard to ignore her red-black hairstyle.

"Welcome aboard. I'm Lieutenant Commander Kearns, Executive Officer on the *Beyond*. We think she's the best station in the quadrant and by the end of rotation, we hope you will, too."

Ava folded her arms across her chest as she listened, impressed. His thirty-five hundred days in the military had essentially hard-wired him for command

and it showed as he reviewed basic station protocol without losing people's attention.

With the notable exception of herself. Ava tried harder to listen instead of just staring and failed miserably. It was all his fault, of course, for distracting her. There was something different about him, something she couldn't put her finger on. Different in a good way. What was it? He was neither taller, nor shorter. He was as muscular as ever.

Her heart flipped as she realized what had changed—he'd gained weight! It was about time, too. He'd been muscle and bone when she knew him in college, lean as a hunting knife and twice as sharp. Now he looked good enough to hug.

His hair was longer than she remembered, too. He'd worn it so closely cropped at their last meeting that his scalp was visible. It was still relatively short compared to the currently popular hairstyles for men, just touching his ears and well above his collar. Certainly long enough to run fingers through, though.

Ava coughed slightly and looked away, wondering if her cheeks were as pink as they felt. For all the time she'd spent dodging unwelcome overtures from so-called business partners, it was startling to realize she wasn't categorically opposed to the idea of romance. *Real* romance, of course.

Why was it that the same men who'd gladly shaken her father's hand to seal a deal assumed she'd be eager to kiss them? It was enough to make her nauseous just thinking about it. So much so that she almost missed that Jean was finishing up.

Reaching the end of the lecture, Jean rewarded them for paying attention with a small joke. "Now, during the last crew rotation we lost a new yeoman for three days." The group chuckled and he indicated the line of waiting crewmembers on his left. "So everyone grab a commband on your way through and get it coded to you. They're how you'll access your company food allotments, shift assignments, quarters, and just about everything else."

Sweeping the group with a final glance, he locked eyes with the redhead. She looked away first and he abruptly realized everyone was staring at him.

"Dismissed." To further impress upon them that the meeting was over, Jean activated the projection display on his own commband. Adjusting the privacy setting to opaque, he opened the list of new crewmembers and scrolled through it. None of the names rang a bell, even after he narrowed them down to yeomen. Remembering her uniform, he eliminated all but the comm officers, which brought the list down to one. "Terina Massuk." He spoke the name softly, testing it for familiarity, but without success. So, who was the mysterious redhead?

Ava, seeing the frown on his face, faltered in her approach. Squaring her shoulders, she reminded herself that she had no choice but to talk with him. He'd never forgive her if she tried to deceive him. Her stomach flip-flopped when he unexpectedly shut down his display and turned toward her.

"What is it, Yeom…" Jean choked on the word, unable to force another microliter of breath out between his lips. Hauntingly familiar orange-flecked green eyes watched him anxiously from either side of a pert nose, above the full mouth he'd dared to kiss once.

The shock of recognition forced him back a pace,

demanding that he look again—which he did, his gaze sweeping her from head to foot and supplying conflicting information. Sigrid Ava Montgomery, who regularly turned intragalactic heads modeling the latest creations of her fashion line, now stood before him looking thoroughly miserable in a yeoman's uniform made of... Well, whatever it was, it looked stiff and scratchy. What was going on?

Chapter 2

The muddle of voices around Jean faded until it was no more than a background buzz, then snapped back into perspective as his mind kicked into overdrive. *Ava* was the mysterious redhead—no wonder she'd caught his attention, even made-up as she was—and the redhead had been standing alone.

"Where's your guard?"

Surprised, Ava shook her head. "I'm traveling incognito. I didn't bring…" His sharp intake of breath stopped her mid-explanation.

"Are you insane?" Hastily, Jean maneuvered them away from the others, at least far enough for a semi-private conversation. The corridor was relatively secure and had a good sightline around them, but there were no good defensive positions. Of course, that might be a good thing, since the wide-open area made it hard to sneak up on someone.

Unless they didn't need to sneak up. Jean studied the group of new personnel closely. He didn't actually know any of them. And for the prize of removing the head of Montgomery Galactic, the challenge of hacking their security system would be dismissed as a trifle.

"Hello to you, too, Jean." Ava wondered briefly if his grip on her arms was going to leave a mark. "And here I was wondering how long it would take you to recognize me." She flinched inwardly when angry blue eyes returned to her face. He wasn't glad to see her, then.

"Have you forgotten what happened?" He cut in harshly, turning his head to look at her. Their first and last private date, sans security at *his* insistence, would live forever in his nightmares.

Her lungs seized under the intensity of his glare, robbing her of her speech. *Forget? He thinks I've forgotten the most wonderful day of my life?*

"Where are your quarters?" Jean swept the area with a glance, already planning their route to the crew's residential sector. Or should he take her to his own quarters? She'd certainly be safe there, except… No. No, he couldn't take her there.

She blinked. "M-my quarters?"

"Never mind, I just remembered." Extreme pressure had a way of sharpening his wits, in this case allowing him to remember that detail from her file. "Let's go."

Ava considered her choices as he began propelling her away from the others. Half of her bristled at his high-handed way. The other half recognized the barely suppressed tension radiating from him as he strode toward the pivotlift—he'd gone into protector mode. Almost instantly, she made the decision to defer to his protection. Within reason, of course.

Jean checked the interior of the pivotlift to be sure no one was lurking inside, then let her precede him. Entering his security code, he overrode any stops between them and their destination, then allowed himself to breathe.

"Well, that was exciting." Ava smiled tentatively. This was her chance to talk him down, convince him there were no trained assassins lurking in the corridors and closets. "Thank you for keeping me safe." When he didn't respond, she tried again. "It's good to see you. You look…" *Wonderful. Devastating.* "As handsome as ever."

"Never mind how I look," he snapped. "What are you doing here? And what are you *wearing*?"

Ava, who'd been innocently—perhaps even a shade eagerly—anticipating a reciprocal compliment, now tightened her grip on the strap of her travel case and drew a steadying breath. "I'm here as part of standard crew transfers. Yeoman Terina Massuk, junior comms officer reporting for duty, sir." She sketched a mock salute with her free hand. "Nobody else knows where I am, not even my personal assistant, Phyl." They'd had a frank discussion about it and Phyl was definitely not thrilled, but eventually the older woman had thrown up her hands in surrender.

"I don't believe that for an instant," he huffed. "If your personal security chief doesn't know where you are, you should fire them. In fact, you should fire them for letting you pull a sapbrained stunt like this."

"Sapbrained stunt?" she sputtered. Her temper rising, she demanded, "How dare you?"

"*How dare I?*" Jean hit the standby button on the input panel so hard his hand hurt, bringing their journey to a halt. Stalking the few steps over to her, he glared. "I am the second officer aboard this station, President Montgomery. It is my sworn duty to protect everyone in here from each other and from everything out there." He flung his arm out, not really caring where he pointed since the station was surrounded by space. "How dare *you* come here without adequate protection? We only have two fighter squadrons and the standard weapons array, scarcely enough to defend ourselves under normal circumstances."

Ava squirmed under his accusing gaze even as she sprang to defend herself. "For your information, Lieutenant Commander, I've traveled half the galaxy, *on my own*, to get here. Every other station and ship I've passed through is still in working order, so don't start acting like I'm a walking, talking security breach!"

"You are as far as I'm concerned," he barked. "Or have you forgotten…"

Jean broke off, suddenly uncertain as to the wisdom of bringing up their one and only proper date. They'd spent a great deal of time together for a few months in college, so much so that he'd worked his way up to a first name basis with her entire security team, not an easy task. He'd used that friendship to convince that team to let them have one day to themselves. No peanut gallery, no distractions. No backup if—make that *when*—he failed miserably at the job of protecting her.

Marla. Edgar. Todd. Yvette. Norman. The others. Not for the first time, Jean wondered what had happened to the members of that team. Were they all fired for their stupidity in trusting him?

For her part, Ava's mind made the leap without further prompting and she turned away. She didn't want to talk about their breakup, either. Not what led up to it and certainly not the event itself.

An examination of the explosive device after the incident had shown it to be expensive, unique, and built for the sole purpose of disabling her personal hovercraft. But they hadn't taken her craft. No, the little bit of freedom had gone to her head, prompting her to yield to Jean's stubborn insistence on arranging the entire night. That decision saved both their lives; which they promptly stopped sharing, for reasons she feared she would never understand.

Finding herself face-to-face with the input panel, Ava pressed the standby button, starting the car on its way again. It hadn't gone far before it slowed, then altered course to go up instead of sideways.

Jean took a few deep, calming breaths, then moved to stand beside her again. "I heard about your father." That was a dumb thing to say. The entire galaxy heard when Edwin Montgomery died. "I'm sorry for your loss." So inadequate.

"Thank you." Ava folded her arms across her chest, trying to deny access to the emotions that inevitably swarmed her each time she slowed down enough to feel them.

"Why change your hair?" Jean threw out the change in subject when he noticed her eyes growing suspiciously moist.

"What?" She looked sharply at him, uncertain she'd heard correctly. His eloquent shrug confirmed that she had. "Oh, I, I don't know. Make myself look different." Shaking her head swung some of the loose hair onto her upper arms. Irritated, she brushed it off. "I tried a couple of colors before settling on this, um, on these. The black for mourning and the red because I kind of like it."

"Makes sense." Except it didn't. Ava wouldn't alter her appearance, assume an identity, and travel 'half the galaxy' incognito without a good reason. What that reason might be, he couldn't begin to guess. He did, however, need to know. "Why did you come?"

"I came because I've spent the last six months completing a, well, a tour of succession, I guess you'd call it." Her voice broke slightly as she remembered why the tour was necessary. Months. Things spoken of in large lumps of time were things folks hoped to forget, or at least get over. The passage of time from special events, times and happenings that they wanted to remember, was always counted in the days spent savoring the memories. "I've made personal visits to every major business concern Montgomery Galactic owns. I shake hands, listen to complaints, and check the books."

"Skip to the part where you went around without your security detail," Jean prodded. He shoved aside the guilt he felt for interrogating her.

"Right." Ava smirked at him. "Because naturally, none of what I just told you could've been accomplished by a mere yeoman." She held up her hand to stop him before he could scold her again. "Jean, relax. I've had the exact same training as any of my investigators. I'm not a bored debutante here on a dare. Just keep running the station the way you have been and I promise I won't be late for any of my shifts. Deal?"

The pivotlift whirred to a nearly silent stop, and the doors slid open.

Confident that she'd won her point, Ava stepped out into the corridor and headed toward her assigned quarters. She was only mildly surprised to find Jean beside her when she stopped in front of a plain, gray door, indistinguishable from all the other doors in sight except for the numbers embedded in the wall beside it.

Holding her commband up to the security panel until the screen unlocked, she selected a room configuration, then leaned one shoulder against the wall to wait while the synthesizers created the furniture for her. Raised an eyebrow at Jean, who'd composed his features but was clearly still mad enough to chew through a blast door.

"The *Beyond* is my last stop on this tour," she explained quietly, needing his approval more than she cared to admit. "Your security chief has just been informed that I will arrive by personal shuttle in twenty days. Between now and then, I'm just one more face in a sea of them."

"You're going to do this whether I like it or not, aren't you." It was slowly sinking in for Jean that he had absolutely no choice in the matter. She'd dismissed his objections and, as his boss' boss' boss' boss' ad infinitum, she could simply order him to stand down. And, while he wouldn't apologize for reflexively ushering her to safety, he did feel a little better knowing she had some training to fall back on.

"I'm afraid so." Ava sighed and pushed her hair back again. Made a mental note to put it up before she went on duty so it wouldn't drive her crazy the whole time. "You can only learn so much by reading reports, Jean. Sometimes you have to get things firsthand."

Her words reverberated in his mind, the echo of something he'd once said himself when asked why he insisted on visiting the front line each time he got a new assignment. He'd never gone incognito, but he'd never reached her equivalent rank, either.

"Then I guess I'd better get out of your way before I blow your cover." He was just straightening from a slight bow when his commband vibrated and the alert light began rapidly blinking amber. Another minor emergency. Turning so his shoulder was to her, a promise that he was leaving, he took the call. "Kearns."

"Sir, this is Command. Security Chief Taylor has a situation that needs your attention, a code 3T." Officially, there was no such thing as a 3T. *Unofficially*, there were some things that the whole station was better off if Captain Donovan didn't know about.

"Again?" Jean grimaced, embarrassed by the groan in his voice. In nearly the same breath, he inquired, "Is it urgent?"

"No, she's, er, everything is okay." The tone of voice was empathetic enough that Jean winced. How he hated having the entire station crew know his business! Or at least, everyone on shift in comms when his six-year-old daughter got up to something. He suppressed another groan when he realized that would soon include Ava.

"On my way." Jean closed the channel and looked over his shoulder at Ava, who'd heard every word. Despite her carefully blank expression, he could tell she was curious. For a microsecond, he considered letting her believe that the 'she' in question was his girlfriend. His wife, even. He could use the distance that would put between them as breathing room, to keep things strictly professional. Except, he'd never lied to her. He'd nearly gotten her killed, but he'd never lied to her.

"Sounds important." Ava risked the two words, hoping they sounded more concerned than curious. She had no right to be intensely curious about the 'she' in Jean's life, yet she was.

"Very." He looked away, gathering himself, then popped the proverbial airlock. "My daughter is adorable, creative, and smart. All of which contributes to her getting into trouble on almost a daily basis."

"Your daughter?" Ava almost jumped when the door to her quarters clicked open, signaling that the synthesizer was finished. "I...I didn't know you were married." She also didn't know why the news was making her head spin. Or, at least, she refused to admit that she knew why.

"It isn't like that." Jean ran his fingers through

his hair, searching for words to explain despite having had this conversation dozens of times before. Thirty-three was an awkward age to abruptly become a father, and apparently even after six years he wasn't used to it. It was the first time he'd had it with Ava and that seemed to make all the difference. "Her mom and I, we were from the same sector on Orpan. Orphaned the same season, taken to the same military school, and sent to serve in the same unit. She was like a sister to me."

His voice dropped to just above a whisper and Ava had to strain to hear it. *Was.* Then, this woman of whom he spoke with such obvious fondness was deceased. Ava wrestled with the urge to run over and wrap her arms around him. Three thousand days was just too long a span between goodbyes and hellos to be sure of one's footing, even with as close as they'd been at one time.

"We survived by relying on each other. I," he shook his head, "I have no idea how many times she saved my life. When I heard she'd died in childbirth, I thought it was a bad joke. Then they told me she'd made me her daughter's guardian." He paused for an instant to steady himself, the shock and pain the memory stirred up still real enough to taste. "I didn't even hesitate."

"Oh, Jak." The sobriquet slipped from Ava without her even noticing as she blinked eyes that stung with tears. "She's the luckiest little girl in the whole galaxy."

"Thanks." Jean tried to chuckle and nearly choked on the lump in his throat. "You know, you're still the only one who's ever thought to call me that." He almost asked if anyone else ever called her Sam, short for Sigrid Ava Montgomery. Then again, how many people knew her full name? He'd shared his over supper one evening when she'd asked about his family, and she reciprocated, resulting in the discovery of their hidden nicknames.

"I'm glad." The subtle change in his expression at her admission set her heart to pounding so hard she could feel it in her fingertips.

"Me, too." Jean cursed himself for a fool before the sound of the words had fully faded. What was he doing? With an effort, he looked away from her mesmerizing eyes. She was the only person he'd ever met with any shade of orange in her irises. And hers were such a bright orange, like a warning beacon to others that she carried a fire within too great to be fully contained. "You're sure you don't want to stay in your quarters until I can whistle up a battle cruiser to take you home?" He threw out the question in a lame attempt to change the subject.

"The *Beyond* is my home, Jean, as much as any Montgomery holding is." She might've been mistaken, but she thought she saw a flash of sadness in his eyes at that. Sadness for her? Why?

"Understood." Jean stopped just short of saluting when he heard laughter coming from somewhere down the corridor. "Then, if you'll excuse me?"

Ava made a shooing motion at him with her hand and shoved her door fully open so she could enter her quarters, close it, and lean against it while she waited for her hands to stop trembling. When she'd used her sobriquet for him, a surge of emotions rushed over her like a sneaker wave from the ocean, threatening to pull her under and drown her.

Of course, after striking upon the idea, she'd never again thought of it so clinically. No, 'Jak' became a one-word vocabulary for everything wonderful: the sound of his deep laugh; the scent of his soap; the feel of his arms around her.

Shaking her head to clear it, Ava pushed away from the door and walked determinedly into the bedroom area. Seeing Jean had rattled her; talking with him only made things worse. She couldn't have avoided the conversation for very long, but maybe it would've been wiser to postpone it. Everything was easier after a hot meal and a good night's rest.

Setting her travel case on her bed, Ava was just about to open it when she heard a chirp, alerting her that someone was at the door. Pausing long enough to strip off her stifling uniform jacket, she tossed it in the reclaimer as she passed it, nodding in satisfaction as it was broken down into its component molecules to be repurposed at some later date.

Tapping the screen by her door, Ava checked to see who was calling on her so soon. The sight of a handful of laughing, chatting crewmembers greeted her. Some of them she recognized from the shuttle. *Hmm.* Remembering how easily the door swung open, Ava took care to stand clear of it as she released the catch.

"Hello?" In keeping with her assumed background, Ava clasped her hands in front of her demurely.

"Hello and welcome to the *Beyond!*" The senior crewmember took the lead. "It's station tradition that your first meal aboard has to be eaten with the rest of the crew, and we're here to escort you to the cafeteria."

"Why, that's—" After days of public transport, Ava was dying for an evening to herself, but she forced a smile. "—nebular! Just let me change and…"

"Nope!" Another of the group interrupted with a laugh. "This is come as you are. That's the other part of the tradition."

"I'm out of uniform!" She protested mainly to see how they'd respond.

"Too bad." The first one spoke again, grinning from ear to ear. "Hey, don't worry about it. The only one who'd care is the captain."

"And he never eats with his subordinates." A woman on the side of the group pulled a face as she stressed the last word, prompting general laughter.

"Well. Alright." As they made their way through a bewildering set of twists and turns to their destination, Ava kept her ears open. The captain was apparently a sore subject amongst them and bringing him up had cast something of a pall on the group.

"Two minutes late for my shift and bam! I've got a month of earlies," muttered one fellow. "Straight off of the over shift, he puts me on earlies to 'teach me the value of punctuality.'"

Someone else agreed, "He's a regular saveus."

Ava flinched inwardly. 'Saveus' was a vulgar term for particularly cruel slave owners. Slave systems were the blank spaces on the Montgomery map, for Ava and her father had agreed to do nothing that might support such cultures. It was hard to believe that the practice of slavery had survived the establishment of galactic peace treaties and trade agreements, let alone the invention and general implementation of service bots, but it had proven a particularly resilient form of evil. The *Beyond*'s proximity to a slave system was the one reason they'd almost decided not to build there.

"Hey, what's on the table tonight, anyhow?" The group leader tried to rescue things by completely changing the subject.

Ava tried to look increasingly alarmed as slang terms were tossed around. After someone assured her she was 'going to love the fly cake,' she tried to duck out of the group. "Maybe I should eat in my room after all."

"Whoa, whoa." One of the younger girls blocked her path, with both hands up in a soothing gesture. "Look, don't take these idiots seriously. All we have here is ordinary food. Now, nobody's going to force you to come, but," she lowered her hands and indicated the corridor ahead, "it's a pretty good way to get to know each other."

Pleased, Ava once again joined the group, though she kept a doubtful expression on her face. The same, nice girl who'd talked her out of leaving now stuck with her through the food line, showing her where to find what, and deftly folded Ava into her private circle of friends when she sat down at the table.

"Everyone, this is Terina, fresh in from Derli. Terina," she indicated the group, "this is everyone."

"Derli, huh?" A woman with pink- and green-striped hair grunted as she sawed at her synthesized steak. "Never been. What's it like?"

"Dull as static." Someone further down the table answered for her. "Only place I've ever been stationed where it was just as boring off-duty as on."

Ava sat back and let the two of them argue about whether or not that was really possible, but pricked up her ears when the conversation drifted back to life on the *Beyond*.

"I'd love to have a boring day here and there."

A man plunked his tray down across from Ava. "Just spent nine hours refereeing impatient ship captains."

"Aw, poor you. It's so hard keeping track of which docking bays are empty, isn't it?" jeered the steak-sawyer.

"Okay, okay." The newcomer laughed with everyone else even as he rubbed his face. "It's just nerve-wracking when Donovan's staring over your shoulder the whole time."

The hair on the back of Ava's neck stood up in response to how quickly the table quieted.

"Yeah. I know what you mean." A few voices up and down the table echoed the sentiment.

"Why does he do that?" Ava couldn't see who asked the question, but those sitting nearest her began shaking their heads.

"Haven't got a clue." The original speaker stirred his soup and sighed. "It was worse than usual today, though. He countermanded me twice."

It was on the tip of Ava's tongue to ask if he remembered *which* two ships were involved—except of course she couldn't. Nope, she had to sit there and pretend not to be intensely curious about the austere captain's idiosyncratic behavior.

Chapter 3

Jean dropped his face into his hand. "Then what did she do?"

Security Chief Taylor coughed into his fist, perhaps trying to clear the laughter from his voice before he continued. People always seemed to think things were funny when they had no personal stake in the matter.

"She dressed them down pretty good. Quoted regs and just generally gave them, er—" He eyed the little girl waiting primly in the chair by the desk in his office. Logically, he knew she couldn't possibly hear what they were saying. Instinctively, however, he chose words he wouldn't be horrified to hear come out of her mouth. "—a bad time." He rubbed his chin thoughtfully. The chair dwarfed her in size, yet she somehow seemed to fill the room with her presence. "Y'know, she'd make a great security officer." Meeting Jean's eyes, even peeking out through his fingers, Taylor backpedaled instantly. "Well, not right now. Don't be ridiculous. She's too young to contract."

"What in the eighteen golden shades of Oktar am I going to do with her?" Jean asked nobody in particular. "She sleeps nine hours a night, goes to school six hours a day, and unless something's wrong in Command, I spend as much of the remaining twelve hours with her as I can."

"Aw, now, it isn't as bad as all that." Taylor hooked his thumbs over the top of his belt. "She might've been swiping candy from the sweet shop instead of rousting a trio of guesters." The crewmembers of visiting ships, unofficially known as 'guesters,' were restricted to certain areas of the *Beyond*. Up to an hour ago, Taylor would've shredded anyone who suggested they could get as far in as the station crew quarters, but thanks to Solène, there was irrefutable proof to the contrary. He already had a team of his best reviewing the situation, and fully intended to join them as soon as he was done there.

"Don't be ridiculous. Solène isn't a thief. But she can't go around lecturing rough-and-tumbles on the rules, either." Even Jean's protest sounded tired. "She's the only child I know who behaves like she's sixty years old instead of almost six." Granted, he cherished each of the two thousand fifty days since he'd adopted her at birth. She just wore him out sometimes.

"Huh. Maybe not sixty, but I see what you mean." Taylor went back to rubbing his chin. "She got any toys? Y'know, dolls, books, stuff like that? My sister's kids have enough toys to fill a fleet of shuttles, and it seems to keep them busy." They still got into mischief occasionally, just nothing on this magnitude.

Jean nodded. "She has a shelf full of story cubes, most of which she picked out herself. And a whole family of dolls. Oh, you'll love this—I get in trouble if I forget to call them by name!" Not that he minded. Teaching respect and civility started young, and how rude would it be to forget a real person's name?

Come to think of it, she'd only wanted two dolls to begin with, a daddy and a daughter. Jean had to coax her to pick out more. The second little girl doll came first, so the first would have a best friend like Solène did. A few months later, she'd hesitantly asked if it was okay to get a mommy doll, too. They'd had a long talk about mommies and daddies, and he'd promised her up and down that he thought it was a wonderful idea for her to get a mommy doll, too. Looking back, he had the distinct impression she'd been afraid of hurting his feelings, as if getting a mommy doll somehow implied that having just a daddy wasn't good enough.

"How's she doin' at school? Her teachers say anything?"

"Huh? Oh, plenty." Jean thought it was important to keep in touch with her teachers, the sort of thing a real parent would do, but lately the short chats were getting longer. "It all boils down to this same sort of thing, though. They don't know what to do about it, either."

"I'd suggest sending her to visit grandma if she had one." Taylor shook his head in defeat. "I'm stumped, I reckon. Nothing much more we can do for her here." Suddenly, he snapped his fingers. "Hey, that's an idea. Send her to school somewhere else! What do they call it? Bored school?"

"Boarding school? I couldn't do that, Taylor." Jean fought down the bile rising in his throat. Maybe that was why things were starting to go wrong. His own family experience ended abruptly at age six, the exact age that Solène was now. A raging epidemic swept several villages off the face of the land, leaving him and hundreds of other orphans in its wake. The government 'generously' made a place for them—in military schools. "No!" He barked when it looked like Taylor was about to argue the point. "I won't and that's final."

Taylor threw up his hands. "Okay, okay, you don't have to go all battle commander on me."

"Good." Jean wet his dry lips and took a steadying breath. "I better get her home. It's almost suppertime." Straightening his tunic, he walked to the door that separated him from his daughter.

Took another deep breath and opened it.

"Daddy!" The sweet, rounded face of the child he loved lit up like a solar flare as she hopped off the chair and ran over to throw her arms around his waist. "I thought Chief Taylor forgot to call you!"

Jean's heart constricted as he realized how long he'd kept her waiting. "No, mareyth." His mother's pet name for all her children fell easily from his lips. He smoothed her space-black waves gently and pulled away enough to squat down to her eye level. "Chief Taylor would never forget something that important."

"But I've been waiting so long." Her bottom lip trembled ever so slightly as she stared up at him.

"I'm sorry." He gave her shoulders a soft squeeze. "Chief Taylor and I were talking about what happened."

"Am I in trouble?" Worry filled her somber gray eyes.

"Oh, not too much. You were exactly where you told me you would be, doing exactly what you said you would be doing." He smiled reassuringly.

"Then what did I do wrong?" Her forehead puckered. "Chief Taylor said you had to tell me."

"Is that what he said?" Jean made a mental note to warn Taylor against leaving children to stew about what they'd done wrong. Their imaginations were powerful things and tended to do more harm than good in cases like this. "Were you very scared?"

"Not very." Her chin came up. "I knew you would come."

"Smart girl. Now." He settled himself into the chair and lifted her onto his lap. "Do you remember seeing anyone in the corridor that should not have been there?"

She nodded vigorously. "Three men, Daddy. They weren't wearing station uniforms and I told them they were going to get in trouble." Her voice trailed off. "Is that what I did wrong, Daddy?"

"Part of it is. I'm proud of the fact that you saw something wrong and decided to do something about it." He paused to organize his thoughts. One of the toughest things he had to do as a parent was explain that the world wasn't always a safe place to live. "What worries me, and Chief Taylor, is that you might have gotten hurt. Not all adults are nice people, mareyth. We've talked about that."

"But they were in uniforms, Daddy. Guesters, I think."

"That's true." He sighed, then perked up as a thought struck him. "Were they in uniform doing what they were supposed to be doing? Were they where they were supposed to be?"

After a moment's thought, she shook her head solemnly. "Does that make them bad adults, Daddy?"

"No, mareyth, not always. But it *does* make them adults that another adult should talk to, not you. Do you understand that?"

"An adult, Daddy? Like you?"

"That's right. Me, or Chief Taylor. Or any of his security officers." He sat up straight and she mimicked him. "So, the next time you see an adult that's breaking a rule, will you go tell them?"

"No, Daddy." Light danced on the obsidian waves of her hair as she shook her head vehemently. "I won't talk to them at all. I'll, um…" Her forehead scrunched up. "I'll tell you or the first security adult I see."

"That's my girl!" Kissing her forehead, he scooped

her up into his arms and got to his feet.

"Daddy!" She began squirming immediately. "Put me down! I'm a big girl!"

"Solène." He waited until she looked him in the eyes. "How does a big girl ask?"

She stilled. "Please put me down, Daddy. I would like to walk."

"Perfect." He set her on her feet, but kept ahold of her hand as he offered, "Would you like to pick what we have for supper tonight?"

She grinned and gave a little skip. "Let's have real food! At Masie's!"

He laughed knowingly. "You just want to see Masie's xintxa." Masie's restaurant boasted some of the finest, heartiest food on the station and, as a bonus, she had a silver-gray xintxa for a pet. While Jean would never understand what made the little tree rat worth the extra money it cost Masie in pet deposit fees, he was grateful for her generosity in letting Solène play with it.

Solène's grin only got bigger as she eagerly hauled him off to the restaurant level.

The *Beyond* rented a square mile of its available space to restaurants and the best were all located in the residential sector. Even though station crew ate there at a reduced price, most of them tended to steer clear of the pricier places except on extra special occasions. Truthfully, eating 'real food,' as Solène called it, was an occasion in itself. Synthetic foods were provided free of charge to the station crew along with their quarters and up to two outfits per lunar cycle.

Still. Synth foods, with all their precisely programmed ratios of this electron to that proton to perfectly simulate the composition of thousands of dishes, never made Jean's mouth water the way the food at Masie's did.

"Extra dumplings, please!" Solène called after the waiter, an older man with twinkling eyes and a way with kids.

"Extra dumplings?" Jean poked her lightly in the side, producing a giggle. "Where do you put them all? Here? Or maybe here?" Her giggles erupted into full-blown laughter, the sound he loved most in the world. He persisted a moment more, then pulled her in for a hug. "I guess you have room for extra dumplings. I should warn you, though. If you eat too many, you'll pop!"

Her laughter eased off enough for her to shake her head and say, "Oh, Daddy. You're silly!"

"Me?" He wiggled his eyebrows at her.

"Yes, you." Masie pushed her trademark cart up to their table, then swooped in to hug Solène. "Look at you! So big! Were you this big last week? Ah, you grow too quick!" She believed that her customers were part of her family and treated them as such. Especially those that had no other family to speak of.

"It's all your fault," Jean informed her dryly. "You're the one who makes the dumplings."

"Ha." Masie shook a friendly finger at him. "I make them, yes. Who pays me to make? You!"

Setting out warm, clean plates for them, she dished out hot, steamed grain and added a ladleful of savory meats and vegetables—heavy on the vegetables. Meat was the most expensive part of the meal because it had to be imported from nearly a system away. The vegetables, however, came from the station's own garden and were priced accordingly.

"Of course I pay for the dumplings." He feigned mild indignation. "I'm a responsible adult who always pays his debts."

Masie hooted as she expertly dipped a little of this sauce and a little of that sauce from small warming containers in her cart to make a winning flavor combination just for Solène. "You save more monies," Masie lectured him, "if you ate more synth food."

Jean pretended to think about it, then leaned over to mock-whisper to Solène, "I think she wants us to leave."

Solène shook her head and reached for her fork. "You're *both* silly!"

Masie laughed so hard she had to stop serving to fan her face with the ruffled edge of her ample apron. "Oh, you little one, you good for my heart." She hugged Solène again, careful of the child's mouthful of food. "You eat, and then you come see my xintxa, okay?"

Jean made eye contact with Masie over Solène's head and gave her a nod of thanks. Every so often he wondered what would happen to Solène if…well, if anything ever happened to him. He should make arrangements, just in case. He simply didn't know many people that he'd want to trust her to. The few friendships he'd formed since leaving the military were mostly skin-deep, like beauty. Someone to chat with at work; someone to eat with in the cafeteria afterwards.

Looking at his daughter, inelegant yet adorable as she gobbled her food so she could go play with Masie's xintxa, Jean knew it was past time for all of that to change. Alas, realizing that was the easy part. Deciding what to do about it was another thing entirely.

"Hello, Solène." A tall, slender woman approached their table, a smile on her face for both of them.

"Captain Cole!" Solène waved enthusiastically. "Want to come see a xintxa?"

The woman laughed kindly at the unexpected invitation. "Do you have a xintxa?" Her eyebrows rose in exaggerated surprise. Chief pilot for one of the *Beyond*'s supply companies, she took care to be on friendly terms with the command staff as much as possible.

"It's not mine, it's Masie's." Solène's smile dimmed for an instant, then she perked up again. "She lets me play with it, though!"

"That's wonderful!"

Something clicked in Jean's head as the two of them talked, and he blurted, "Will you join us?" Judging by the abrupt widening of her eyes, Captain Cole was as startled by the invitation as he was.

"Daddy." Solène tugged at his sleeve until he leaned down. Quietly, or at least, as quietly as a child of only two thousand days could manage, she whispered, "Does that mean I can't go play?"

"Oh, um." Feeling twice the idiot, Jean straightened up. "Excuse me, Captain. I misspoke a moment ago. Solène has finished her supper and is ready to go play, so," he narrowly avoided pausing to swallow, "I guess you'd be joining just me." His palms began to sweat as he waited for her reply.

"You're sure?" She waited for his nod, then took the seat opposite him before it even occurred to him that he should have helped her with it. "I'd love to."

"All done. Bye, Daddy!" Solène wiped her mouth and ran off, abandoning him to his fate.

"They're so energetic at that age." Captain Cole's mouth curved upward even as she sighed. "I wish I could borrow some of that."

Good, a topic he could handle. "You sound

like you've had a long day."

"Well, I," she hesitated, "don't mean to complain. It's only that docking delays negatively impact our schedule."

"Of course." By listening and answering carefully, Jean was able to keep the conversation on neutral topics. It wasn't all that different from what he was used to, except that he didn't have an established rapport with her from spending a nine-hour shift together in the same room.

"Mm, that was delicious." She touched her mouth delicately with her napkin and laid it aside. "Now. What was it you wanted to talk to me about?"

Jean blinked. "Why, nothing in particular."

"Nothing? Well, that's a first."

Something about the way she raised a carefully shaped eyebrow at him made Jean nervous. He didn't know why, just that it did. A familiar voice interrupted his inner musings.

"Lieutenant Commander." Ava stood at attention by his table, hands at her sides. Her brain hadn't quite caught up with her heart, so she had no idea what she was going to do next. Seeing Jean sitting there, chatting comfortably with a beautiful woman had short-circuited her logic, plain and simple.

"Excuse me." Jean offered his most-polished smile to the captain and rose to face Ava, of all people. "Yeoman. What's so important that you have to interrupt my supper?" Taking her by the arm, he walked her a few steps away from the table.

"I, um." Ava struggled to keep her confusion from showing on her face. This was completely unlike herself. "I don't know."

"You don't..." Jean looked away from the table

and stifled a chuckle. "Then this isn't an official summons?"

Ava shook her head, not trusting her voice when her cheeks were already betraying her.

"Mhmm." Jean 'accidentally' bumped his shoulder against hers as he turned to smile pleasantly at the captain. "Thanks for the rescue."

Her eyes flew to his face. "Rescue?"

"Yeah, I was floundering over there." He blew out a breath and admitted, "I'm out of practice." From now on, he was going to stick with the families of Solène's friends. He was less likely to find himself out on a limb with a saw in one hand that way.

Ava bit the inside of her cheek to keep from laughing aloud. The source of the relief bubbling up inside of her was a mystery, but there was no debating its existence.

"Wait here, please." Jean returned to the table, where he thanked the captain for her time and bid her a good evening. Making his way back over to Ava, he motioned for her to fall in with him, which she did.

They hadn't gone far when she ventured to ask, "Where are we going?"

"Around the corner." He pointed. "I have to pick up my daughter."

"Your daughter?" Ava missed a step. "You want me to meet her?"

Jean turned toward her even as he paused and she nearly ran into him. Everything he knew about Ava raced through his brain and touched his heart. "Yes. Yes, I do."

Chapter 4

Ava entered the little home with all her senses on alert. The lighting was tuned to a warm yellow, casting a soft glow over the round end table and two-seater sofa on one end of the long front room. It even managed to take some of the bite out of the brilliantly colored rug that covered most of the floor, stopping just short of the closed door on the right and the ceramic tiling in the kitchen to the left.

In the center of the rug sat a lovely little girl. Chin-length black hair swung loose about her face as she focused intently on the sleek animal sharing the rug with her.

Ava watched in fascination, as the animal—as long from tip to tail as Jean's arm though not nearly as large around—raced back and forth along the rug in relentless pursuit of a tiny dot of light.

"Daddy, watch!" exclaimed Solène. "Watch what happens!" Deliberately, she slowed the dot down until the xintxa pounced, trapping it under its front paws. Except, of course, the dot shone on top of its paws.

Confused, the animal tried a few more times to capture the dot, but each time the obstinate point of light refused to behave. It barked once, then settled back on its haunches with a noise between a huff and a howl.

"Alright," laughed Masie, appearing in the kitchen doorway with a long spoon in her hand. "That's enough for now. We don't want to wear Tandu out."

"Yes, Masie." Obediently, Solène hung the narrow beam emitter on a hook on the wall, then chirped at the xintxa.

Ava cringed at the way the animal scurried up the child's bare arm and was astonished to see that it hadn't left a single claw mark on its way. It circled her shoulders and shoved its narrow nose into the girl's hair, chittering all the while.

Giggling, Solène said, "I love you, too, Tandu." Looking up at last, her gaze settled on Ava. "Who're you?"

Jean cleared his throat. "Solène, this is my friend." Pausing, he shot Ava a look. He'd never lied to Solène, either, and didn't like the idea of starting now. He should've thought of this and discussed it with Ava before they got there! Or vice versa. Actually…why hadn't she thought of it? No, that didn't make sense. Solène was *his* daughter.

Ava's stomach and heart switched places for a moment, then woozily resumed their proper positions. During her training, they'd taken pains to emphasize the rule, 'Never break cover!' And she never had. Jean didn't count because he already knew her, so it would be safer to take him into her confidence as quickly as possible.

These and other thoughts swirled through her mind as she knelt to be at the girl's level. Serious gray eyes studied Ava's face, tugging at her heart. She shouldn't even be considering this. Her instructor would express his horror at the idea in terms of her physical exertion. Twenty laps, at least.

"Can you keep a secret?" Ava waited breathlessly for the answer.

"I keep lots of secrets." One shoulder rose and fell as if to say secrets were nothing new.

"She does," Jean confirmed, kneeling as well

despite a hitch in his knee, an old war wound that would never quite heal. But as for Solène, there was secret and then there was *top secret*. "She's never once told me what she's gotten me for my birthday." He checked Ava's face to make sure she got his message.

"Oh. That's very impressive." Inhaling, Ava got a rush of Jean's scent and almost forgot what they were discussing. "I, um." She was never at a loss for words, she couldn't afford to be.

"I keep good secrets, too," inserted Masie, an interested twinkle in her eyes as she looked back and forth between the two adults kneeling on her rug. "I don't tell nobody you got a girl for a friend, Jean."

Ava ducked her head to hide a smile and snuck a peek at Jean. His face, pale despite the mandatory time spent under a sunlamp, reddened slightly at Masie's words.

"Thanks, Masie. So much." Jean wasn't sure how else to respond to that. Speaking more quietly in the hopes of a semi-private conversation, he suggested, "Maybe we should finish this conversation at…" He went from eyeing Masie to looking at Ava and abruptly realized how close their faces were to each other. Drawing back, he wiped damp palms on his slacks. Suddenly, inviting her to his quarters seemed like a really, really complicated decision. "I mean. Somewhere else."

Ava inadvertently swayed toward him when he started to move, realizing belatedly that he was just getting to his feet. "Good idea." Her cheeks burned as she copied his actions and she faked absorption in checking her uniform slacks for animal hair or lint or anything so long as she didn't have to meet Jak's—no, *Jean's* eyes.

Solène gave a heartfelt sigh and tickled Tandu's tummy. "I'll come play with you again, okay?" she promised. Tandu chittered at her, making her smile.

"Thanks again, Masie." Waiting until Tandu was secure in Masie's arms, Jean opened the door, allowing Ava and Solène to precede him into the corridor.

"Where are we going, Daddy?" Solène slipped her hand into his and began swinging it back and forth.

Jean hesitated. The best, most private place on the station would probably be an empty loading bay. He knew that because Chief Taylor was constantly complaining about how hard it was to patrol all of them. Unfortunately, they were on the other side of the station and his knee was a tad stiff after kneeling.

"How about the garden level?" Ava suggested.

"It might work." Jean rubbed the back of his neck. The garden was enormous, occupying the largest circumference level in the sphere portion of the station. It was practically perfect for private meetings, except that there was no clear line of sight, which meant… "Except we couldn't be sure we had the place to ourselves."

"This must be a scrumptious big secret," observed Solène gravely. "Why don't we go to the library? Everybody whispers in the library."

Ava fought back a reflexive smile. Secrets apparently meant whispering to the little girl. Looking at Jean over Solène's head, she nodded her approval.

"Good idea, mareyth." Jean changed direction. "It's just one level down."

The library wasn't large. Its primary function was the maintenance of the available digital content, a handful of research stations, and a few devices that station guests could check out during their stays. Nevertheless, as Solène said, all communication was conducted in whispers.

Ava followed Jean who followed Solène to a short table in the back. Solène drew out a chair and seated herself.

"This is where I do homework," she explained in a sotto voice.

"Ah." Jean knew that, of course, but now he eyed the short chairs with some trepidation. He was sort of accustomed to them from his visits to her classroom. Ava was not. "I can get some adult-sized chairs, if you'd prefer."

"This is fine." Ava shook her head and perched herself on one of the pint-sized chairs. Watched in astonishment as Jean gracefully did the same, dwarfing the seat so completely that he looked as if he was hovering in midair.

"Shall I call the meeting to order?" Jean cocked an amused eyebrow at Ava, who was staring at him as if she'd never seen him before. Surreptitiously, he stretched his legs out under the table and almost sighed in relief.

"Oh. Um." Ava cursed herself for blushing a second time in less than an hour. "Right. If we're all ready?" She looked at Solène to be sure and found the girl watching her so intensely as to be disconcerting. Was that how she'd been looking at Jean? Heavens. If her face got any hotter, her uniform collar was going to catch fire.

"I think we're ready," Jean offered. If they had to wait much longer, Solène was going to spontaneously combust from sheer curiosity.

"Right." Ava took a deep breath. "Solène, do you know what undercover means?"

Solène scrunched up her nose as she thought,

then shook her head.

Jean jumped in to help things along. "You don't know the word, but you've seen it happen. Remember when Chief Taylor changed his uniform and went down to work in the docking bays?" At Solène's nod, he explained, "He was undercover, pretending not to be the security chief."

Wide gray eyes focused on Ava again. "Are you pretending to be someone else?"

This time, Ava allowed herself a small smile at the adorable phrasing of the question. "That's right. While I'm undercover on the *Beyond*, people call me Terina Massuk."

Her nose scrunched again. "So everyone knows you're pretending?"

"No." Jean answered quickly. "That's the secret. You know." He pointed to her, then to himself. "And I know." Leaning closer, he whispered even more softly. "We're the only two people on the whole station who know!" Eyebrows raised impressively, he nodded and straightened up.

Solène's mouth formed a perfect 'O' of surprise and for several seconds she just sat there, absorbing the weight of the new information.

"Will you always be undercover?"

Ava shook her head. "Just for a few weeks."

"Can I meet you again when you're you?" Solène pressed.

Ava shot Jean a look, unsure of how to respond. When he folded his arms across his chest instead of helping her, she took a deep breath. "I'd like that, but I'm usually very, um…" Her words trailed off under the continued scrutiny of those piercing gray eyes. What was it about the gaze of a child that stripped away excuses? Because even though Ava knew she would be swamped with all the catching-up she'd have to do, the unshakeable conviction remained that she could make time to spend with Solène. Just like Ava's own father had made time to spend with her when she was a child.

"Solène." Jean, worried that Ava's identity as the owner of the *Beyond* might be too big of a secret, intervened. "Will you keep this secret?" Relief coursed through him at his daughter's solemn nod.

"Thank you." Ava swallowed hard. "And yes. You can meet me again when I'm 'me.'" Jean's frown caught her eye and she turned to face him. "If it's alright with Dad." Her lips curved upward at the last word. The more she got used to the idea of Jean as a 'dad,' the more she liked it.

Jean's heart stopped, then thundered on. Somewhere in the depths of his memories was the recollection of his parents calling each other 'Mom' and 'Dad' in place of their real names. How desperately he'd wanted that for himself. And just now…had there ever been a sweeter sound than Ava's voice calling him 'Dad'?

Slowly, he became aware of a tugging on his sleeve. A sweet little voice calling him. "Daddy? Daddy, can I? Please?" Snapping back to himself, from where exactly he refused to ponder, Jean plucked Solène off her chair and set her on his knee. "Do you truly want to, mareyth?"

"I do, Daddy. Positively."

Gently, Jean smoothed the 'v' from between Solène's eyebrows with the tip of his forefinger. "Then let's plan on it."

"Thank you, Daddy!"

He looked at Ava over Solène's shoulder as the little girl engulfed him in a hug. He needed to be sure that Ava knew how important this was. 'She'll be counting on this,' he mouthed.

Ava nodded. 'Don't worry,' she mouthed back.

Don't worry? Jean almost laughed aloud. Loving a child might be fifty percent of parenting, but worrying was the other half.

"Meeting adjourned?" suggested Ava aloud, noticing that Solène had begun to sag in Jean's arms.

"Good idea." Rising carefully, Jean slid his chair back in with his foot.

"Put me down, Daddy. I," a yawn interrupted her, "wan-oo waaalk."

"I'm not Daddy," he teased, winking at Ava, who had already taken care of the other chairs. "I'm Ametsen, come to guide you to the land of dreams."

Ava felt particularly alone as she watched Jean carry his daughter out of sight, regaling her with promises of dreams about a wild forest full of adorable little xintxas that all wanted to play with her.

Rubbing her arms in an effort to calm the tingling running along them, Ava forced her thoughts back to business. She'd done her research on the *Beyond* and knew the official complaints by heart. Finding herself in the wrong frame of mind to try coaxing unofficial complaints out of the crew, she made her way back to the restaurant section.

Veering away from those offering cloth napkins and handprinted menus, Ava strolled toward the smaller cafes, the ones that weren't fancy but still had wait staff. They were all clean, well-kept, and even though she'd just eaten, the delicious smells that filled the air were worth noting for later.

So. Why weren't they busier? Station guests might prefer the fancier spots, but these should be exactly the type of places station personnel would frequent. Real food, not synth, at prices they could easily afford.

She would've taken a seat and ordered something, tried to talk with the staff, if she hadn't eaten her fill in the cafeteria. Ah, wait. Up ahead she spotted a restaurant with a dessert-only menu. Perfect.

Easing herself into the booth, she studied the wall menu with growing amazement. Eighty-five dups for a single scoop? Did they import the ingredients and make it themselves?

"What can I get ya?" A man approached the table, commband arm raised, the projection of an order blank already up.

"A dish of chocolate custard, please." She watched as his fingers stabbed at the display, then hovered there as if waiting for her to complete her order. How many people could afford to order more than that? She allowed the silence to stretch until he gave in.

"Anything else?" He arched an eyebrow.

"That's all, thanks." She watched him head behind the counter and dish it up, a glum expression on his face.

"Here you go." He slid a bowl of the frozen dessert in front of her.

"Thanks!" She accepted with a big grin. One of the greatest discoveries of the last few centuries, in her opinion, was that of a plant from a distant moon that had the bizarre property of mimicking the flavor of any spice without adopting any unhealthy attributes. It allowed her to eat the desserts and rich foods that she so enjoyed. "Kind of slow tonight, huh?"

"Kinda." He'd been about to turn away, but now he leaned against the back of the bench facing her. "You're new aboard."

"Just got here today," she confirmed.

"Figures." He glanced gloomily out at the corridor. "Transfers and transports bring business. Everybody's gotta try all the spots at least once."

The discouragement in his voice made it hard for her to swallow, even the slippery custard. "This is fantastic." She got another big scoop and held it up. "I know I'll be back."

"Yeah?" A funny look crossed his face. "I mean, yeah. Great." He cleared his throat. "You'll, uh, tell your friends?"

She licked her spoon while she pretended to think about it. "I probably shouldn't. Once the word gets out about this place, it'll be tough to find a seat."

"Oh. Well." He shrugged and swiped at the table with a cloth he'd produced from somewhere. "That's no problem. I...I'll save you a seat. Sure. No problem."

The custard soured on her tongue. He was practically begging for her help. According to the reports, nearly every restaurant on the station was suffering. But why? Though Montgomery charged a steep price for the restaurant slots, it was always with the expectation that the proprietors would earn far and above the rent. In short, the prosperity of the businesses aboard meant prosperity for Montgomery.

"So." He was still watching her closely. "You'll tell folks?"

"Happy to." It wasn't easy forcing a lightness into her voice. "And I'll be back. As often," she grimaced, "as I can afford to."

His face fell. "Right. I get it."

She toyed with her custard. It wasn't easy,

gauging how direct to be in a moment like this. "You look like a man with troubles."

"You know somebody without troubles?" He swiped at the table again, polishing the same spot as earlier. "Eh, I guess you wouldn't know. Comms, right?"

Perplexed, she just nodded.

"You'll find out soon enough, but it's like this. I got a contract with Montgomery Galactic, the company that built this place." He waited for her acknowledging nod to continue. "I pay for the space, the lights, all of it. Heh, sometimes I think they charge me for the air I breathe. Anyhow. I pay. They promise."

"Promise what?" Her heart rate picked up even as her stomach took a nosedive, aided by the supper and custard she'd just eaten. She'd encountered grouses before, they were nothing new. This man, though. He didn't come off as a crank about to unload a shuttle's worth of perceived grievances.

"They promise a lot of things, but what they don't do is deliver the supplies."

"Supplies?" She was back to being perplexed. More so than before, in fact. Nothing in corporate records indicated a breakdown in the supply chain. Things of that magnitude were usually listed on top of the report, in big red letters, so to speak. A station like this, suspended in space, was painfully dependent on outside resources. The garden level supplemented their imports, but it could never hope to support the entire station's population on its own.

"Things were okay at first." He sighed and rubbed the back of his neck. "Thought I'd finally picked a shooting star."

"What happened? When did all this start?"

These were key questions. If he could answer—
really answer it, not guess or make wild accusa-
tions—she could start fixing things for him and,
apparently, every other restaurateur aboard.

"When? Huh, when that guy died. Y'know, the
one that owned this place?" He threw up his
hands. "Since then, if the shipment ain't late, it's
spoiled. If it ain't spoiled or late, we only get some
stuff, but not all of it."

She opened her mouth. Shut it. 'That guy' he
referred to was her father, Edwin Montgomery.
Sorrow squeezed her heart, but she shook it off
with an effort. She still had a lot to learn if she was
going to fix things. "Wow, so. Do you get a re-
fund?"

"Depends." His narrow shoulders rose and
fell. "Sometimes, the charge is barely enough to
cover what they were able to get."

Ava dropped her gaze to hide the anger flaring
up inside her. Whomever was pilfering the supplies
was hurting the businesses on both ends—driving
up prices, which cost them their customers, while
stealing from their ever-dwindling financial re-
serves.

As Sigrid Ava Montgomery, she itched to dig
deeper into the problem, to sort it out, and above
all, to make things right. As Terina Massuk, all she
could do was sit there and offer her sympathies. It
felt like trying to warm a room using only a candle
as a heat source.

Chapter 5

Once safely in her quarters, Ava updated her files with what she'd learned over dessert. Somehow, she'd managed to choke down the last of the custard, despite the lump that grew in her throat as the man shared detailed information with her. The price of desserts had only risen as a result of the shortages—the price of meat had skyrocketed. Most of the restaurants couldn't even afford it anymore.

He'd confided that he suspected some chefs had begun using synthesized meats in their food, while still charging their regular price for the meal, which she found quite disturbing. While she wouldn't make changes based solely on his theory, if it proved true, it would require punitive action.

For now, she simply instructed her assistant to quietly investigate the shortages, the spoilage, etc. It was easy to suspect the transport companies of carelessness or, though she hated to think it, deliberate theft. Likewise, some of the goods might've been mishandled from the beginning, badly processed and packaged. In that case, the contracts would be declared broken. New contracts would be drawn up with different suppliers, the merchants on the Beyond would be compensated, and life would go on.

Unless that wasn't the problem.

Yes, unless. That doubt was what got under her skin and stuck there.

Rising from her desk, Ava paced her small quarters. The unavoidable truth was that none of this had been officially reported. Why not? This matter could hardly be described as reflecting badly on the station itself. The *Beyond* was still new, brand new in terms of its expected lifespan. Also, some of the companies used to supply were new to Montgomery. Reporting their deficiencies would've allowed for swift rectification of the situation, one way or another.

If no one on the *Beyond* was being protected by remaining silent, why do it? Unless there was some other, less altruistic reason guiding the mind that faked those reports.

Groaning, she sank back into her chair and massaged her temples. Every question led to one or two more. Exactly whose mind was responsible? Someone on the station, or someone down the line? Reports were filed digitally; though they were not supposed to be altered, they were vulnerable to those with the right skills and the wrong inclinations.

After a few more minutes of considering, she decided against adding a request to have the digital histories of the reports reviewed. She should poke around in the station logs before doing anything that might tip off the culprits. Once she logged in to her workstation tomorrow in Command, there would be ample opportunity to do so.

Linking into the galactic network via the station's comm system, she pulled up a shopping site that was popular with Montgomery employees and logged in. Navigating to the customer service section, she selected an icon that was only visible to herself and her assistant, Phylis. A few more clicks and an encoded copy of her message was on its way, recorded in station logs as an ordinary request for product information.

"Now it's your turn," she told her commband as she removed it and powered it down. For all intents and purposes, there was no way to physically connect it to another device. Why would there be? Ordinary updates were automatically received over the station's comms system. It didn't even connect to the galactic network. However, Ava's plans required a little something more than standard functionality, which meant an upgrade was in order.

So, she rummaged in her travel case until she found the tools she wanted, then gingerly connected a small storage device to her commband. The alert light flashed through its normal colors of green, orange, and red, then began flashing blue.

Satisfied that the software installation had begun, Ava hurried through a hot shower, then returned to reverse the process, removing the storage device and replacing the screws.

"Not bad," she complimented herself as she closed the wall panel. "Better than Poilys II. Never did find that last screw after I knocked them all onto the floor."

Tossing the now-empty storage device into her travel case along with her tools, she paused to stretch and was surprised to notice a green light blinking on her commband. Picking it up, she rubbed the screen with her thumb while she scolded her heart for skipping a beat. Just because the green alert was reserved for benign communications that didn't mean this was a personal message. It was probably a general update, a recounting of progress on pivotlift repairs, that sort of thing.

At some point during her deliberations, Ava must've begun to pace, for she abruptly halted in front of her bed. Taking a seat, she shook her head to clear it. She could sooner expect the captain to show up in his dress uniform to take her to breakfast tomorrow morning than she could to receive a message from Jean when she'd only just seen him.

Resolutely, she lay back on her bed and hit the play button. A child's sweet voice filled the silence, the last thing Ava expected.

"Hi, this is Solène. Daddy says you might not be able to sleep tonight. I don't like not sleeping, it makes me tired." Ava shifted into a more comfortable position, her muscles relaxing further as she smiled at the simple logic. "This helps me, sometimes. I hope it helps you, Miss Terina. Night."

The message ended and a voice Ava didn't recognize began softly singing. She caught a word here and there, enough to identify the language as Orpan, Jean's native tongue. The lullaby conjured up images of Jean holding baby Solène and singing to her.

Something about that made her feel suddenly, achingly alone. The darkness loomed up around her, the sheer emptiness of it at once mocking and menacing. Curling up into a ball, she closed her eyes and tried to remember the last two thousand days…to picture the next. She wouldn't complain about the past—at least she'd had her father for company.

She still had Phylis, her personal assistant and occasional confidant. Now, though, she felt a bone-deep longing for something more. Deeper, consuming even.

The thought made her frown. There were times when she feared her present responsibilities were going to consume her whole. Was it even possible that she might find the strength and energy for another, equally demanding endeavor? Or was she only wishing? And, if so, for what, exactly?

She knew plenty of men, but none of them appealed to her as someone she cared to share her life with, day in and day out, let alone as the father of her children. Her thoughts ground to a halt as a familiar face came to mind.

Rolling onto her stomach, she put her pillow over her head and squeezed her eyes shut. She couldn't fall in love with Jean again. Her heart wouldn't be able to take it when he walked her to her shuttle and slammed the door between them.

Perhaps she should say 'if' instead of 'when.' As her father often reminded her, it was foolish to presume to know another's mind. That bit of wisdom had saved her on many occasions, prompting her to plan not just for cooperation or resistance but both. Having a Plan B and even a Plan C could flip even a failed business deal on its head.

She kept turning the question this way and that, like a jeweler inspecting a precious stone under the light before making a cut, until her mind succumbed to the peaceful music that she'd allowed to continue playing.

The recording must've run out at some point during her night, because her alarm was the only thing she heard when she woke for her shift. She still had more questions about her future than answers, but she found that oddly exhilarating. After all, where there was indecision, there must be options. It had been far too long since the most exciting decisions in her personal life were those of choosing what to eat and what to wear.

Entering the cafeteria in her newly synthesized plyfiber uniform, Ava helped herself to about half of what she wanted to eat and sat next to one of the girls she recognized from the night before. Omitting the part of her evening where she'd interfered in the life of an old flame and risked her mission on the secret-keeping skills of a child, she skipped straight to an account of what happened at dessert.

"Are all the restaurants that expensive?" she half-asked, half-complained as she reached for her glass of juice.

"The synth places aren't so bad," shrugged the other woman, wiping her mouth on her napkin.

"Synth? I can get that here, and for cheaper." Ava pouted. "Coming here, to a new station, I was set on trying some fancy places."

"Yeah, well, you'd need a captain's salary for that these days. I mean, we grow most of our own fruit and veg, so that helps, but the specialty stuff the restaurants order? They're paying like it's premium and lucky to get passable."

"Wow." Ava chewed a bite of bread and swallowed. "You know a lot!"

"We're not supposed to know much about stuff, but when you work in Command you can't help it. You kinda know everything."

Widening her eyes in feigned surprise, Ava leaned closer. "Like what?"

"Like prices started going up ten standard cycles ago, same time as the supply trouble. Spoiled food. Half-packed containers. Mislabeled shipments. Junk like that." Shrugging, she got to her feet. "C'mon. No way do you want to be late on your first day."

It wasn't until Ava rose to follow her new friend that she spotted the woman from the shuttle—the security officer—seated in a far corner, apparently minding her own business. Except that the last time Ava had seen her, she'd been waiting to enter a pivotlift. And, though a roll was in several small pieces on her plate, it looked like none of it had actually been eaten.

Tucking the information away for later, Ava hurried to catch up. It didn't take much prompting to hear more of what everyone said last night. Captain Donovan was either an excellent officer cursed with a rotten crew or a terrible person who'd alienated most of the station purely on his own merits. She wanted to believe the first scenario, because it was difficult to accept that a villain had reached the rank of captain on one of her stations; yet she couldn't, in good conscience, discount the second. No, she couldn't be sure until she'd met him herself and seen him in action.

"Same layout as everywhere else." Her friend and now guide pointed at the stations around the room. "Sensors, station-keeping thrusters, comms, Captain's office, XO's desk, weapons platform controls, the usual."

"What're those empty desks for?" Ava pointed, playing the neophyte.

"Those? Emergency access for department heads. Hospitality, maintenance, docks, security, you name it. Something goes colossally wrong, and they get up here by hook or by crook." With that and a nod, she left Ava to report to her own station.

"Yeoman Massuk." A man roughly twice her age beckoned to her. "Let's get you logged in."

Ava obeyed quickly, taking the seat he indicated and entering her codes.

"Looks alright." He directed her to open a number of programs, then nodded. "You're ready to go. Just remember to change your codes before the end of day."

"Change them?" Ava pretended to be confused. "But they work."

"Sure, they work. But it's company policy." He rubbed a hand over his head, mussing what was left of his ash-gray hair. "New posting, new codes."

She knew from his elevated eyebrows that this was all the explanation she was going to get, so she nodded quickly. "New codes, yessir." Turning back to her monitor, she watched him from the corner of one eye as she made the change and got to work.

It wasn't long before her supervisor became engrossed with an unscheduled merchant ship, which gave her the chance she'd been watching for. Activating the program she'd installed on her commband the night before, Ava hastily minimized it on her monitor and blew out a breath. In just a few minutes, the commband would be updated to give her access to anywhere on the station.

She could've designed it differently, had it trigger as soon as she installed it on the commband, but that was far too dangerous. Anyone who got ahold of the program could add it to a device and walk around Montgomery Galactic structures as if they owned them. This way, all the pieces were technically separated. And, even if someone got ahold of both the program and the codes, they'd still need a command-level station.

"You." A harsh voice sliced through the steady hum of conversation, severing it. "With the hair."

Ava froze. This was it. She'd finally gotten caught. It was already too late to turn toward the voice as if from natural curiosity. Her hesitation was as good as a confession that she was up to something.

"Yeoman! Look at me when I'm talking to you!"

She whipped around to face…*the captain?* Captain David Donovan stood in the middle of the floor, staring down his nose at her.

"Your hair is a disruption, Yeoman." He jerked his chin toward the door. "Go pick a color."

"My hair?" Stunned, she found herself reaching for the end of her braid. Was he kidding? "It's… I'm in mourning."

"I don't care." He advanced a step. "Get out and don't come back until you look presentable. Oh, and I'd be quick about it if I were you. I'll be docking your pay, starting," he lifted his commband, "now."

Ava's own commband vibrated, alerting her that the upgrade process was completed. Hastily, and without taking her eyes off Donovan, she ended all the programs currently open at her station and got to her feet.

"Begging your pardon, sir." Ava put her hands behind her back as she faced him. "My hairstyle reflects the fact that I'm in mourning. Which makes your order a direct violation of Regulation 1219 paragraph H, which guarantees Montgomery employees the right to engage in their cultural practices unless or until their own safety or the safety of others is compromised by said practice." When he snorted, she clenched her fists to keep from 'promoting' him to guest on the spot. "That includes mourning rituals, sir."

"I don't care what it includes," he retorted. "I won't have anyone in my command center looking like…" Words clearly failed him, because he ended lamely, "Like *that.*" He struck a haughty pose, and the overhead light glistened off tiny beads of sweat on his forehead.

"Captain." Jean spoke from where he sat at his desk, watching. He was afraid to stand up. If he started moving, he wasn't sure he'd be able to stop himself until he'd put his fist through Donovan's bigoted face. "According to the regulation just quoted, she cannot be forced to abandon this ritual or punished for observing it. Any attempts to do so would naturally be reported to corporate." Donovan's complexion began edging toward purple and Jean jumped ahead before any more hateful words could explode out of him. "She can, however, be assigned duties outside of the command center. If it pleases the captain." He tacked the last on at the end more for his own amusement than anything else.

Donovan expelled his breath in yet another snort. "It pleases the captain very much," he mocked. Waving at Jean, he ordered, "See to it." And stalked into his office.

Jean took a deep breath of his own, then motioned for Ava to join him at his desk. "You know your regs, Yeoman." As she approached, he pulled up the duty roster. "Let's take a look at your skills." His request brought her around the desk to stand at his side and soon as she was close enough, he lowered his voice to ask, "Are they listed accurately?"

"Yes, sir." Aware of their audience, for the drama had captured the attention of everyone on the floor, she added more quietly, "I was going to go exploring after I finished my shift, but this is even better."

"Hmm." Jean wisely refrained from remarking further than that. Scrolling down through the list of low-priority assignments, he paused and tapped one, enlarging the text for her. "Could you do this job?"

"It's a minor repair." She caught herself before she could shrug. Wouldn't do to seem too familiar with the XO on her first day. "Yes, sir, I can do that."

"Right." He updated the assignment with her name. "When you've finished this job, check your commband for the next one."

"Understood. Thank you, sir." The words, spoken for the benefit of all the listening ears, felt weird coming out of her mouth. So stiff, so formal. Judging by the faint crease in Jean's forehead, he didn't like it, either. Her hand was reaching out to smooth the lines from his forehead when something moved on the wall monitor behind Jean's chair. Captain Donovan's reflection, watching them closely.

Jean reflexively returned the crisp salute she gave him, then blinked. For an instant, when his hand fell to his thigh, he half expected to feel the slick, cool coating of battle armor beneath his fingertips. Except, he wasn't in the military anymore. He certainly wasn't in college. In fact, he didn't feel like he was much of anywhere at the moment.

His past and present had never overlapped to this extent before. Meanwhile, the future he'd been edging up on, day by day, seemed strangely shapeless and dark. Why?

Did it have anything to do with the sinking feeling in the pit of his stomach as he watched her walk away?

Chapter 6

Over the next couple of days, Ava completed menial tasks that took her from one end of the station to the other. In keeping with her cover story as a Derlite in mourning, she said little. To further the ends of her investigation, she listened a lot. Strange how a utility belt and drab uniform made her more or less invisible.

Everything she heard pointed to odd goings on, but the theories ranged as wildly in shape and color as the stars outside. One senior steward confided to a maid that the missing supplies were being stolen by fairies that lived in the space between the stars. A group of dockworkers loudly asserted that Montgomery Galactic was just too cheap to get them quality spare parts. Add to that a security guard, who all but shrieked aloud when she startled him by coming out of an access tube, then warned her sharply that bad things happened in the station's more remote areas.

Ava huffed in irritation as she plunked her utility belt back into the storage locker at the end of her shift. She was slowly building a picture of what was going on and she didn't like it.

A cursory comparison of the bills of lading against the reported inventory on station revealed that they were short on everything here, from food to soap. Ava had quietly broken into the dock's storage area the night before and confirmed via scans that the spare parts were decidedly inferior to the orders placed and paid for by Montgomery. Granted, the parts *could* be synthesized, like ninety percent of everything else aboard the station, but heavy jobs like that ran the risk of burning out the synth system and then where would they be? Generally speaking, it was safer and more sensible to transport such things.

As for the food situation—per Phyl's reports, spot-checks confirmed that the food supplies were being meticulously prepared, packed, and shipped. Poor Phyl. She was running the poor woman ragged with all her requests for information. A yawn escaped her, and she chuckled. It wasn't doing much good for her own sleeping habits, come to think of it. Phyl was nothing if not thorough, which often meant her answers amounted to pages of information, all of which Ava had to read and understand.

Ava looked up, startled, when someone cleared their throat. Her heart skipped a beat, then wobbled a bit before regaining its rhythm. Due to the fright, naturally, she told herself.

"Haven't seen you in a few days. Thought I'd come see how things are going." Jean kept his distance as he discreetly looked her over. The staff was pretty evenly split between males and females, but Ava was the only woman aboard whose figure did as much for her uniform as it had for any gown or athletic costume he'd ever seen her wear.

"Hey." Relaxing, Ava leaned back against the lockers, unwittingly inviting him to come closer. "It's going." She flashed a small smile at him. "Some problems are easily solved. Others, well," she tried not to sigh, "take more time."

"Yeah, I've noticed that myself." He moved to stand beside her, resting his shoulder on the wall by the lockers. "Getting good reports on your work." Looking closer, he spotted bandages on her hand and face. "What's this?"

Her heart did a triple flip when he took her chin in his hand, angling her head so that he could see her cheek better. "Nothing." Incredibly, her voice didn't shake. Feeling braver, she lifted her chin free and shrugged. "I was flushing a hydraulic line on the docks and caught a little spray. Could've been a lot worse."

A lot worse. Jean's chest tightened unbearably at the thought of her getting seriously injured. It shouldn't happen, not if safety protocols were followed; but he'd never heard anyone use the word 'accident' to describe something they planned on having happen. And, judging by the faint circles under her eyes, she hadn't been sleeping well, which only increased the odds of things going wrong.

Ava's breath stuttered when his hand lifted to trail one fingertip along her cheekbone. She knew, in her head, that whatever they might have had was long gone. Now she just had to convince her heart. The same heart that kept prodding her to start her own future—with Jean.

"You're tired." He didn't know why that surprised him. She'd been working hard since leaving Command, actual physical labor.

"Oh." The moment lost any and all of its romantic blush and she stepped away from him. "Sure, I guess." So that was why he'd been staring at her. Counting the lines around her eyes, probably. *Men.*

Caught flat-footed, Jean stared after her for an instant as she strode away, then hurried to follow. "I imagine you're hungry, too."

"And?" She hit the call button for the pivotlift with more force than was strictly necessary. Frustration simmered in her veins, fueled as much by the mysterious termination of their relationship three thousand days ago as by the rejection of mere moments ago.

"We'd like you to join us." He reared back when she turned to face him again. Their faces were even closer than before, and he had to fight to maintain his thought process. "Solène sent me particularly to find you." And just as suddenly as she'd walked away a moment ago, she was all smiles, warming him from head to toe like a burst of sunshine on a cold day.

"She did?" The irritation drained away, leaving her with only a tired ache and a firm resolve to go. "That's quite a young lady you've got there."

"She is." Jean tore his gaze away from her shining eyes to check the corridor. He needed to remember he was just one more officer in her empire, a speck of stardust in her universe. A snap of her fingers and he could be replaced with someone…

"I'd love to." Ava moved to enter the pivotlift and hesitated as to what destination to enter. "I should probably clean up first, though." She'd spent four hours doing maintenance on the gardening drones, which were stored far too close to the central water reclamation unit for her delicate sense of smell. No doubt the odor lingered on her. Her gaze flicked to Jean, who gave no indication that he noticed.

"Perfect." He joined her and pressed the button for her level. "I'll wait for you."

"In my quarters?" She frowned. Though she had every reason to trust him with her life and her reputation, which she did, it still wasn't strictly proper for him to be alone in her quarters while she showered and dressed.

"Unless that's a problem?" Puzzled, he studied her face for some clue as to her dissatisfaction with the idea. He could hardly wait out in the corridor, to be noticed and remarked upon by every passing person.

Belatedly, it clicked in his head. "I'm a fool," he muttered under his breath. Apparently, she heard him anyway, if the upward quirk of her lips was any indication. "I sometimes forget that I no longer live in the barracks." Privacy was at a premium in barracks, with lavatories and some sleeping areas pretty much the only off-limits space.

She shot him an amused smile. "Jean, you don't have to worry. I never doubted your intentions for an instant." The answering look that he gave her both confirmed her beliefs and sent prickles raising along her arms. No, he would never do anything untoward. However, if she was impossibly lucky, he just might kiss her again. Someday.

"Thank you. That means a lot to me." Clasping his hands behind his back to keep from reaching for hers, he suggested, "I'll meet you there. I can help Solène set the table."

"Mhmm. Or..." She squinted as though to see her thoughts more clearly. With her expanded access to the station systems, it would be child's play to open and read the security files. Except that she was one child who was eagerly looking forward to an early bedtime. Maybe she knew a shortcut? "I've learned a lot, and I've heard a lot, some of which I'd like to discuss with the station security chief. I'd rather do it as Terina, but I doubt he'd answer her questions."

"He'd answer my questions." As much as he would rather allow himself to be distracted by her protracted nearness, Jean forced himself to focus. Right then, he'd have offered anything to speed up her investigation and get her safely back behind her glass wall of power. "What do you need to know?"

Ava rubbed the back of her neck, which was stiff from staying in one position too long while she worked on the drones. "Tell him you've heard rumors that 'bad things' happen around the edges of the station. I," she blew out a breath, "have no idea what that's supposed to mean. It might be ghosts stalking the corridors, or maybe malevolent sky fairies."

"Taylor's a good man, a good officer." Jean did his best to keep a straight face. He could make an argument for the existence of plant fairies, maybe. Water fairies, even. But sky fairies? What rot. "He'll tell me what he can." Suddenly, he frowned as a thought occurred to him. "Has someone tried to hurt you?"

Reminding herself that the concern in his voice was nine-tenths professional, Ava shook her head. "No, nothing like that. It's something a guard told me yesterday when I surprised him. He was so rattled I'm not sure he even realized what he'd said."

"That's not good." Jean folded his arms across his chest and scowled at the wall. "Which officer was it? And where were you?" He nodded when she told him, then resumed scowling. "Taylor usually lets me know when something new happens, and he hasn't mentioned anything so…" His voice trailed off as he grappled for the right words.

"So vague and creepy?" she supplied, lips twitching. "It's possible nobody's told him. I mean, how would you like to have to justify writing 'bad things happen' in a report?"

"No, thank you." Jean couldn't help chuckling.

"Still, Taylor's hands-on. Routinely accompanies his officers on their rounds, takes his turn manning the overnight monitors. The more I think about it, the more I'm convinced he'll know something about it."

"I hope you're right." Ava lifted her chin and pushed her shoulders down until something popped. "Oh, that's much better." Finding Jean looking at her, she blushed quite unaccountably. "What?"

"Nothing. I, um." He ignored the vibration of his commband. "I'll track Taylor down and have a chat with him before supper." His heart shot to his throat when she reached out to put her hand on his chest.

"Thank you." Her mind spun like the time her ship had gotten sucked into a space swirl, only nicer. Good grief, what was she doing? More importantly, why did it feel like her hand was fastened in place? Unable or unwilling to try explaining it, she dropped her gaze instead.

Jean inhaled shakily and told himself to step back. His legs remained frozen in place. The silence was slowly becoming electric when the pivotlift slowed to a stop and the doors opened. It felt like she ripped his heart out through his uniform when she lowered her hand at last and stepped into the corridor.

The doors closed behind her, and he found himself gasping for air. He'd known he still cared about Ava. He just hadn't realized how much. It was several seconds before he recognized he hadn't entered a destination, and so was just standing in one place.

After he'd punched the right buttons, he scrubbed a hand through his hair, frowning with irritation when he felt how long it was getting. He didn't have time to get a haircut, not while Ava was on the station. She'd practically ordered him to stand down as far as her security was concerned, but the thought of sitting in a chair listening to a barber spouting drivel while she was out poking her pretty little nose into station affairs—and eventually getting into trouble—was enough to make his stomach ache.

No, he needed to be available, ready to move and move quickly if the occasion called for it. He…he needed to focus. Her safety had factored into every assignment he'd given her, taking pains to keep her in range of a camera at all times. So, what business did he have almost kissing her?

Jean scowled at his reflection in the highly polished glinsen rock that lined the pivotlift interior. What would it take for him to remember he wasn't good enough for her? Another, this-time-successful attempt on her life?

All he'd wanted was a night off. An opportunity to relax, to see what they were like when it was just them. She'd been breathtaking in a simple cream-colored tunic, flame-orange belt, and black slacks. Twice she'd commented on how odd it was to not be able to see her security team, though each time she'd slipped easily back into conversation with him.

Oh, how they'd talked, discussing everything and nothing until the waiter despaired of them ever leaving and began working the other tables. And then, when they did leave, Jean saw her personal hovercraft waiting for them.

Somehow, he'd persuaded her that it would spoil the whole evening if they took her vehicle and flagged a paid vehicle down instead. A decade or more old, the conveyance was dented on the outside and smelled overpoweringly of scented cleanser on the inside.

He'd laughed off her complaints, assuring her, 'It has character!' Wrapped an arm around her as though it was all the protection she needed. And perhaps he'd actually believed that—right up until the explosive detonated.

Clenching his fists, Jean would've slammed both of them into the wall if he hadn't felt the pivotlift begin to slow. As it was, the group of chattering, cheerful station personnel waiting to use the pivotlift went silent when they saw him, then stepped aside to let him pass.

Retreating to an alcove to avoid scaring the guests, Jean began clawing his way out of the memory and back into the present.

A soft rippling sound like the tinkling of thousands of tiny bells drew his attention to the moss that lined the upper half of the alcove. Native to Moisme, the moss clung tenaciously to the rock imported from the same planet, purifying the station's air and water supply at a phenomenal rate.

In the center of the wall, a reservoir of clean water waited for thirsty people, and Jean took advantage of it now, filling and draining the cup three times before returning it to its sterilization chamber.

"You okay?" Taylor asked from where he leaned at entrance of the alcove.

Jean barked a laugh. "Close enough."

"Good. I was just coming to find you."

"Oh? That's quite a coincidence." Jean smiled tightly, knowing that neither of them put much stock in the idea of coincidences. "I was on my way to talk with you."

Taylor grunted, then shoved off from the wall. "My office or yours?"

"Yours, by all means." Jean fell in beside the security chief as they walked the few hundred yards to his office.

Some complained that the main security office should be on the same floor as the higher-end shops or situated just beneath the station staff residential floors, but Jean agreed with Taylor that the more central location allowed greater response flexibility.

"Alright." Taylor closed the door behind them and gestured for Jean to sit. "I'm guessing this isn't about what I just sent you."

Surprised, Jean glanced at the blinking orange light on his commband. "How did I miss…" He stopped abruptly as he realized it must've come in while he was talking with Ava. Clearing his throat, he met Taylor's eyes. "Guess you'll just have to tell me in person."

Taylor quirked an eyebrow, then shrugged. "You first."

"Alright." Jean shrugged. "This won't take long. I'm just here to follow up on some disturbing rumors about station security." The intensity of Taylor's answering glare was enough to freeze a woolly praegra, and he instantly recognized his mistake. Smoothly he added, "Naturally, I came to you straight-away." Nobody liked to be interfered with, and a touch of deference was just what the diplomat ordered.

Taylor relaxed, marginally. "Rumors are just hot air. I could clear that up with a desk fan."

"You're not wrong." Jean hesitated. "It's a little more complicated when the hot air comes from a security officer, though."

They went back and forth a few times before Taylor relented and opened his files to review them for overlooked details.

"It's not much." Taylor leaned back, steepling his fingers as he studied the officer logs displayed in the air between them.

Jean, reading the same logs thanks to the alternate view function, had to agree. But what was he supposed to tell Ava? He doubted she'd be satisfied with 'inconclusive.' Speaking of which, nearly twenty minutes had elapsed since they'd parted at the pivotlift. She'd be showing up at his quarters soon, and he'd forgotten to let Solène know she'd agreed to come for supper.

"Which isn't the same as not being there." Taylor drummed his fingers on the desk, then slapped his hand down. "Only one thing for it. I'll have to talk with Briggs directly. Go on a few rounds with him, try to get a handle on what he's picked up on but can't fit into a report."

Jean nodded. "Thanks. I appreciate you taking the time to follow-up."

"Forget it." Taylor shut the display down and looked at him directly. "I know I got all frosty when you first sat down. I don't like finding out there's something going on without my knowing about it. Particularly," he grumped, "when it involves someone else telling me about one of my people."

"Perfectly understandable." Jean made a show of starting to rise, then caught himself as if remembering something. "Oh. What was it you wanted to talk to me about?"

"This." Taylor opened the display again and pressed a button on his desk.

Jean jerked violently as the empty space before him was abruptly filled with three rows of mighty teeth and a long, thick tail.

How had it gotten in? No, not in—*on*. How had it gotten on the *Beyond*?

Chapter 7

Sweat beaded on Jean's brow as certain details began filtering through the shock. He wasn't dead. He hadn't been bitten or stomped. Across the room, Taylor wasn't screaming or trying to run away. And, the creature was see-through.

"A projection." The ache in his hands eased remarkably when he forced himself to release the chair arms.

"Hmm?" Taylor's eyes shifted to focus on him for an instant, then returned to examining the image. "Yeah. I had to call in a few favors to get this much." Reaching down, he tapped a command.

Jean almost jumped out of his chair when the image abruptly grew larger.

"I've gone bigger," Taylor explained, "but the resolution is so bad it's useless. You can't even tell what the thing is."

Bigger? Jean worked his tongue in his mouth, trying to get the saliva flowing again. Not being able to tell what it was sounded fine to him.

"It's a…"

"Tokarian Terrabeast." Jean cut him off and was confused at how neutral his own voice sounded. Catching sight of the corner of a house in the image, he continued, "A small one, not more than two years old. At a guess, it's a thousand pounds and measures twelve feet from tip to tail." Getting to his feet, he stood a moment to make sure his legs weren't going to fold under him, then went to the water dispenser.

Meanwhile, Taylor's gaze flicked from Jean's face to the beast, confirming that none of those details were present on the display. He muttered to himself in surprise when he located the correct section in the file and read it.

"How did you know all of that?" he demanded. "First I ever heard of them was two weeks ago, in a news piece from a dustbowl." 'Dustbowls' were planets that had so little water of their own that they had to import it. "I dug for over an hour to get anything useful."

Small settlements blossomed and died on such planets, lasting only so long as whatever they were mining held out. The remotest of them were occasionally claimed by slavers and smugglers, and decent folks had to be careful to steer clear or risk falling prey to their heinous laws.

Jean sloshed the last gulp of water around in his mouth, savoring it, then swallowed. Putting the glass on a half-full shelf, he slid the door closed and watched the sterilizing light come on.

Meeting Taylor's eyes at last, Jean explained, "I lost a lot of good people on Tokar."

"*You* lost?" Taylor looked more confused than before. "What was the Orpan military doing on Tokar?"

"The dirty work." Jean had spent over a year on Tokar, scaling boulders, slipping through stinking slimepits, and watching people die until their masters said 'a sufficient quantity of land has been rendered free of predators.' "I don't know exactly who for. Never cared." Sensing that Taylor still wasn't following him, he retook his seat with a sigh. "One of the disadvantages of having the largest military in Orpan history was the cost of upkeep. So, on occasion, they hired some of us out to make ends meet."

Taylor's mouth dropped open slightly when understanding hit him. Closing it with a snap, he powered down the display. Leaning forward, he rested both forearms on his desk. "You're just the man I've needed to talk to."

Jean listened in growing disbelief as Taylor outlined a pattern in the news articles he'd been reading. "Have you told anyone else about this?"

Taylor snorted emphatically. "I clipped it all together and sent it to every galactic force I could think of—including Tilknan's Rovers and the Pikmut Force. Even found some group that's pushing for a law to prevent creatures from being taken off their homeworlds."

"Nobody believes you." Brow furrowing, Jean considered. "If identical 'murder' sprees on five planets doesn't rate their attention, what does?"

"That's where the terrabeast comes in." Taylor's finger hovered over the button that would power up the display, but he changed his mind. "The one I showed you. That image was taken less than a minute before they killed it. It's all there in the article, how somebody suggested the claws reminded them of the murder weapon, the tests, and voila. A whole bunch of murders got closed."

Jean's stomach heaved. "Terrabeasts, loose in a neighborhood? How?" His mind raced ahead, trying to figure out why they hadn't decimated the local population in each case. Caution, born of an unfamiliar environment? Insane good luck, in the form of fatal accidents before the creatures could get a proper foothold? Once, or even twice, he might believe that 'things just worked out.' But not five times.

"Actually, the how is pretty obvious." Taylor scowled. "Xenocreature smugglers."

Jean's face hardened. "That opens up a whole different line of discussion." And introduced the possibility that the ring was somehow responsible, both for allowing the creatures to escape and for either killing or recapturing them in time to prevent further fatalities. "How stupid do you have to be to let a terrabeast get away?" It was such a ludicrous thought that he could barely form and speak the words.

"Here's my theory." Taylor adjusted the display to show all of the news stories at once. "There are a lot of moving parts in a xenocreature smuggling ring. You've got to get the animal, sure, but then you have to transport it, feed it, and most importantly you have to offload it."

"So?" Jean quirked an eyebrow at him.

"So most of the people in smuggling rings are there because they can't keep any other kind of a job. Which means that the cages are most likely being left in the tender care of someone I wouldn't trust to remember to wash their own face in the morning."

Jean nodded slowly, then voiced the question that had been forming in the back of his mind since the initial shock of the terrabeast projection. "Why did you want to talk to me about this? You were already planning to before I told you about my time on Tokar." He believed there was a good reason—Taylor wasn't the type to waste time—he just wasn't sure he wanted to hear it.

Taylor's entire body stilled. "I think they've been coming through here." Taylor switched files and turned the display on again, this time with an image of the galaxy. Tokar and exactly five other planets were marked with scarlet rings.

Startled, Jean looked down at his vibrating commband. "Excuse me. This is probably Solène, wondering where I am."

Rising, he stepped out into the hall and answered. After apologizing to his daughter and promising that he would be there in a few minutes, Jean took a deep breath and went back into Taylor's office.

"Have you told Donovan any of this?" As he'd expected, Taylor shook his head. "Good. Send me a meeting request. I want to see every scrap of proof you have that this is true. If I'm convinced, I'll make sure someone listens." He was turning to leave when Taylor cleared his throat.

"I was hoping you could help." Dousing the projection again, he stared at Jean intently. "I'd stake my career on this, Jean."

"It won't come to that." Jean offered a small smile before hurrying away. There wasn't a doubt in his mind that Ava would bring her considerable power crashing down on a smuggling ring criminally stupid enough to use a Montgomery concern in their dealings. Or that he would enjoy watching her do it.

Still distracted, Jean walked through his door and stopped abruptly. Stared in horror at the checkered cloth draped over the table. All three place settings included multiple utensils, white plates with green vines curling around their edges, and ornate glasses. Venturing a step closer, he touched one of the glasses, making it ring. *Real glass?*

He backed away hastily. These weren't his quarters. Simple as that. Something had gone wrong with his commband and, not paying close enough attention to where he was going, he'd walked in on someone else's supper.

As he retreated, he experienced a slight pang of jealousy at the pretty picture the table made. Somebody was awfully lucky to come home to this. Growing up, he'd eaten most of his meals at the military academy with a knife and fork. Plates and glasses were made of the same sturdy metal as the utensils, easy to maintain.

Curiosity overcame him and he risked glancing into the living area. Doubt rippled through him and he stood there, welded to the spot.

Solène stood in the middle of the room, but not *his* Solène. This was a young woman, a diplomat's daughter or perhaps even a princess. Her straight, black hair had been expertly swept up and pinned into a knot at the nape of her neck, just loose enough around her face to soften the effect. The rich sapphire blue gown had wrist-length sleeves while the skirt hovered just over the tips of her bare toes.

"Welcome home, Daddy."

Jean's stomach slowly unclenched. This was no aloof stranger. This *was* Solène—and a hint of what she'd grow into. Meteorites, but she was going to have to beat the boys off with a stick! He might even have to help.

"Thank you, mareyth." He held out his arms and she rushed into them, her head nestling against his chest without a hint of concern for her carefully arranged hair. Grateful that she was still her carefree self, he bent to press a kiss to the top of her head. "You look absolutely beautiful."

Giggling, she leaned way back to look up at him. "It was Miss Terina's idea."

Ava? He looked around the room for her. The sight of her standing in the doorway to Solène's bedroom took his breath away. She'd resumed her naturally pale blond hair, and wore it in the same style as Solène's. Her pastel orange dress brought out the flecks of color in her eyes while its lines flattered her in all the right ways.

"Welcome home, Jak." *Oops, she'd meant to say Jean!* Nevertheless, Ava dropped a low curtsy, something Solène had forgotten to do, then nearly fell over when she saw the longing in his eyes. Her heart began pounding so hard it pulsed in her head and she was barely able to straighten up.

"Come on, Daddy." Solène tugged on his arm. "You dress up, too."

"Hmm?" Jean was at once grateful for the distraction and reluctant to stop staring. "Dress up?"

"Yes!" Releasing him, she clapped her hands. "Miss Terina let me pick out what you're going to wear, but I can't tell you what it is."

Chuckling, he spun her in a circle, the last of his meeting with Taylor sliding off his shoulders and into a lockbox he would reopen later. "If I don't know what it is, how am I supposed to put it on?"

"Silly, it's in your room!" The instant her feet were back on the ground, Solène began pushing him in that direction.

"I'm going, I'm going." He made eye contact with Ava again and nearly changed his mind. The soft, white curve of her neck was begging to be kissed. Fortunately, Solène didn't relent until he was inside his room.

"Hurry, Daddy. Supper's almost ready!" And with that, she slammed the door in his face.

Stripping off his jacket and stepping out of his boots, Jean headed for his washroom, where he plugged the sink and stuck his head under a jet of ice-cold water. He needed to get a grip. Even if his boss was willing to kiss him, he shouldn't be wanting to kiss a subordinate.

Except, his reflection reminded him when he

came up for air, *she's not actually your subordinate.*

Taking a deep breath, he plunged his head into the water again, determined to stay there until he was thinking straight.

Meanwhile, Ava and Solène giggled and chatted as they synthesized the food they'd discussed earlier. Ava hadn't had this much fun in a long time. She laughed so hard that she cried when Solène snuck a taste of the puce-colored sauce as she carried it to the table.

"That's yucky!" Solène announced after her mouth had been rinsed.

"By itself, yes." Crouching down so she was the same height, Ava lightly tapped Solène on the nose. "But a little bit on the fish will taste delicious."

"Maybe." Solène frowned, uncertain after such a bad experience. "What do you think, Daddy?"

What did he think? Jean thought he'd died and gone to heaven. Coming into the kitchen to find his girls huddled in conference… Whoa, back up! *His girls?!* He had no right to think of Ava that way. Even if she was blushing adorably.

Ava swallowed hard at the way his chocolate brown suit coat strained around the shoulders when he offered her his hand to help her rise. Did her best to ignore the heat that swirled through her veins at his touch, right through the heavy gloves she wore to protect herself from the hot dishes. Somehow, she couldn't think of him as Jean when his thumbs were gently stroking the insides of her wrists. The royal blue edging on his lapels made his eyes an even deeper blue than she remembered.

"*Daddy!*" Solène erupted in laughter. "Your feet!"

"What? Is something wrong?" Delighted by

her response, Jean wriggled his toes. "I thought the order of the day was fancy dress and bare feet."

Ava suddenly looked down at her own feet. "Oh, my." Pressing gloved hands to her rapidly warming cheeks, she realized, "We were so distracted with trying new hairstyles that we forgot all about shoes!"

"It's okay, Miss Terina," Solène piped up. "We go barefoot lots of the time."

Jean ran his fingers through his hair, standing it on end, then shrugged. "She's right."

Ava felt as though the temperature had just gone up a few degrees and had to resist the urge to reach out and smooth the hair he'd just rumpled.

"You have to pull out our chairs, Daddy," Solène innocently asserted, breaking the silence. "That's what gentlemans does."

Ava tore her gaze from Jak's face to smile at the little girl's mispronunciation. She wanted nothing so much as to kiss him right then but wasn't at all ready to explain such an occurrence to his wide-eyed daughter.

"It is?" Jean's attempt at a steadying breath was thwarted by the subtle scent of Ava's perfume. Exerting superhuman strength, he managed to turn away and smile at Solène. "I mean, yes. You are absolutely correct."

He seated Solène first and helped her arrange her napkin, which was made of the same fabric as the thick tablecloth. Eyeing the bowls of soup and recalling past meals with his daughter, he could only hope the fabric was fantastically absorbent. Despite his best efforts, Solène remained an impatient eater, capable of spilling nearly anything she intended to eat.

Jean's stomach tightened as he moved to assist

Ava with her chair. Manfully, he resisted the urge to take advantage of his proximity and took his seat instead.

Together, Ava and Jean helped Solène with which utensil to use for which dish. In return, she kept things from getting too serious.

"Somebody must've been awfully bored," she announced in disgust when they insisted she use yet another fork for a different course, "when they made up all of these rules."

Ava's gaze met Jak's and they both collapsed into laughter.

"You know, she's probably right?" Ava dabbed at her eyes with her napkin. "Can you imagine going to all of this trouble for every meal?"

Jean shook his head as he reached for his water glass. "We were glad to get a fork and a knife apiece with our meals in the mess hall."

Surprised, Ava dropped her gaze and pretended to focus on spearing a stubborn vegetable. He'd been reluctant to discuss his time in the military when they'd first met. Perhaps the passage of time had eased his memories somewhat?

"I'm eating, I'm eating." Solène shoved a bite into her mouth.

Puzzled, Ava observed, "Yes, we can see that you're eating."

Solène started to speak around her food, caught herself, and swallowed first. "He's always telling me stories about what they made him eat when he was a boy. Then he says I don't know how lucky I am."

Jean stirred his vegetables briefly, then met Ava's concerned gaze. "I might be making it sound worse than it was. This one," he tipped his head toward Solène, "is practically perfect. Unless she doesn't like what we're eating."

Ava nodded as if she believed him, but her heart went out to the heartsick, orphaned little boy who'd been herded off to a military school.

Jean filled the tines of his fork with the rest of his vegetables, then stuffed them into his mouth and held both hands up at shoulder height. Swallowing before the vegetables were more than half-chewed, he announced, "I win!"

Solène giggled and began gobbling her vegetables so fast that they bulged her cheeks as she chewed.

Ava wasn't sure what was going on, but she dove in anyway, finishing just a hair's breadth after Solène, who threw her hands up in the air.

"You, my dear," Jean grinned at Ava, "have to clear the table."

Relieved that the penalty for finishing last was so mild, Ava saluted him and got started. By the time she'd finished, Jean was slicing a freshly synthesized pie. Solène insisted that they eat dessert in the living room, where she cheerfully plopped herself between Ava and Jean on the couch—and fell asleep between bites.

"Here." Jean handed his and Solène's plates to Ava, then scooped up his little girl, intending to put her to bed. The rustle of her skirts stopped him, and he asked, "Can she sleep in this? I mean, comfortably?" He wasn't worried about the dress. He could drop it in the reclaimer anytime. They lost a little energy in the process of reclaiming and synthesizing, but it saved a lot of water and out here, that was the main thing.

Ava chuckled as she got to her feet. Setting the plates aside, she whisked the pins out of Solène's hair, smoothing it as it fell, and kissing the crown of her head softly. "She can now."

Chapter 8

As Ava stood there, Jean's lips unresponsive against her own, mortification began bubbling in the pit of her stomach. It was like kissing an ice statue. Slowly, she lowered her heels to the floor. "Sorry." Her arms wanted to curl around her waist when she removed her hands from his cheeks, but she refused to let him see how deeply his rejection cut. "Stupid of me."

Clamping her lips closed, Ava took a step back. People who were calm and in control didn't chatter aimlessly, which she was in serious danger of doing. She had to go, to get away before she said anything she couldn't take back—like demanding an explanation for his utter lack of a reaction to her kiss.

Turning to leave, she stiffened when his hand grasped her elbow.

"You can't go like that." Jean frowned when she looked up at him, confusion and pain in her eyes. Releasing her before he lost the battle with himself and pulled her close, where she belonged, he coughed to clear his throat of any words he'd regret saying. *I love you. Forgive me. Stay.* "Dressed like that, I mean." Gesturing vaguely toward his bedroom, he offered, "You can change in there. I need to catch up on my communications, anyway. Oh, and don't forget your hair."

Fury mounted within Ava, warding off the numbness that might have settled in if not for his magnanimous intervention. The world seemed tinged with red as she stalked into his room, hating every rustle and swish of the skirt she'd enjoyed up to that moment, and only concern for Solène kept her from closing the door to his room with a slam worthy of the galaxy's most spoiled brat.

It was easy enough to override his synthesizer with her commband and trade the dress for her uniform, but recoloring her hair was another matter. Not until after she'd singed three fingers was she able to take a deep breath and force her thoughts away from what had just happened.

Ja…Jea…*He* had closed Solène's door and smiled at her as he thanked her for a pleasant evening. And what had she done? She'd lost her infernal mind.

Well, he didn't need to worry that it would happen again. His lips just now had been like…like kissing a cake of ice! Cold, hard, and utterly indifferent.

Which begged the question of how she really felt about his stopping her in time to correct the significant discrepancies in her appearance.

Setting the follicle stimulator aside to cool, Ava sighed. Grateful. A little. How else could she feel? She'd crossed a line in kissing her subordinate, the ultimate gamble in a way. Yes, she should be grateful, and more than a little, that he'd chosen to overlook her inappropriate behavior long enough to protect the investigation.

On the other side of the door, Jean paced the combined length of the living room and kitchen, trying to get his emotions under control as he relived the sweet torture of Ava's lips pressed against his. If she'd waited even another heartbeat to retreat, he would've kissed her back and…and then what? They'd live happily ever after?

A wall loomed up before him and he glared around at all of the walls as he turned to continue stalking around the limited space. It was the first time he'd ever sympathized with the caged terrabeasts he'd seen on Tokar.

He froze mid-step and nearly fell over sideways as old memories and new thoughts rammed into his brain. Fumbling with his commband, he keyed an outside channel and dictated a short message. Sent it, then sank onto the couch. He had to be wrong—he hoped.

That was where Ava found him, staring blankly at the far wall, his face the same shade of light gray as his pillowcases. Whatever she might've planned to say faded from her mind, except... "I wanted to apologize for kissing you. If you decide to file a formal complaint, I won't contest it."

With that and a nod, she strode toward the door, head high. There was no reversing time and taking the kiss back, but it was her experience that the neglected mistakes were generally the ones that grew fangs and claws and chased her through her nightmares.

Time slowed for Jean as he watched her walk away, the length of recently restored black hair swaying with each step. This wasn't the first time such a thing had happened for him.

"Miss Montgomery." He wielded the formality like a shield. "Before you go?" Getting to his feet, Jean clasped his hands behind his back as though at parade rest.

Ava paused, mere inches from escape. "Yes, Commander?" Not knowing what to expect, she didn't turn to face him. Besides, she didn't want him to see the tear sliding down her cheek.

"My meeting with Security Chief Taylor was inconclusive. But he has promised to investigate."

"I see." She wanted to laugh almost as much as she wanted to cry at how ridiculous it was to stand there, discussing business with her back to him. "Very well."

"He also brought something to my attention, something he's already looking into." Jean hesitated, debating how much he wanted to tell her. There wasn't that much to say, just a few educated guesses. "But I'll have more on that later."

"Excellent." Another tear surrendered to gravity, tracing a cold, damp trail down her cheek and neck to where it was absorbed by her shirt collar. She needed to leave, quickly. "Anything else?"

"That's it."

"Very good." Ava pushed herself forward only to hesitate at the last instant. "I brought you something tonight. It's on your bed. Just…be careful, it's only a prototype."

Slack-jawed, Jean watched her back as she vanished. Curiosity compelled him to investigate and there, sitting on the foot of his bed, sat a small black box. A prototype box?

Chuckling ruefully at his attempted humor, Jean reached out to open it. Frowning, he ran his hand around the front and sides of the box only to discover that the surface was smooth. Picking it up to examine it more closely, he had almost concluded that it in fact *was* a prototype box when he heard a muted click and whirring noise.

"Identified: Jean Antoni Kearns," a voice announced politely. "Welcome to Project Security Suit."

He barely had time to register that the surface beneath his right ring finger was glowing when the lid slowly lifted to reveal two circlets held in place by metal clips, the smaller circlet nestled inside the larger. Twisting the clips aside, Jean removed the circlets, then nearly dropped the box when a beam scanned his face and shoulders, only to stop about halfway down his torso.

"Scanning error." The voice was back. "Please place the box on a flat surface two to three feet from your person and stand perfectly still while you are scanned."

"Scanned for what?" He asked the question automatically, then rolled his eyes when the machine began repeating itself word for word. Recognizing that the process couldn't move forward until he complied, he sighed. "Alright, alright, you blasted push-button program." Setting the box back on his bed, he retreated the required distance and held still while the white beam took his measure.

Then the beam vanished, and a display window suddenly popped up. "Scanning complete. Please watch this short, instructional video while your Suit is configured for you. This video will provide you with the information you need in order to…" An image of two circlets appeared while the voice droned on, explaining how to wear them, how to activate them, what to expect from the Suit, and so on. "Thank you for watching this video. Enjoy your Suit, but please remember that this is just a prototype. Should you choose to attempt any activities outside of those explicitly outlined in this training video…"

Jean tuned out the last of the verbal fine print and focused on the box, the lid of which was finally opening. Tilting it, he shook two black circlets onto the bed. Approximately an inch wide, they gleamed even in the artificial light as he picked them up. The smaller one slipped over his hand to rest comfortably on his left wrist. Bending to buckle the larger one around his right ankle, as the video indicated, he remembered that he was still wearing the fancy suit.

The jacket he tossed into the reclaimer, along with the belt and then the collared shirt. Catching sight of himself in the full-length mirror on the back of the bedroom door, he snorted. "One security suit, partial coverage only." Even though he'd seen the slow-motion demonstration on the video, he struggled to imagine the two slender, slightly stretchy pieces that he now wore forming a complete protective suit. On the other hand, this was a Montgomery Galactic prototype. That meant Ava believed in it—right?

Frowning, he looked more closely at the mirror. If this worked, he wanted to see it with his own eyes. "To activate the suit," he mimicked the dry voice of the recording as he reached for the wrist bracelet, "pull here." The suit covered him before he could even begin the admonition that came next. "And hold completely still," he went on a bit weakly, his voice sounding strange as it filtered through the helmet, "for a minimum of one second."

Rapping on the arm of the suit with his gauntleted hand, Jean heard nothing. Running in place produced the same result. "Stealth mode, check."

Overcome with curiosity, he began experimenting with the suit's options, becoming more impressed with each success.

"Whoa!" He bumped his head on the ceiling when he tried out the antigrav unit. "Sensitive." Gingerly, he eased himself back down to the normal grav setting.

Eventually he ran out of things to test without going for a walk outside the station or checking out a weapon from the station armory, so he opened his helmet and tried to catch his breath. His nose twitched, and he stifled a laugh at how strange his room smelled after the oxygen mix provided by the suit.

His commband vibrated and he automatically tried to take the call, only to find his access blocked by the hybrid metafabric of the suit. Grimacing, he clicked his heels together and the suit retracted as quickly as it had covered him.

"Kearns." Thankfully, the call was an easy one, the sort of minor emergency that required verbal authorization of the solution, but nothing else. Reminded of how late it was, he completed a hasty toilette, then set his commband on the charger.

As he sank into his self-healing bed of plant-gel, exhaustion warred with excitement about the suit and frustration at how things had gone with Ava. With some difficulty, he organized his thoughts into mental rooms and closed the doors so that he would be able to sleep. He only had to lock one door that night, the one with Ava's kiss behind it. And despite his best efforts, it escaped the locked door to haunt his dreams.

Ava tried a prototype of her own that night, a gadget that claimed it could promote healing in surface injuries, such as she'd sustained on her hand and face while working. She couldn't tell if they were working or not, but they made her palms itch so badly it distracted her from the fiasco at Jean's and she was eventually able to drift off to sleep.

Her alarm jolted her awake a few hours later and she stumbled to the bathroom, where she rinsed her eyes with water until the feeling of grit beneath her eyelids faded. Dressing for the day, she checked her commband for her assignments and sighed.

"At least you're not stuck at a desk," she reminded herself as she boarded a pivotlift. Too tired to deal with even the simplest menu, she went to the crew cafeteria where the buffet stretched around all four walls, with grudging breaks in its lines to allow for doors. She loaded up her tray with scrambled eggs, bacon, and even indulged in a stack of fragrant pancakes, which she smothered in delectable berry jam. Eaten hot, it was hard to tell it was all synth.

"I don't care," muttered a voice sharply. "I'm putting in for a transfer."

"Okay, okay." Two trays hit the table behind Ava, the sounds startling her so badly that she nearly choked on a bite of bacon. "You're gonna transfer. The best pay, the fastest promotions, the newest station in the Montgomery biz, and you're too good for it."

"I didn't say that," protested the first voice. "I said Donovan was a…"

"Hey, not so loud. Bad enough you said it the first time."

"Whatever. I know I'm not an officer, but nobody screams at me, especially for not knowing about an unscheduled transport. I'm putting him down as my reason for transfer."

"Sure you are. Tough guy. We're all very impressed."

Ava tuned out the rest of the conversation, hyper-focused on the 'unscheduled delivery.' For a thoughtful moment, she rubbed the ring on her right hand, barely noticing that her palms had stopped itching. She'd deliberately seated herself in the middle of the sea of rectangular metal tables, just in case there was something to overhear. Now success had caught her flat-footed. She couldn't access her commband out here in the open, where any chance passerby would be able to see what she was doing.

Resignedly, she stuffed a final bite of deliciousness into her mouth and headed for the reclaimer. From there she boarded a pivotlift and, content to ride along wherever the other passengers were going, stood with her back to the wall while she pulled up a list of all transports that had arrived in the last nine hours. Eliminating the routine stops left her with four entries, one of which stood out from the others in that it claimed to be returning from uncharted space.

Backtracking through station logs, Ava confirmed that the vessel had never docked there on its way out, which was highly unlikely given the *Beyond*'s strategic location. Most Captains preferred to replenish their supplies before striking out into the relative unknown. On a whim, she ran the silhouette without names or dates.

"Jackpot." Saving the search, she forwarded it to Phyl and Jean and finally stepped forward to enter a destination via the control panel. Her role as a floating handyman was the perfect cover, one she embellished by checking out a utility belt from the level's lockers before she entered the docking area.

The corridor around the pivotlift fairly vibrated with activity, people hustling this way or that, and at first Ava had no trouble blending in with the traffic. As groups peeled off to work on this dock or that ship, she began getting odd looks from those walking the opposite direction.

Ignoring them, she assumed a bored expression and choked her gait down to a half-hearted walk. Even when she couldn't see or hear anyone, she maintained the guise. It was good practice, though she couldn't help wondering how long she had until someone noticed she wasn't at any of her assigned work locations. Assuming anyone bothered to check, of course.

Slowing further, Ava came to a stop beside the bay where the unscheduled transport was docked. Leaning against the wall as casually as she could, she tried to come up with a good excuse for being there, doing absolutely nothing. It was as good a way as any to pass the time while she watched and listened for any signs of life.

Then, taking a deep breath, she strode through the bay doors. A stack of cargo containers grabbed her attention. No one challenged her as she made her way over to inspect them. Less than fifty feet further into the bay, the door to the craft stood wide open, tempting her. Her nose twitched at the foreign odor emanating from it, something earthy and raw that she had no name for.

Only her training held her back. The containers were a sure thing—the ship wasn't. Tapping her commband, she brought up the scanning function and aimed the beam at one of the codes.

Her heart leapt to her throat when the commband emitted an obnoxious error noise, piercing the silence. It would've been wise to step further behind the stack, but her feet wouldn't move.

"I tell you, I heard something."

Ava caught a glimpse of a thick, scruffy-looking man as he stomped into the bay from the ship. Her throat constricted painfully, squeezing her heart back into her chest, and suddenly she could move again. Easing back behind the stack, she wisely put her commband on silent.

"Sure you did." A deeper voice growled, indicating a second man had entered the bay. "You heard me say it was time to pay me back." There was a short pause, then the voice continued. "Don't think I'm gonna forget just because you pretended to hear something!"

Ava rested her forehead against the cool, smooth side of the container, willing the first man to respond. He would, unless he was still suspicious. He'd say something rude to the second man, they'd argue, and then they'd go back into the ship.

Any second now.

She dried damp palms on her pant legs and took a deep breath. Something was wrong. Impulsively, she grabbed one of the loading rungs on the containers and pulled herself up, intending to climb the stack and hide at the top.

Suddenly, a hand grabbed her calf. "Well, well, well. What have we here?"

Ava looked down into brown eyes hard enough to pass for polished stone. "Hey! Let go!" Kicking at him, she dropped back down to the deck. "Are you nuts?! You could've given me a heart attack or something."

"Yeah." The man agreed absent-mindedly, his mind tracking with his eyes as he looked her up and down.

"Who're you?" demanded the second voice from behind her.

"Me? I'm the one who's come to inspect your cargo." Shifting mental gears, she snarled as she stepped out from between them, then turned to size them up. They were both thickly muscled, with scars on their cheeks that reminded her of her bare-knuckle fighting instructor. What turned her blood to ice, though, was the braided cord one of them wore around his neck, an unofficial symbol of the pro-slavery groups——the sort that prowled the edge of their space hunting for victims. Particularly rich ones. "Now if you'll be so kind as to get out of my way, I'll do this as quick as I can and get out of yours."

"Yeah." The second man scratched his shaggy beard. "That's not gonna happen."

"Seriously?" She rolled her eyes even as her brain jumped ahead like a checker on a winning board. They weren't buying her story. She didn't stand a chance against them in a fight, so that left one course of action. "Do I need to call station security?"

Faking a lift of her left wrist, Ava bolted for the corridor. From the corner of her eye, she saw a fist slash through the air, nearly stopping her before she got started, and spurring her on to greater speed. It was hard to tell with the echoes, but it sounded like only one of them was following her. Which meant the other one was…what? Alerting the rest of the crew?

She didn't have to make it all the way to the pivotlift, she reminded herself, listening to the heavy footfalls behind her. She just needed witnesses. They wouldn't dare do anything to her in front of…

Two large men came around the curve in the corridor. In an instant, she'd pegged them as being from the ship by their style of dress. They grinned when they saw her.

Chapter 9

Cold. Ava scrabbled in the dark for her blankets, without success. She yelped and jerked awake when she ran a finger into something hard and unyielding. Blinking, she tried to see the room around her, then realized it was pitch-dark. "L-lights." Her voice sounded strange. Clearing her throat, she tried again. "Lights. Ah!" She flung up a hand to cover her eyes, which had indeed been wide open.

Cautiously, she opened them again, mere slits this time. She was lying on deckplate. There was a wall an arm's length away from her. As her eyes continued to adjust, she was able to confirm two more bare walls and a ceiling without moving too much. Wherever she was, the room was barely big enough to stand up in, let alone lie down in.

Pausing, she assessed her physical state. Moved her legs. Flexed numb fingers. Her head was pounding, and yes, there was definitely something digging into her back.

Taking a deep breath, Ava rolled onto her stomach and dragged her knees and arms underneath her. The drums in her head turned into huge gongs being beaten with sticks the size of hundred-year-old trees. Her stomach roiled and she slumped onto her left side, focusing on controlling her rebelling body.

That was when she noticed the sticky, sweet smell. Shoving aside the mental fog, she pawed through her training to come up with a name for it. "Ondoegi." A favorite of human traffickers, even a tiny amount of the drug, sprayed in the face of a victim, could incapacitate them for hours. Worse, so long as it remained on the skin, it kept them disoriented and nauseous.

Hours. How long had she been out? Was anyone looking for her? Where was she? The room didn't seem to be moving, but she couldn't be sure. As her memory gradually returned, another thought occurred to her, one that made her feel even colder. What if they'd taken her onto their ship and she was now lightyears away from the *Beyond?* They could have already crossed into the Puer system, where the law would declare her a slave and all that she possessed would become the property of her new owner.

Not happening. She had to escape. There was no other choice.

When her stomach ceased trying to crawl up and out via her esophagus, she became aware of a pain in her left side. It felt like…like she'd rolled over a small mountain and a peak was stabbing her. With an effort, she forced herself to keep taking shallow, even breaths as she studied the rest of the room.

Two short, squat droids lined the far wall, the kind that cleaned docking bays between uses. Some of her fear faded at the familiar sight of the Montgomery Galactic emblem on their sides. The fact that she was still on the *Beyond* greatly improved her odds of survival. She nearly sobbed with relief at learning she was still aboard her own station.

Wait. She was in a room on the *Beyond.* Rooms had doors. Yes. Yes, she'd seen a door, it just hadn't meant anything to her at the time. Where was it now? Tilting her head, she ruled out the three walls that she could see, which left the wall immediately behind her.

She tried getting up on her knees again and yelped when the stabbing pain in her side intensified. "What is…" Looking down at herself, she sucked in a startled breath of delight, along with another dose of the ondoegi. It was doing most of its damage by absorption now, yet the fumes contributed to a lightheadedness that nearly put her back down.

"Easy does it," she whispered to herself. Flexing her fingers, she got some feeling back into one hand, which inched up her leg to her waist, where it fumbled with the catch on the utility belt that her captors had carelessly left with her. Released from the weight of the pokey, lumpy articles arranged around the belt, she regained her knees with relative ease.

Lunging to her feet, she nearly ran into the door. Bracing herself against it, she rested for a moment. Refusing to make the mistake of breathing deeply again, Ava endured several uncomfortable moments before her heart and stomach settled again. Then, gripping the handle, she pushed down.

It didn't budge. Confused, she mustered her strength and tried again. The third time, she used both hands and leaned all her weight on it until she slithered down to the floor in exhaustion.

Locked. Of course it was locked!

Resting her head in her hands, Ava reasoned that she shouldn't be surprised. What was the point of drugging someone and tossing them in a room if they could just walk out when they woke up? Then again, what was the point of leaving her alive on the *Beyond?* Befuddled as she was, it still seemed obvious that they'd decided she wasn't much of a threat to them. Why not? She'd seen faces. Her commband would've automatically recorded an image of the container's designation.

Her commband! She could open any door on the station with… Her right hand slapped her left wrist. Opening an eye, she peeked to confirm what her chilled fingers were telling her. Her commband was gone.

"Swell," she muttered and rubbed her empty hands on her knees.

One of three fates had befallen her significantly altered commband: it was on the unknown ship, headed for an equally unknown destination; they'd been thorough enough to destroy it; or, they were careless enough to simply toss it in a corner or trash bin aboard the station. Under the circumstances, the third option seemed the most likely. They hadn't destroyed her or taken her aboard their ship, so why bother with an apparently standard-issue commband? She hoped.

Speculation wasn't going to get her out of that room, though. If only she could think! The ondoegi really needed to come off. Eyeing the droids, a thought floated to the surface, and she latched onto it. *Water. They synth their own water while cleaning.*

From where she sat, she couldn't see a way to get at the synthesizer, so her next task was to stand up again. Putting her palms on the floor, she pushed, expecting to come right up on her feet. It didn't work. Her legs remained stretched out before her, as if they hadn't realized they were part of the effort.

Odd. Concentrating, she bent her knees one at a time, then tried again. One foot slid forward, leaving only one leg to support her hips, which had at least managed to leave the floor this time. After a few wobbly seconds, she collapsed back into a seated position, frustrated.

Alright. If she couldn't walk, she'd crawl. Clumsily, she shifted herself until she was in position, then made her way ponderously across the room to the nearest droid. Hooking her fingers around the handle, she brought one knee up to her chest and lurched upward.

"Ow!" Not daring to bend down enough to rub the knee she'd just smashed against the droid's side, she allowed herself a moment to be grateful for the numbing effects of the drug. By now she probably had a dozen fresh bruises forming, and only the latest was bad enough to penetrate the haze.

Anyway. Ava swiped at her forehead with the back of her hand. At least she was warming up. "Here," she punched the power button, "we go!"

Wincing at the bright, lime green lettering that appear on the black background, she began scrolling through the menu. A stroke of delayed genius sent her back to the first option, CORRIDOR CLEAN. Pressing it, she looked eagerly toward the door.

A flashing error notification brought her gaze sorrowfully back to the droid. Whatever they'd done to lock the door, it exceeded the droid's remote command access. Disappointed yet again, Ava read through the rest of the menu carefully until she discovered a way to skip straight to the rinse portion of the mopping function.

Adding a tic to the 'success' column and doing her best to ignore the 'failure' column entirely, Ava started the process. Counted to five, then aborted it before the droid began spilling the precious water onto the floor. Calling up the maintenance submenu next, she instructed the droid to unlock its main compartment.

A whoosh of relieved air escaped her lungs when the front panel popped open. For all its hours of service, the interior of the droid glistened and gleamed, as pristine as an operating room. It had to be out here, where unchecked germs posed as real a threat to station personnel as any fire.

Tugging the reservoir out to where she could reach in, she wet the cuff of her sleeve and used it to scrub the area around her nose and mouth. Ah, the relief! She took a deep, glorious breath for the first time since waking up.

It was harder than she expected. She tried again, but met with the same strange resistance from her lungs. A moment later, the continuing struggle set off an alarm bell in her gradually clearing mind. Her gaze darted around the room, confirming the utter lack of vents. And the door, like most of the doors on space-going vessels, was designed to withstand sudden depressurization, including being absolutely airtight.

Wait… A thought caught up to Ava and she frowned. She was locked *inside* droid storage. That shouldn't be possible. Unless someone had deliberately tampered with the lock.

Well, well, well. Maybe they'd decided she was a threat to them after all. It made a gruesome sort of sense, leaving her to die without any marks of violence. Cause of death was probably supposed to be accidental asphyxiation as the result of drug use. Tragic, yet not unheard of, even in their advanced civilization.

Unfortunately for them, she was Sigrid Ava Montgomery. This was *her* station and she had no intention of dying here.

Unfortunately for her, the synth mechanism on the droid didn't include parameters for anything outside of its primary functions.

Stripping off her jacket, she tossed it aside and reached into the reservoir again for a drink while she considered her situation. It didn't take long. That locked door was the only way in or out of the room. Except it was made of solid durasheet alloy, right down to the dozen hinges embedded in the wall like three-inch thick metal binding combs.

Her gaze dropped to the utility belt, which lay on the floor where she'd left it. It was a miracle she hadn't tripped on it while crossing the room earlier. Sliding it over with her foot, Ava clung to the droid with one hand while she squatted down to pick it up, then spread it out on top of the other droid. Methodically she opened every pouch, checked every tool.

When she got out of there, she was going to have to recommend that the investigator training courses include a scenario similar to this one. She'd learned a bit about locks, including how to bypass the highly popular electronic locks, but only from the outside. The cheaper varieties needed a mere six-inch piece of sturdy wire to defeat the internal workings of... The, um... Oh, what word was she looking for? She knew it was something all locks had.

Why was that important? Scrubbing a hand over her face, Ava struggled to dredge up what she'd learned in her classes. Maybe if she recited what she could remember, she could figure out what her brain was trying to tell her?

"Lock mechanisms," she began, "include levers, springs, pins, and other moveable parts. These parts, whether digital or physical, can be manipulated if all else fails."

Her head snapped up. Moveable parts! Nothing

could move inside a truly solid door. Therefore, the door was not truly solid. There had to be a pocket of space to allow them to function. Yes! It would take a loading crane to rip the door out, but if she could just access the lock mechanism, she'd be free!

"Moveable parts don't function well when they're cut in half, either," she muttered to herself. Turning to the utility belt, Ava double-checked the tools. When she was satisfied that she had what she needed, she buckled the belt and draped it over her shoulder. It threw her off-balance when she started walking, but at least she wouldn't have to come back for any of the tools.

At the door, she hung the belt from the handle. As she paused to rest, her thoughts shifted to Jean and his prediction that she'd get into trouble. Blast the man, he'd been right. Naturally, that intensified her need to get out of it on her own. She'd never live it down, otherwise.

Unsteadily, she nudged the water reservoir over to where she'd be able to reach it. Then she knelt, drill in hand, and set to work probing the door around the handle.

Meanwhile, on the other side of the station, Jean was talking quietly with Chief Taylor when his commband went off. Shaking his head, he accepted the call.

"Kearns."

"Sir, this is Corporal Griffith. I'm sorry to bother you, but protocol said I should. Call you, I mean." The sound of a forced laugh was followed by, "I had to look it up."

Jean rubbed the bridge of his nose, trying to ward off the tension headache he could feel building. "Look what up, Corporal?"

"Oh! Um. The system was running its usual station scan, sir, and it threw an error. It says a commband has gone silent."

"Silent?" Jean silently forgave the corporal for having to look that one up. Commbands were nearly idiot-proof. "Whose?"

"It's, um." An uneasy feeling settled over Jean as he waited impatiently while Griffith scrambled to find the user designation. "YTM000…"

"Their name, Corporal." Jean interrupted brusquely.

"Uh, right. Massuk. Terina."

An ice comet lodged in Jean's stomach. *Sam!* Hearing that she was in trouble ripped the sobriquet from his soul. He couldn't speak. He couldn't even move, except to meet Taylor's eyes.

Taylor snapped into action. Activating his own commband, he added himself to the conversation via a security override. "This is Security Chief Taylor," he barked, no doubt startling the poor lad out of his wits. "Give me the last reported position on that commband."

"Yessssir!" The rattled corporal hit the keys so hard they would hear him operating the machine. "Outer ring. Section F, Level 12."

"Section F, Level 12." Taylor's face paled, but his voice remained steady. "Keep monitoring for that commband, Corporal. If it comes back up, contact me the instant you hear it. Understood?"

"Understood, sir!" Their commbands blinked off as the channel closed.

Jean forced the words past stiff lips. "Section F is the fuel processing section."

"And level twelve," Taylor continued grimly, "is barely more than a handful of corridors connecting the repair droid docking bays. Easy access to the outside."

Outside? Jean's breakfast clawed its way up from his stomach, but he choked it back down. "She's not dead."

Taylor eyed him briefly, as if considering reminding him that one sure way to shut down a commband was to expose it to open space, then shrugged and spoke into his commband instead, ordering a security team to sweep the area.

"Time to wait." Taylor leaned back his chair. This was the part he hated, but with such cases there was nothing he could do that his team couldn't do just as well.

"I have to go." Jean was halfway to the door before he registered that he'd moved. "Something's wrong."

"Hey!" Startled, Taylor came to his feet. "Go where? And do what?" His eyes narrowed. "Commander, do you know something that I ought to know?"

Jean paused. There was nothing to be gained by telling Taylor Ava's real name, but another truth slipped out before he could stop it. "I love her."

"You…" Taylor raked his fingers through his hair and sat back down. "Get back here."

"Taylor, I." Jean began to protest.

"Now!" Taylor snapped. "I just had an idea." Turning to his computer, he began rapidly typing and clicking.

Jean *knew* it was a waste of effort to rush out and start opening doors at random, but he still had to drag himself back to Taylor's desk. Holding still while Sam was in trouble might well drive him mad enough to chew nails.

"We don't track commband location," Taylor explained as he brought up a display so Jean could see it, too. "But the computer records every time a commband is scanned, whether you're buying something or just accessing a secure area. Here's the last scan." He pointed at the screen. "Massuk entered F12 over two hours ago. Could be anywhere by now. Huh."

Jean scanned the screen, then his friend's face. "Huh what?!"

"It doesn't make sense." Taylor frowned as he pointed at the grouping of records just above. "See? The last scan before that was docking level seven."

The comet in Jean's gut dropped in temperature. "That's impossible. At the very least, she'd have to scan in at the pivotlift." Next to the command levels, the fuel-processing levels were the most closely guarded on the station.

"So if she didn't, who did?" Taylor changed the search parameters and scowled at the results. "Nothing in our time frame. Hmm."

"That's not possible." Jean racked his brain for another explanation. "Computer error?"

"Could be." Sympathy for his friend prompted Taylor to keep what he was really thinking to himself.

Jean drummed his fingers against his thigh, then nodded sharply. "I'm going down there."

"What? Where?"

"D7. I'll try to figure out what she was doing there. Maybe I can find something that will tell us where she went on F12." He stared intently at Taylor. "Keep me updated."

"I can do that." Unease threaded through him as he watched Jean go. "I must be gettin' soft in my old age," he muttered to himself. "Oughta chuck him in a cell so he can't get in trouble."

Jean headed straight for the pivotlift where Sam started on D7. The *exact* pivotlift. The time he spent trapped in a mobile box, hiding his emotions from his fellow passengers, served to further infuriate him and at the same time, instilled an icy calm. This was hardly his first search and rescue. A methodical approach was best, so he stood a moment in the corridor just to the side of the pivotlift.

Why had Sam come here? Quickly checking her assignments confirmed that D7 wasn't on that list. Curiosity, then? Or, something related to her investigation?

Sam, where are you? Now that his sobriquet for her had resurfaced, he couldn't seem to shake it.

His heart tugged his gaze to the left. There was no reason for it, none that he could explain, yet he began moving in that direction. As he walked, he tried to make sense of it, to intuit what had brought Sam here of all places.

D7 was a perfectly ordinary docking level, essentially identical to the other fourteen such levels the *Beyond* boasted. The top five, as the closest to the business and residential levels, were typically reserved for use by passenger vessels. The bottom five levels served the vessels that were in a hurry to be unloaded and refueled. Overflow from either category could, and often did, spill into the middle levels, but even a cursory glance at station logs showed a quiet day.

An unscheduled docking caught his eye. At first glance, there was nothing special about the *Mandoa*—except that it was assigned a berth on level D7 and left approximately the same time as Sam's mysterious scan on F12.

He told himself it was absurd to think that Sam

had been deliberately kidnapped. Why would anyone kidnap a mere yeoman?

Realistically, however, the possibility did exist.
And that possibility was enough to give a man
nightmares.

Blast the woman! When he found her, safe and
sound, he was going to give her a lecture she'd
never forget. He'd warned her about traveling
without a security team!

Chapter 10

Too many holes later, Ava wiped her forehead as she set aside the hand drill, then marked the final hole. Wearily, she probed the hole with another tool, trying to get a sense of how deep she should cut to get past the frame without damaging the lock mechanism.

Helping herself to another drink of water, she fumbled for the laser-beam cutter. On her second try, she squinted down at it and realized it was being held in place by a safety loop.

"I've got to get out of here," she muttered. Freeing the cutter at last, she positioned it carefully, then paused. The cutter wouldn't use up any oxygen or, by itself, contribute any more noxious gases. Heating the metal, however, was risky.

Given how she already felt, her window of opportunity for cutting away the metal and successfully manipulating the locking mechanism before she asphyxiated was minuscule. Surely someone was looking for her by now. Should she wait and hope they found her before she succumbed to carbon dioxide poisoning?

The cutter slipped and she skinned her knuckles hard on the door before she caught herself. Pain radiated up her arm, making her smile grimly.

Who was she kidding? Setting the cutter back in place, Ava switched it on and began dragging it, right to left, across the gap between the two top holes. Then down to a third hole and back across, this time left to right.

Somewhere in the back of her mind, an alarm began sluggishly building, but it wasn't enough to penetrate her concentration.

Almost...there...! Reflex prompted her to shut

off the cutter even as she raised her arms in victory. And watched in consternation as the piece of metal teetered on its bottom edge before falling out of the hole she'd just created.

Dropping the cutter, she reached out to catch the metal—then screamed as the hot edges seared into her unprotected palms. Throwing it aside, she plunged her hands into the water reservoir. Her lungs ached for air while her head spun with carbon dioxide and fumes from the cutting process.

Get. out. of. here.

A surge of survival instinct, combined with hours of training, kicked in like the reverse thruster on a heavy freighter. Her gaze jerked toward the freshly exposed mechanism, searching out the weakest point. Grabbing the heaviest driver from the tool belt, she inserted it and heaved.

Unnoticed, the utility belt shifted on the door handle. Slowly it inched forward, its weight rotating the handle downward as the mechanism shifted.

Ava suddenly realized she'd risen to her knees without changing her grip on the driver. Spotted the belt as it was about to slip off the handle. Throwing her full weight onto the driver, she lunged to her feet and grabbed the handle.

***

Jean, still following his heart, suddenly found himself juggling a human being that erupted out of a door he would've otherwise disregarded. Once he'd steadied them both so they wouldn't fall over, he risked a glance at their face.

"Sam?" The sight of her too-red face and unfocused eyes sent his heart to his toes. "No. Not again!"

Scooping her up, he slammed his commband against the nearest wall, activating the emergency beacon. And then, he wavered. Was the smoke he smelled in the present or the past? A faint *pop* and *hiss* seemed to grow louder, until he was convinced that if he turned around, he'd see the bombed-out remains of the hovercraft where they'd nearly died that night, so long ago.

"Lieutenant Commander, this is Command." The concerned voice echoed in the corridor, snapping Jean out of his memories. "What is the nature of your…"

"Medical. Send a team to D7." Shaking his head to fully clear it, Jean sprinted toward the emergency station in the nearest bay. "Bay 23. Hurry!" Lowering Sam gently to the floor, he ripped open the medical cupboard and yanked out the diagnostic bracelet.

Once the bracelet was on her wrist, he forced himself to pull his hands away so he wouldn't interfere with its processing. Unable to just sit there, even for the few seconds before the diagnosis, he located the oxymask and a see-through case of prepared syringes.

"A medical team has been alerted. Do you require security personnel as well?"

Jean nearly choked on the word 'no' as he abruptly changed his mind. "Yes. Inform Security Chief Taylor of my whereabouts. That's all." Ripping the sterile packaging from the oxymask, he placed it carefully over Sam's nose and mouth. He didn't hesitate because he'd seen carbon dioxide poisoning before. Who in space hadn't?

"Yes, sir." The commband channel closed, leaving Jean alone with a glassy-eyed Sam and a med bracelet whose display flashed an angry orange, warning him against taking further initiative.

He relaxed fractionally when the display resumed its standard gray and the oxymask's indicator light turned a solid blue, confirming a successful link with the bracelet.

Next, he reached for a see-through kit that held vials of medicine. Breaking it open, he prepped the needle attachment and followed the directions from the medical bracelet to inject a vial of blodren into her thigh to help cleanse her system of the CO_2 build-up.

"Your color's getting better already." He spoke as though she could hear him, more for his own sake than hers. Believing she was going to recover was critical to his ability to keep going. Just as it had been that ill-fated night so long ago.

Ears ringing, vision fading in and out, he'd gathered an unresponsive Sam in his arms and staggered to a safe distance from the hovercraft. He didn't remember doing it, but the police had been quick to point out that there was only one set of footprints in the damp grass. Which, they'd reasoned, meant that the five bodies scattered around where he and Sam were eventually found must've come from another hovercraft.

From the corner of his eye, he saw the bracelet display change to yellow and begin flashing. Blast, he'd missed seeing the next step come up. Leaning closer, he read the instructions for tending her hands.

That was when he noticed not one but *two* lines on the toxicology report. "Ondoegi." It registered as a trace amount, but it was there. Burn cream suddenly spurted from the tube he'd opened, landing uselessly on the deckplate. Cursing himself for a fool, he summoned his self-control and began tending her hands carefully.

Even so, his thoughts kept straying to the report. He'd first heard of ondoegi in the news reports. Originally developed on a low-tech planet for medical purposes, it was easily made, easily transported, and far too easy to use, making it an instant favorite with criminals. Which begged the question— what was it doing here, on the *Beyond*? And how had it gotten into Sam's system? How *much* of it had gotten in?

His hand shook a little as he reached out to smooth her hair, and he wished she was awake enough to answer questions. At the same time, part of him was glad she couldn't hear him whisper, "I love you, Sam. I always have." He'd lost people before, starting with his parents and siblings when he was a child. Without Sam in it somewhere, though, the galaxy would be a much colder, emptier place for him.

The pounding of boots on deckplate brought his head up. Three white-tunicked personnel jogged through the door a moment later, following the emergency beacon on his commband. He started to move out of their way and bit back a word his mother would've been ashamed to hear him speak when his knee nearly gave out on him.

"Commander!" One of them veered in his direction, propping him up and moving him clear while the others got to work on Ava. "Where are you hurt?"

"Just in my pride." Jean managed a tight smile and leaned back against the wall. After fifteen rotten years of dealing with the injury, he ought to know enough to be careful of it. "Really, I'm fine. This is ancient history. She's the one who needs you now." Ignoring the doubtful expression on the medic's face, Jean persisted until they were all focused on Ava.

He answered their questions the best that he could while they prepared her for transport to the medical level and was glad that Taylor arrived in time to hear most of the answers.

"All set? Okay, let's go." The head medic initiated the travel bed's levitation and they all started toward the door.

"Let me know the minute she's available for questioning," Taylor instructed as he moved aside. Turning to Jean, he ordered, "Show me exactly where you found her."

Jean gave his leg a final stretch while he watched Sam out of sight. Then, he took his myriad fears for her, muscled them into a box, and slammed the lid down tightly. He hadn't had much call for that skill since leaving the military, thankfully. Well. Except on Solène's first day of school. Every year.

"This way." They walked in silence, a lot longer than Jean expected. Of course, he'd been running before. And thoroughly distracted. He might've thought he'd gone the wrong way, except that the closet finally came into view.

"This is it?" Taylor eyed the still-open door with interest. Half a dozen minidrones deployed from their slots on his belt and began buzzing around the door, a few slipping inside the room itself. "Did you touch anything?"

Jean replayed the moment in his mind to be sure, then shook his head. "I very literally had my hands full."

Staying clear of the minidrones as they scanned for prints, recorded images, etc., Taylor moved to where he could see into the room. "Your girlfriend is in some kinda trouble."

Jean bristled instantly. "On what grounds? Since when is there a regulation against..." He broke off when Taylor looked at him over his shoulder, one eyebrow raised sardonically.

"Who said anything about the regs?" Taylor pointed into the room. "I don't know all the facts yet, but I do know these doors don't lock themselves. Not from the inside, anyway. Whatever happened here was deliberate."

Jean blinked. "What?" Moving closer to Taylor, he stared in shock at the rectangular hole in the door with a driver still sticking out of it. Noted the overturned container and the puddle of water spreading lazily across the floor.

Taylor's frown deepened as he consulted the feed coming in from the drones. "They're picking up a foreign chemical in there. Not sure what it is yet."

"Ondoegi," Jean supplied flatly. At Taylor's questioning look, he explained, "The med bracelet found it in her blood."

Taylor whistled softly. "This is worse than I thought." The minidrones returned one by one to their slots and he stepped into the room. "Bad things do happen on the *Beyond*."

"Find whoever did this," Jean ground out as he watched Taylor bag Sam's sodden jacket. "You find them, and I'll bring them in."

Taylor grunted as he got to his feet. "Doesn't work that way, Jean. But don't worry, Security will get these guys." He made a mental note to keep an eye on Jean. Girlfriends had a way of messing with even the sanest man's equilibrium. "She'll be okay. You gave her emergency treatment as soon as you found her. A few hours in the infirmary and she'll probably be released to rest in her quarters."

A wave of relief swept over Jean when Taylor's commband went off, and a voice informed them that Sam was ready to be interviewed.

Taylor refused to leave until two of his officers showed up to take over, then began trying to figure out how to keep Jean out of the way until after he'd spoken with the yeoman. It would be simplest to force the issue with an order, but a security chief didn't have that many friends. Sure, the civilians were nice to him, as long as things were going well. He'd been in the job long enough, though, to know how quickly that could change and what a treasure a real friend was.

So, as they entered the pivotlift, Taylor cleared his throat. "I'll make a deal with you. You promise not to interrupt, and you can come in for the interview." He held up a finger to stop Jean's response. "I'm serious. You get in the way, and I'll toss you into a cell overnight." Exactly what he should've done earlier, but he decided to forgive himself since things had turned out alright.

Jean knew Taylor didn't make idle comments, particularly when it came to his cells. Not trusting his voice, he just nodded gratefully. Taylor might not think it much, but it was far more than Jean expected. After the bombing, while she'd lain unconscious in the hospital, he'd been in a corner room getting badgered by the police officers. *Sure you don't remember anything else about it?* If he'd heard that question once that night, he'd heard it a hundred times.

"Alright." Taylor led the way when the pivotlift doors opened. He didn't miss the way Jean stutter-stepped as they crossed into the infirmary, but Jean didn't say anything, so neither did he.

The charge nurse pointed them in the right direction and a moment later, Taylor knocked on the frame of the open door, then walked in as soon as her eyes met his. "Yeoman Massuk, I'm Security Chief Taylor. Looks like you had a close call." He was pleased to see she'd already graduated to a half-mask, leaving her mouth free for speaking.

"I'll agree with that assessment." She smiled tightly. "Shall I start at the beginning?"

Taylor considered briefly, then nodded. "Go ahead. Alright if I record it?" She was the most self-possessed victim he'd ever encountered, and he was curious to see how the interview would go with her in charge. He could always interrupt or backtrack as needed.

"Please do." With an effort, Ava shifted herself higher on the pillows. She smiled gratefully at Jean, who reached around her to stuff another pillow into place. "I overheard something this morning that…" She broke off to stare at the door.

Jean's jaw dropped in shock when he saw none other than Captain Donovan hovering in the doorway. Hastily, he closed his mouth.

"Excuse the interruption, Chief." Donovan breezed into the room. Stopping by the bed, he gazed down at Ava with an almost fatherly expression of concern. "I heard the alerts coming in and had to come hear what happened myself."

"Of course, sir." Though Taylor kept his tone carefully neutral, he didn't believe it for a second. In the three years that they'd worked together, he'd never known Donovan to give more than a passing thought to the station personnel. "We were just getting started."

"Yes." Ava agreed politely, but it wasn't butterflies stirring up her stomach, it was icicles of fear. "Thank you for coming to check on me, Captain."

She might not have put it together so quickly if Donovan hadn't made a point of coming to see her. It all made a horrible, sickening kind of sense. And she didn't dare let him know, which meant not cringing away when he reached down to pat her on the arm.

"Yeoman?" Taylor spoke up after a few silent moments had passed. Concerned that she'd forgotten why he was there, he prompted, "Why don't you start with what you were doing on D7."

"Yes, sir." Ava wanted to laugh at how meek she sounded. "I wanted to explore a little before my shift today. Haven't been here long, so I sort of picked a deck at random."

Jean disciplined a frown so as to not give away the fact that she was lying. He instinctively trusted her to have a good reason for it—was it Donovan's presence? Everything changed the instant she'd seen him.

Ava sketched a loose tale about how she'd stopped to peek into one of the bays. "Things are kind of…confused after that. I don't remember going into a droid storage closet, or falling asleep, but," she shifted uneasily, "that's where I woke up."

With Taylor's coaxing, she relayed the rest of the story of how she'd broken out of the closet, making sure to punctuate the retelling with hazy pauses and guilty glances at the captain.

"That'll do for now." Taylor saved the recording. "I may have more questions later, after we've had more time to examine the room."

"Um." Ava paused deliberately, twisting her hands in the bedsheets. "Will I have to pay damages?" That was something a yeoman would worry about, right?

Donovan chuckled, looking from Taylor to Jean as if they were all suddenly old friends. "You can put that worry out of your mind, Yeoman. I personally guarantee that you won't have to pay for a thing." He made a small gesture at the room in general, no doubt to imply that her visit to the infirmary would also be 'free.' It might've fooled her into thinking he was somehow to be thanked for it all, except that she already knew company policy on workplace accidents and injuries.

"He's right," Taylor agreed. Then, looking directly at Ava, he remarked, "Fact is, Montgomery will be lucky if you don't file against them for the faulty latch."

"Me?" Ava did her best to switch from acting relieved to acting shocked when truthfully, she was almost too tired to care. "Oh, I couldn't."

Donovan's smile had slipped at Taylor's suggestion and now he hastily asserted, "What you need to do is get some rest, young lady. We've stayed too long."

At that moment, Taylor realized Jean hadn't had a moment alone with the woman he'd confessed to being in love with. With that in mind, he winked surreptitiously at Jean, then turned to the captain. "I'll put a rush on our investigation into the malfunctioning lock, sir. Hope to have it finished by the time you get an E74 form filled out."

"E74?" Donovan repeated blankly.

"Right." Taylor kept talking as he shifted position to block Donovan's view of Jean, and subtly herded the man into the corridor.

Jean stepped closer to Sam's bed. "You can trust Taylor," he promised quietly. "Just tell him."

Ava nodded slowly. "I was going to." She also kept her voice down. "I mean, I will, as soon as I get the chance. Wait." Her hand touched his arm when Jean moved to go. "My commband. Did you find it?"

"Yes." He allowed himself a wry smile. "You don't have to worry about getting charged for that, either."

"Haha." She wrinkled her nose at him. "This is no joke, Jean. I need that commband, that *exact* commband, back as quickly as possible."

"I'll do what I can," he promised. "But I don't know what kind of shape it's in. It may need a complete wipe or even repair."

She bit her lip. "A wipe would be alright, I guess. As long as it is a *comprehensive* wipe."

"Why are you so worried about a commband?" He couldn't help frowning. "Sam, you nearly died. Less than an hour ago."

Looking down at their now-intertwined hands, she had a hard time remembering what they'd been talking about.

"Coming, Lieutenant Commander?" Donovan reappeared in the doorway.

"Sorry, sir." Ava sprang verbally to Jean's defense even as he hastily pulled his hand away. "It's this extra pillow. I can't lie back, and…"

"Allow me." Jean lifted the pillow clear, straightened away despite the ache to hold her, then asked solicitously, "Is that better?"

"Yes. Thank you." As she lay back, he tugged the covers up around her shoulders, making her feel safe and protected. She managed to keep her eyes open long enough to mouth, 'Thank you,' then allowed the fatigue to win.

Chapter 11

It ended up being Jean who filled out the E74 form, which surprised no one but amused Taylor immensely.

"I'll never understand how people like Donovan make captain," Taylor muttered as he added a digital copy of the form to the investigation folder. "It takes more than a personal appearance now and then, y'know?"

"What have you found so far?" Jean eyed Taylor's opaque display, so different from their last meeting. While he respected Taylor's obvious decision to keep him on the periphery, he didn't have to like it.

"It's only been a couple of hours," Taylor reminded him as he shut the display down. "In fact, all we've established so far is that the lock is in good working order."

"That's not possible." Jean objected automatically. "She said she was locked in."

"Oh, I'm inclined to believe her, if only because of the ondoegi in the medical report." He turned his hands palms up. "Nevertheless, the locks are programmed to lock people out, not in. And, I got a strong sense that she was hiding something during the interview." Taylor squinted at Jean as a flicker of indecision crossed his friend's face. "But, then—you already knew that."

"I did." Jean didn't hesitate to admit it. "She told me that she was going to tell you the whole story, as soon as she got the chance."

Taylor's frown deepened. "Are you saying she didn't feel comfortable talking with Donovan around?"

"That's my guess, though she didn't have time

to tell me." Jean looked over at shelves that ran along one wall. An assortment of items were carefully laid out on one shelf and he indicated them with his thumb. "Is that her commband?" He still hadn't figured out why it was so critical that she get that *exact* commband back. Well, unless it got wiped.

"Yeah, that's it." Taylor was puzzled by the change in topics. "Why?"

"Because it's one more reason to believe her." Jean smoothly shifted mental gears. "Or have you figured out how it ended up on one level while she was almost dying on another?"

Taylor drummed an impatient beat on his desk before admitting, "Not yet."

"Fair." Jean nodded. The investigation was only a few hours old.

"You got any ideas?"

"Just one." He resisted the urge to fiddle with the band on his left wrist, lest he accidentally trigger the Suit. "Let me talk to her. Donovan'll get wind of it if you go, and then you've wasted a trip. Tell me what you want to know and I'll bring back a full report."

"What if he catches you there?"

"I'm just visiting my girlfriend." Jean shrugged as if he was perfectly secure in his relationship with Ava. "Fraternization between officers is a minor infraction, one he might even choose to overlook." Not a chance. Donovan would like nothing better than to nail him. But it was worth that risk to try to get the whole story from her.

Taylor hit him with the tough question next. "And you'll tell me everything she says?"

Jean took a deep breath. "I'll even record it for you."

In the end, Taylor's list of questions boiled

down to, 'Get the full story.' On his way to talk with Ava, Jean arranged for Solène to go straight to Masie's after school, freeing his mind for the task at hand.

His steps slowed as he approached her quarters. He'd never enjoy a trip to the infirmary, he'd woken up in such places too many times, usually feeling more dead than alive. But it would've been easier to remain professional there, with the nurses and doctors bustling about.

He dismissed the idea and pressed the chimer at the same time. They were both adults. And, after what happened when she'd kissed him in his quarters, there really wasn't much danger of things getting 'unprofessional.'

The longer he stood, waiting for her to answer the door, the more worried he became. Should he chime again, in case something was wrong? Or had she understandably gone to sleep after such an ordeal, and he was disturbing her?

Just when he was about to turn and walk away, the lock clicked, and the door swung open an inch or two. The corners of his mouth turned down as he entered the room, its lights barely on fifty percent lumination.

Not that there was much to be seen. The table. The couch. The woman curled up on one corner of the couch, lovely despite the bruising visible on her hands and legs. His hands curled into fists and if the responsible parties had been before him in that instant, he'd have cheerfully given them bruises to match hers.

Ava regarded him with mild curiosity. A pang of regret pierced her weariness as she concluded that he was going to remain standing. Her mind had cleared to the point that she was starting to think about all the things she would've left undone if she'd died. At least she could count things between them as closed, the only good thing to come of her foolish attempt at kissing him the other night. "Hi."

"Hi." Jean eyed the last few inches of couch but stayed where he was, trying to smile despite the growing ache in his chest. "Love what you've done with the place."

A half-laugh, half-sob escaped, and Ava wiped away a tear she hadn't realized was so close to the surface. "Yeah, I, um." She managed a more convincing laugh as she waved at the bare gray walls and pile of prototypes in one corner, then curled her fingers around the palm-sized bandage she'd momentarily forgotten about. "I use the same interior decorator as the queen of Yoplan."

"What a coincidence." He shifted closer without realizing it, drawn by her obvious need for companionship. Who could he send over after he was done? Masie? Yes, perhaps. "I thought about hiring her myself, but she's a bit pricey for a mere lieutenant commander."

"Did you come to ask for bargaining tips?" Ava's eyes settled on his hands, where he was rolling a narrow tube around and around.

Following her gaze to Taylor's recording device, Jean decided to blow the airlock. "Taylor sent me to get the rest of the story."

Nodding, Ava took a deep breath and swung her legs off the couch. "Want something to drink?"

"No. I can get it. Whatever you want, I mean." He stepped between her and the synthesizer, but she was already on her feet.

"Thanks." The temptation to 'trip' was strong—anything to be in his arms again. With an effort, she shoved the idea away. He'd put her right back on the couch, then scold her for good measure. "I've got it." This was the perfect opportunity to show him she was stronger than he thought.

His eyes followed her as she limped over to the synthesizer.

"You're sure you don't want anything? Not even a wee yagg of væske juice?" Her hand hovered over the buttons, waiting for his response.

"Well." Pleasantly surprised that she remembered his favorite, he surrendered. "If you insist."

The synthesizer hummed briefly, then the glass door slid aside, allowing her to reach in and retrieve their glasses.

"I hope you like it." She handed him his glass, careful to keep their fingers from touching. "I've been playing with the recipe, trying to get it just right."

Intrigued, Jean took a sip. "Hey, that's pretty good!"

"Yeah?" Ava smiled and her malaise lifted slightly. She *had* survived. The memories of the ordeal would fade, given time. "As good as Eyd's?"

"Mmm, no." Jean softened the blow with an unpremeditated wink. "Nothing is as good as his. Of course, he cheated. He made it from fresh væske pods."

"That's true." Relaxing further, Ava slid back onto the couch, legs stretched out before her. If he wasn't going to sit down, she might as well use the room to baby her knee a bit. The pain level was markedly reduced since her visit to the infirmary, but she knew from past experience that it would still take longer than she wanted for it to fully heal. "So. Shall we?"

Twirling a chair so that it was next to the

couch, Jean set the recorder on the seat, turned it on, and listened. As he'd expected, she gave it to him straight, starting with how she'd overheard the conversation in the cafeteria. When she got to the part about her encounter in the docking bay, Jean clasped his hands behind his back to keep from hitting the wall.

But it wasn't until she was describing waking up without her commband that she cleared her throat and eyed the recording device long enough for him to reluctantly press pause.

"Alright, go ahead." He arched an eyebrow at her. "What's so confidential that you can't tell your own station security chief?"

"I, um." She didn't particularly want to tell Jean, either. But, she needed his help in getting her commband back, so she blurted out the truth about the upgrade.

"You…" He shook his head in disbelief. "Are you actually sitting there, telling me that you turned a commband into an all-access pass? For the entire station?!"

"It's not like I was planning to have it stolen, Jean." Ava fiddled with her glass, trying to prepare for him to give her the dressing-down she'd already given herself.

His glare didn't abate. "You should've. Yes, you heard me. If that ever got into the wrong hands…"

"Exactly. I'm glad you agree we need to get the commband back as quickly as possible." She bit her lip and watched in concern as he covered his face with his hands. It sounded like he muttered something under his breath, something about 'wandering around without a security team,' but she chose to ignore it.

After a few more moments and a steadying

breath, he turned the recorder back on and gestured sharply for her to continue.

She sketched in a few more details, then shook her head. "I definitely remember burning myself. It's a little fuzzy after that." Ava studied the bandage on one palm, her other hand loosely clasping the now-empty glass that she still held. "The doctor said it won't even scar. I'm not sure how I feel about that. I mean." She bit her lip unsteadily. "I went through all that and I won't have anything t-to sh-show for it?"

"You're alive," he cut in brusquely. What an idiot he was! He should've waited at least until morning before coming here to force her to relive the experience. Reaching down, he shut off the recorder and jammed it into his pocket. "If that's everything, I should go." Before he lost the last vestiges of control and took her in his arms to show her just how glad he was that she hadn't died.

"Stay." Ava whispered huskily. "Please. Y-you didn't last time." Blast, why did she have to keep stuttering?

"I couldn't." Jean knew instantly that she was referring to the night of their date, yet another near-death experience she'd somehow survived.

"Yes, you can. You don't have to report back for duty until…" She broke off when his eyes abruptly met hers.

"That's not what I meant."

"Oh. Oh, you meant…you meant then." Too tired to play games or act like she didn't care, she blurted, "But why? I've…" She tried unsuccessfully to swallow the painful lump in her throat. "I've wondered that every day for the last three thousand, two hundred and twelve days." There. She'd finally said it. And how!

"*Days?* You count in days how long it's been since…" It hurt too much to finish the sentence, to think that she cherished the memory of the end of their relationship, so he just stopped speaking.

Exasperated, Ava fisted her free hand on her hip. "You listen to me, Jean Antoni Kearns. Yes, I know to the day how long it has been," she raised both eyebrows for emphasis, "since *our first solo date.*" Something flashed in his eyes, something just as quickly extinguished, leaving her to wonder if he was as invulnerable as he'd been acting since her arrival. "Those were the best hours of my life, Jak."

His shoulders sagged. "I knew this day would come. I even tried to plan for it. Used to lie awake at night when the nightmares got too bad, arranging and rearranging words that were never quite good enough." And now, when he needed it, he couldn't remember a single line.

"Good enough? Jean." She reached out to touch his hand, and he jerked away.

"Yeah, good enough." He stalked away as far as the wall, but refused to let himself turn toward the door. He'd never get another chance at this and maybe—*maybe*—he could set some old ghosts to rest if he went through with it. "I don't know any words that make it alright to be responsible for contributing to the near death of the person you love." He all but choked on the last few words.

Mouth agape, Ava said nothing. Not because there was nothing to say, but because he'd landed a stunner, and she was positively reeling.

"It was sheer luck we didn't die that night." He looked at the carpet, flicked a glance at her, then went back to the carpet. "They got sloppy. That's all there was to it. And that's why I never…"

"Who told you that?" She leaned forward, the orange standing out in her eyes as she studied him intensely. "Because they were lying."

Those four words hit him like a ballistic missile, screaming through his mind as it leveled entire mountains of his reality. *"What?!"*

"Listen to me." She rushed on, more than a little frightened by the way the color drained from his face. "You saved my life that night. Repeatedly." His frown of disbelief drove her to insist, "It's true! It was your idea to take a public hire. It was you, alone, who got me out of it after the explosion. You kept your head and administered first aid. Then, when they sent someone to finish the job…" She broke off, throat tightening with emotion.

"We would've been safer in your personal vehicle." He recited what he'd been told semi-automatically.

"We would've died." She grimaced. Outright murder wasn't all that common in the corporate world, cutthroat though it was. "They ran a full-scale security sweep after the attack and discovered similar explosive devices on my father's vehicle as well as mine." If the coup had succeeded, she and her father would've died within hours of each other. Which could be interpreted to mean that, in saving her life, Jean had saved her father's as well.

"But yours was strategically shielded. A public hire isn't." Jean felt a hundred pounds lighter as she refuted each of the points her security chief made against him all those years ago.

"The public hire was a completely unknown, unexpected quantity. They had to scramble to plant an explosive after we'd left."

"You can't possibly know that!" he argued.

"Not even if I've seen a video of them scrambling to get the explosive in place during a strategically created traffic jam?" Her security team had scraped together enough personal and public security cam footage to prove when and where it was planted—among other things. "And, they failed to account for any modifications to the vehicle by its owner."

She paused, vividly recalling the clatter of the engine, stains on the upholstery, and just how reluctant she'd been to get in. "That broken-down rattletrap was covered with haphazard repairs, including the flooring. A thin sheet of metal covered a gap well enough to pass inspections, but was about as effective as a piece of paper against the explosion. So, instead of the bomb's force being channeled directly up to us, most of it blew through that weaker point."

"It was a bit of a beater, wasn't it?" He turned in a circle, needing somewhere to go, something to do with the energy building inside him. Silent seconds crawled by as Jean tried to wrap his mind around this new information, but he had one more stone to throw—at himself. "It's a good thing the police arrived when they did. I had a head injury. I was useless."

"Yes. You had a head injury." She'd never forget the terror of watching him engage in hand-to-hand combat with assailants the police later identified as professional hitmen. If they'd attacked in a rush, it would've been a completely different story, but they'd grossly underestimated Jean's military training. "Which probably explains why you don't remember any of this clearly, including the fact that it was I who was useless and *you* who single-handedly fought off their footmen."

Though his mouth opened and shut a few

times, no sounds came out.

"Honestly, Jak, the police barely got there in time to pick up the pieces and start the paperwork. I suppose their presence might've discouraged further attempts, but that's about all the credit I can give them."

Without realizing it, he shifted closer. His world was reshaping itself and it seemed only fitting that she be at the front and center.

"Come with me when I leave," Ava invited recklessly, "and I'll show you the footage." She'd watched it more than once while she was coming to terms with the fact that he wasn't coming back. Now that she understood his precipitous exit from her life, she couldn't help wishing that their story might realize its potential.

At last, taking a seat on the couch, Jean scrubbed his hands over his face, then let them fall to his lap. "He lied."

"Yes." She didn't bother asking who; she had a pretty good idea. Less than a year after the attack, they'd discharged the lead agent on her security team for a pattern of unprofessional behavior toward the men she interacted with.

He looked down when one of Ava's hands slid into his. "I've missed you."

That did it. Two huge, hot tears escaped, scudding down her cheeks at record speed. "Oh, Jak. I've missed you every day."

He risked a look up, then reached out to gently wipe the tear trails away. The corner of his mouth tugged up in a lopsided smile as his gaze strayed to her hair. "Red just isn't your color."

"Neither is black." His hand cupped her cheek for a moment, then she leaned forward to meet him halfway.

This was the Jak she remembered, fingers in her hair as he gently turned her world upside down with his kisses.

"Sam," he whispered, hands cupping her face as he drew back. "Sam, are you sure?" Jean hated himself for asking, but not half as much as he'd hate finding out later that she regretted even a moment of this. "It's been a long time. There's no one else?"

Shifting free of his hold, she wrapped her arms around him and rested her head against his chest. "I belong to the corporation, Jak. Aside from that, I'm all yours."

He huffed a laugh and kissed the top of her head. "That's pretty stiff competition."

"It doesn't have to be." She snuggled even closer, deliriously happy to be in his arms again. "I'm not in love with the corporation, Jak; just responsible for it. And it's a lot smaller now that my father's will has come into play."

"Hmm." He brushed his lips across her forehead, her cheek, the curve of her neck. It felt so right to hold her. But it wasn't just his heart—or even hers—on the line. Even more important than whether or not *he* could be satisfied with the leftovers of her time, how would Solène fit into her already-bursting schedule?

"Jak?" Ava sensed a change, almost as if he'd let out a huge, heartfelt sigh. Straightening away from him was torture, but she needed to see his face. "What's wrong?" She was relieved when he didn't try to deny it.

"I don't know." That sounded lame. "Maybe nothing. Maybe…" Realizing he already had one foot on a rambling path to nowhere, he stopped himself. "It's hard to put into words."

"No hurry." Smiling, she resettled herself comfortably, head on his shoulder.

Jean was surprised enough to laugh softly. "I do love you, Sam. I… Oh, bother."

They both looked around as the door chimed, and nearly bumped noses when he turned back to her, making them both smile. Mischievously, Ava stole another kiss, then grumbled when the door chimed again.

"Maybe they'll go away." Ava sighed and allowed Jean to help her to her feet.

"I should probably go, though. I'm supposed to be here on official business." Jean patted the pocket that held the recording device as the chime sounded again. "Looks like we'll have to answer after all." He smoothed her hair, then accompanied her to the door.

Ava reluctantly put some space between them and adopted the straight face that had seen her through so many dull parties. "Open." When she saw who was there, her eyes widened in surprise.

"Uh. Hi." Steinberg's eyes flicked back and forth between Ava and Jean.

"Hi." Ava faked a yawn so she wouldn't have to pretend to be happy to see him. They hadn't spoken two words to each other since the shuttle arrived, so what was he doing here now?

"We, um. We all heard what happened." Steinberg shifted his weight from foot to foot. "I was elected to come check on you."

"Oh." Ava tried to hide her puzzlement. She'd bumped into a few members of the impromptu welcome party from her first night, but since she wasn't assigned to any one crew, she hadn't made any real friends. So, who was 'we'? "I'm fine. That is, I will be. In a few days."

"Great!" Steinberg shot another glance at Jean, then lapsed into silence.

"Thank you for your time, yeoman." Jean cut through the awkwardness like it didn't exist.

"Sorry I wasn't more help, sir." Ava responded sheepishly.

Naturally, Jean played along. "I'm surprised you remembered as much as you did. But, don't worry about a thing. I'm confident Chief Taylor's investigation will fill in the holes." He stepped into the corridor, forcing the stranger to retreat. "In the meantime, you've just gone through quite an ordeal. I recommend getting some rest."

"Yes, sir." Ava looked expectantly at Steinberg, whose face flushed.

"Good idea," he agreed hastily.

"She's had a long day." Jean offered the stranger a bored senior-officer-big-brother smile, the condescending kind that he'd always hated.

"Yessir!" Steinberg took another step back. "I'll tell everyone you said hi." Wheeling around, he bolted down the corridor.

Safely hidden behind the door frame, Ava shook her head at Jean, prepared to tease him until she saw the thoughtful look in his eyes. "What is it?"

"I'm not sure." Jean nodded in case anyone was watching. "How well do you know him?"

"I don't. We came in on the same shuttle, but that's it." She paused. "Come to think of it, he was acting very strangely just now. On the shuttle, he was confident, suave even. Do you think it means anything?"

"I'll tell you later," he promised. "You really should get some sleep, though. You'll recuperate more quickly." He couldn't kiss her, but he did add softly, "Love you."

"I love you, too." Ava obediently shut the door behind him as he walked away, then leaned against it for a moment. Sleep wouldn't come easily with his kisses lingering on her lips.

Chapter 12

This time, Jean closed the door when he entered Taylor's office, and they listened to the recording together. If Taylor noticed the disparity between the length of the recording and how long Jean had been gone, he didn't say so.

"Wonderful." Taylor scrubbed a hand over his face and glared at Jean. "Now I suppose you want me to investigate Donovan's role in all of this."

"I don't see how it can be avoided." Jean answered diplomatically. "I can confirm what she overheard in the cafeteria—he does have a peculiar habit of overriding docking assignments for supposedly unexpected ships."

"Sounds like something he'd do, just for the fun of it." Taylor hedged. In his experience, space station captains did *not* appreciate being investigated.

"I never thought much about it until today," Jean agreed. Then, he nodded at the recording device. "If I were you, I'd put that somewhere safe."

"And if I were you," Taylor retorted, his fingers curling around the item in question, "I'd steer clear of this whole thing, so I wasn't in anybody's way. Get me?"

Jean hesitated. "In that case, there's one more thing I have to tell you. I wasn't going to mention it yet because all I've got is suspicion." When he'd finished explaining, Taylor scratched his chin thoughtfully.

"That's too thin to make soup with," he said at last. "I couldn't justify pursuing it without more evidence."

Jean turned that over in his mind for a moment,

then smiled. "That means I won't be getting in the way if I make some inquiries of my own."

"Just watch that line, Kearns." Taylor leaned back in his chair. "I don't want to have to investigate you for crossing it."

"I understand." Jean appreciated his friend's warning. It would be all too easy, especially now that he had hope of a life with Sam again, to lose his temper with whomever had nearly killed her.

He kept that at the top of his mind while he checked in with Masie, who was more than happy to watch Solène a bit longer. Returning to his desk in the command center, he sifted through the available information, hunting as much for disparities in the records as for blatant indicators of trouble.

Finally pausing to rub tired eyes, he glanced down at his commband, then stared in disbelief. How many notifications had he missed? The indicator light was blinking rapidly and switching color between orange and green. Grimacing, he began sorting through the messages, determined to finish before he was late for picking up Solène.

It hit him as he was rising to leave—he'd forgotten all about retrieving Ava's commband! Grumbling to himself as he went, Jean made his way back to the security office, where he was only mildly surprised to find Taylor still staring at his display.

"What do you want?" Taylor grumped. He'd never enjoyed the sensation of chasing his tail and at the moment, he was dizzy from doing just that. It should've been as simple as typing in the request to get the names of all ships docked on D7 around the time of the incident, but one thing led to another and now he was trying to determine exactly how many times a particular make and model of ship had visited the station, and under how many different registrations.

"I came for her commband." He'd decided on the way over to present it as his request, not hers. "By now you've checked it for biotraces and pulled all the digital data it has to offer." He was proud of himself for not overemphasizing that aspect of the investigation. If he tipped his hand, Taylor would hang onto the commband and, without a doubt, discover the 'upgrade.'

"Yeah, sure, take it." Taylor waved his hand. "The last thing I need is a cluttered office."

"Thanks." Striving for nonchalance, Jean scooped up the commband—then nearly dropped it as an unnerving thought occurred to him. Taylor wasn't the only person who'd had unrestricted access to the commband. Given the choice between Taylor or the thugs, Jean would choose to have the secret discovered by Taylor. But was there even a way to tell that Ava had been poking around inside it? If there was, Taylor and his crew would find it.

"Something else?" Taylor eyed Jean suspiciously.

"Huh?" Jean forced a smile even as one horrible repercussion after another occurred to him. "Oh, no. Just." Sucking in a deep breath, Jean ignored his instincts screaming at him to hide the commband and instead held it up for Taylor to see. "Somebody must've wanted her dead pretty badly to leave this on another section as a decoy."

Taylor grimaced. "Makes you wonder what she saw in that docking bay."

"Or whom." Jean's thoughts darted to Captain Donovan. Could *he* have been there? Ava hadn't mentioned it, but she'd also been drugged. She might've seen him or heard him without knowing exactly who it was…

"Jean." Taylor glowered at him, not liking the ferocious look in Jean's eyes a moment before. "We'll figure it out. You go take care of your girls."

"Right." Jean backed up a step. "Good advice." Pivoting, he marched out the door, deep in thought. He hadn't learned a single thing during his research today. Well, tomorrow he was going to go at it from a different angle—specifically, through Donovan's records. Cleverly, of course. It would never do to tip him off.

All of which he kept to himself as he and Solène took Masie out for dessert, then stopped by one of the smaller shops to buy a get well present for Ava.

"Do you think she'll like it?" asked Solène, skipping along at his side as they headed home.

"I think she'll love it." He'd given Solène the deciding vote between a hovering backscratcher with a remote and a 3D story cube, and now he was curious to see how Ava reacted.

"Can we give it to her tonight?" Solène tugged on his hand while they waited for the pivotlift.

"I think she's probably asleep right now, mareyth." Noting the disappointed expression on her face, and remembering the commband he was still carrying, Jean hesitated. "I suppose we could go and see, though."

Solène grinned and tugged him into the pivotlift as it arrived, then entered their destination as he instructed her.

On the *Beyond*, where 'daytime' was dictated by one's assigned shift, Montgomery Galactic had made it childishly easy to block out the rest of the station by silencing the door chimer and commband. Excepting in the event of an emergency, when such measures were of a necessity overridden, this was sufficient to ensure the opportunity for sleep to all who truly desired it.

"It's actually a good thing if she doesn't answer," Jean told Solène as he pressed the chimer when they arrived. "That means she's asleep and recuperating."

Solène nodded solemnly, then focused on the door with such intensity that she seemed to be willing it to open, which it suddenly did. "Terina!" She threw herself forward, catching the object of her exuberance completely by surprise.

Ava inhaled sharply at the jolt of having her bruised knee enthusiastically squeezed, then reached down to touch Solène's shoulder. "Golly." The word came out as a pained wheeze, so she cleared her throat and tried again. "Have you missed me?"

Jean gently pried his daughter loose and carried her around the corner to the couch, swinging her legs back and forth until she giggled. Depositing her with the aid of a 'plop' sound effect, he tousled her hair while he looked anxiously to Ava.

Ava nodded to him that she was alright, and was silently glad that she'd taken a moment to run a brush through her hair before answering the door. Pillow-hair might work for some women, but she'd learned long ago that she couldn't concentrate on anything else when she was busy wondering what her hair was doing.

Jean pressed the gift into Solène's hands, winked, and hurried back to check on Ava. "Sorry about that," he murmured, too softly for Solène to hear.

"It's fine." Ava patted him on the arm reassuringly. "Honestly, I think it's a good sign."

"A good sign? I don't follow." That was an understatement. How could hurting her be good?

"Things will be a lot easier if she likes me, silly." Ava felt herself begin to blush.

Jean's heart did a funny little jig in his chest and it was all he could do to not steal a kiss. Instead, he slipped an arm around her waist and carefully picked her up. It was only a few steps to the couch, where he gently placed her next to Solène.

"We come bearing gifts," he announced as he seated himself on Ava's opposite side, casually slipping the commband into the space between them. That accomplished, he stretched his arm across the back of the couch hopefully.

"Gifts? You didn't need to…" Ava cut herself off when she noticed the package in Solène's hands. Smiling, she abandoned her protest in favor of, "What a sweet thought." She didn't remember getting very many *gifts* as a child. Rewards, usually agreed upon in advance, were common enough, but over time she'd learned to cherish the thrill of achievement for itself and extra time with her parents became simply an added bonus.

Emboldened by Ava's smile, Solène shyly pressed the package into her hands, then clasped her own hands in her lap.

"Thank you." She remembered to include Jean in her smile before popping open the lid and peeking inside. "Oh, my." Swiftly, she loosed the catches on the sides of the box and bent them underneath to form a four-legged platform, which she set on the nearest chair. "Is this a story cube?"

Solène nodded vigorously and launched into an explanation of how to use it.

"I get to make choices in the story? Are you sure?" Ava pretended to be in awe of the idea, despite having authored a few such stories herself. They'd started as college projects, then lingered with her until she'd finally surrendered and completed them properly.

"Yes! It's so much fun. You'll love it!" Solène was fairly glowing with excitement as she gave her unqualified endorsement. She didn't stop there, either, but went on to demonstrate how to interact with the story and so forth.

Ava leaned on Jean's shoulder a little and stifled a yawn. She aimed an interested smile at Solène even as her fingers closed around her commband.

Bringing his lips close to her ear, Jean murmured, "Tired?" He only asked to be polite. A common aftereffect of carbon monoxide poisoning and its treatment was a day's worth of weariness.

"Yes." She shivered lightly as his breath tickled her neck. "But I'm so glad you came."

"Me, too." With a wink, he leaned forward and began laying the groundwork for their departure. "Solène picked out the story herself."

"Wow!" Ava played along. She'd slept for a while after Jean's last visit, then got up to eat something. After foolishly checking for communication from Phyl, she'd spent the last hour putting out fires. It was incredibly irritating when department heads refused to acknowledge Phyl's authority. "Excellent choice!"

"I'll be busy most of tomorrow." Jean cocked an eyebrow at Solène. "And so will you, mareyth. You're already late getting to bed, and you have school tomorrow."

"But Daddy!" Solène protested. "I don't have school tomorrow!"

"You don't?" Jean scratched his cheek as if trying to remember, but Solène knew him too well to be fooled.

"Silly Daddy." Stepping carefully over Ava's legs, Solène climbed up into Jean's lap and faced him, hands on his shoulders. "I could come keep Miss Terina company."

"You could?" Jean raised both his eyebrows. Ava had the day off to recuperate. Pity he didn't have it off as well. "I mean, I suppose you *could*, but…"

"I'd like that." Ava jumped at the idea. Aside from supper the night before, she'd barely spent any time with the girl. This was the perfect chance to begin building a lasting friendship with the daughter of the man she fully intended to marry.

"Oh?" His gaze dropped to Ava's lips and his pulse quickened. For an instant, he regretted picking Solène up before bringing the commband over.

Guilt hit him like an iceball to the head. He'd just wished his precious daughter was somewhere else.

Straightening away from Ava, Jean tried to give himself the benefit of the doubt. He didn't want Solène to go away. Quite the opposite. She needed a little time to get used to the idea of someone new in their lives before he complicated things further with the discussions that his having a 'ladyfriend' would undoubtedly bring about.

Belatedly, he returned to his previous thought. "Well, then. If you're sure you don't mind?"

Puzzled by Jean's withdrawal, Ava nearly missed her cue. "I'd love to have you come for a visit, Solène." She relaxed when Solène did, grateful the delay in her reassurance had apparently gone unnoticed by the child.

"I'll be very good company," Solène promised them both.

"I know you will, mareyth." Heart melting, Jean dropped all pretense and tapped her lightly on the nose. Then, to Ava. "How early is too early?"

"Ah, um." It was on the tip of her tongue to say right after breakfast, but there were a few remaining communications she needed to answer as soon as she could see straight again. Naming a slightly later time, she was relieved when they both smiled their approval.

"To be here that early," Jean hopped to his feet, "you had better get to bed, young lady."

Solène giggled as he swung her onto his shoulders, her relaxed air speaking volumes about her whole-hearted trust of her adopted father.

Ava laughed, too, as she rose to accompany them to the door. Jean's near hand gently cupped her elbow as she walked, offering to support her if she needed it.

"Goodnight." She paused in the doorway and lifted her hand in a wistful wave. If their earlier proximity had been awkward, it was now almost painful to watch him walk away, even with the promise of his swift and frequent returns.

Had her mother felt this way about her father? And vice versa? Ava couldn't help but believe that to be the case, which only served to underscore how terribly, terribly brave one had to be to risk falling in love.

Down the corridor, Jean responded to Solène's chatter even as he grappled with the imminent realization of his most precious dream—having a family like the one he was born into.

Now that he faced the prospect directly, though, he questioned whether he was up to it. The memories of his parents and siblings were faded with time yet tinged with gold, as memories often are when they're all one has left. While he might reason that his parents made mistakes, his first few years of raising Solène were fraught with the fear of making a wrong decision.

And there had been *so many* decisions. The decision to stop attending school full-time. The decision to sign on with Montgomery Galactic and keep taking courses. Leaving Solène in someone else's care for the first time had nearly broken him.

What would the future be like if he married Ava? Wonderful? Awful? Or some of each?

There might be more children, someday. Which undoubtedly meant more mistakes. Hmm. Was it easier to raise children with a partner? Some couples made it look easy, like his parents. Others either argued constantly, split up, or one dominated the other.

Oh, bother. That reminded him of joint operations while he was in the military. It seemed almost an unwritten law that such things *had* to go badly. If he tried to be agreeable, the other commander tried to run over him. The few times he'd asserted himself as the senior commander, he was met with resistance at every turn. Eventually he'd learned to smile to their faces, stand his ground when necessary, and make backup plans while they weren't looking. As awful as those short-lived instances were, they paled in comparison with the horror of living that way for the rest of his life.

For an hour after climbing into his bed, Jean lay awake pondering these and other questions. In the end, he gave it up as futile. No, worse. Far worse. How many times had he watched another soldier torture themselves by contemplating all the ways they might get hurt in an upcoming battle? Now here he was imagining all the ways a future with Ava could go wrong.

No more of that! Applying a concerted effort, Jean smashed all the fear into the confines of a mental 'box' and slammed the lid shut. They'd face what came together.

Chapter 13

In a ship light-years away from the station, a rough group sat around a metal table, cards in their hands and drinks of varying sizes within easy reach. A rapidly growing pile of gaming buttons sat in the approximate center of the table as the betting between three of the players reached a crescendo, each refusing to yield. The four players who'd already folded watched with interest, and two other crewmembers began privately betting on the outcome of the game.

A meaty hand casually tossed a large, yellow button into the pile, and a deep voice growled, "And fifty."

"Hang on." The narrow-shouldered, squinty-eyed man who'd folded first spoke up. "Can't do that. Max bid is…"

"Shut up," barked one of the remaining players. "You're out of the game." Selecting two smaller blue buttons, each worth twenty-five, she dropped them on the pile. "I'll call."

All eyes swung to the third player. Cards folded in one hand, Erq Vyl calmly reached for his drink with the other, took a sip, then replaced the glass on the table.

As anxious as they all were to see how the game would end, nobody breathed a word of complaint when he delicately plucked a cloth napkin—stained, but clean—from the table and dabbed at his lips. Nobody dared hurry the captain.

Ah, but Vyl enjoyed demonstrating his power over them. It was even more amusing than beating them at poker, winning back money he hadn't even paid them yet. After a few rounds of rurik, only the best players could afford to continue playing.

He chuckled inwardly. Another day or two of peace and quiet, sheer torture for a group that stupidly believed risking their lives was the 'easy way' to earning their fortunes, and someone would probably try to coax the winners into playing a high-stakes game of circu to relieve the boredom.

"I'll see you and raise you." Selecting a red button no larger than his fingernail, Vyl slid it over to the pile with one finger. He didn't have a high hand, but it didn't matter. "Two hundred."

The whispered betting resumed, loud in the silence while the remaining card players considered their options. There were only two—put up or shut up—yet ponder they did, weighing the potential loss of everything they'd already risked *plus* another two hundred against the slimmer chance that they might win.

Zikin's thick fingers curled protectively around what was left of his future earnings before he muttered something under his breath and threw his cards down. He was out.

Vyl raised sleek eyebrows at Paella. Next to himself, he considered her the smartest person in the room, the very reason he'd made her his second. Tough, too. She'd recovered from wounds that made even veteran doctors shake their heads.

"What's it going to be?" he prodded. He watched her eyes narrow before she moved to cover his bet. Interesting. Almost surprising. Had he done something to tip her off to the fact that he was bluffing?

One by one she laid her cards down, revealing three gailen dragons and two king's castles. Then, her face impassive, she rested her forearms on the table and looked at Vyl expectantly.

Vyl clamped down on the irritation rising in

himself and laid out his four ordered numbers and lone spy. With five consecutive numbers or a higher anchor card, he could've beaten her. He barely heard the whistles and congratulations from the rest of the crew as he tipped his head in a slight nod. *Till next time.*

A movement by the door attracted his attention and he realized it was his cypher, Albo, exiting the room. Interesting. Albo had been holed up in his quarters ever since they left the *Beyond*. He'd even missed a few meals. Not a gambler, he hadn't been there to watch the outcome of the game.

Erq got to his feet and swept his remaining buttons off the table into the cloth napkin he'd been using, then sauntered out of the room. The *Reus* wasn't a large ship, but it still took him five minutes to catch sight of Albo, blast his longer legs.

Coming around a corner hot on Albo's tail, Erq stopped abruptly. The corridor ahead of him was empty. Where had the other man gone? He no longer heard the distinctive thud of boots on deckplating and there were no adjoining corridors close enough to disappear into, even for a man of Albo's height.

Unless…Erq's head jerked up sharply. "Get down out of there now." He glared up into the shadows.

A pair of boots appeared, then descended until Albo hung at full arms' length from the hatch of the maintenance tunnel built into the corridor ceiling. Without even extending the access ladder, he dropped to the floor.

"Most people don't look up," he told his boss blandly.

"Well, I did." Erq clung to his temper for the

sole reason that Albo was the best cypher he'd ever had, capable of bypassing the average security system in seconds and possessing an almost eerie ability to find information in the confusing jumble that was the galactic network. "What were you hiding for, anyway?" His grip on his napkin full of buttons tightened.

"I was being followed." Albo could've been wearing a wax mask for all his expression changed.

"Yes." Erq relaxed fractionally. A bit of paranoia could save a life on a ship such as this. "Can't blame you for taking precautions." That was the closest he could bear to come to an apology. "But it's just me. And I only wanted to ask about your latest project."

Albo smiled suddenly, displaying a shocking number of teeth in such a narrow face. "You'll have to see it to believe it." Jerking his head in a 'follow me' gesture, Albo resumed his trek back to his quarters.

Erq hesitated at the door, if only for an instant. There was something so…almost clinical about the cypher's space. A single, comfortable chair sat at a metal desk that took up a large portion of one corner of the room—arguably Albo's favorite spot on the whole ship. The only other piece of furniture was the perfectly smoothed plantgel bed. Every reflective surface was at a high polish so that when Erq did step into the room, he saw four different angles of himself in motion.

His mouth tightened at one particularly unfortunate memory. He'd been celebrating when Albo came to get him, not quite drunk but well on his way. Forgetting the mirrored surfaces for an instant, he'd drawn his weapon and blasted a hole in the closet door.

"Remember that commband we picked up on the *Beyond*?" Albo knew nothing of how the item came into his hands, only that it had. "The one you made me leave there?"

Dragging his thoughts back to the present, Erq stepped around the end of the narrow bed and over to where Albo already had his display up and was typing away. "What about it?"

"I cloned it." Focused on his display, Albo completely missed the way Erq's eyebrows shot up. If he'd noticed and asked about it, he would've just laughed at Erq's surprise. A two-minute pivotlift ride was more than enough time for an expert cypher such as himself. "I know we've got access and all, but I've got this new code that I wanted to test out."

"Code? What kind?" Erq was understandably concerned. The last thing they needed was to make their contact on the *Beyond* angry.

"Nothing to worry about," soothed Albo. "Just a little tunneler. Something to help me get at extended Montgomery schedules. Y'know, in case we ever want to expand the procurement side of the business."

Erq was still annoyed that he hadn't been consulted, but he settled for a nod. Since nothing had gone wrong yet, he had the luxury of listening to the whole story before he decided how mad he was.

"Right, so I plugged it into the commband copy and started messing around to see how well it worked. And that was when," his fingers flew over the keyboard, then he abruptly stopped and poked a glowing red dot on his display, "I found this."

Erq stared ignorantly at the lines of code on

the display, then at Albo. "What is it?"

Albo allowed himself a tiny sigh. *This* was why he was lonely. He'd tried talking to everyone on the ship, but none of them were as smart as he was!

"It's a skeleton key code." He shut the display down and faced Erq. "With this program, I can open any door on the *Beyond*. And that's not all." He folded his arms across his chest. "I think it might work on any door at any Montgomery facility." Watching Erq closely, Albo was gratified to see interest in the man's face. "It's a genius bit of programming…"

He kept speaking, outlining the finer points of the code, but Erq had stopped listening. In fact, Erq had actually stopped breathing, his imagination staggering under the weight of the implications of Albo's calm announcement. His greedy little mind was running rampant around the galaxy, selecting a plum target, then discarding it for an even richer one. No!

Then, the best plan of all struck him like a spanner to the back of the head—a coordinated attack! Why limit himself to *one* facility when he had three ships? And he knew half a dozen captains who'd trade their own ships to be in on a raid like this. They could all retire on this one.

"Erq?" Albo shoved a chair behind him just in time, for Erq sat as if his knees had given out suddenly. No one who knew Erq would've been the least surprised to see that his grip on the napkin filled with gaming buttons had only tightened. "You okay?"

"Hmm? Fine. Just thinking." Erq shook himself free of the fevered dreams of a moment before.

"Yeah? Thinking what?" Albo eyed him suspiciously.

First things first. "What would it take for you to test your theory about the code? Properly, I mean."

"You mean, see what doors it'll open?" Albo's forehead scrunched up in obvious confusion. "You're not serious."

"Deadly serious." Erq leaned closer. "What do we need?"

It took some doing, but Erq finally hounded specifics out of Albo and sauntered off to his own quarters. Montgomery facilities littered the galaxy, everything from spaceship docks to scientific laboratories.

Now there was a thought! Industrial espionage!

Erq dropped his napkin of buttons on the table by the door as he entered his cabin. The largest suite available on the *Reus*, it boasted a lounging room with two couches, a room for his exercise equipment, and a bedroom besides.

Toeing his boots off, Erq stretched out on the nearest couch to think. Rushing around, being sloppy was an excellent way to wind up on the receiving end of the galaxy's 'hospitality' for two to five years. This would take careful planning and handpicked crews.

His next thought deepened his frown. Was this a windfall or a trap? Suspicion was so ingrained in him that the real surprise was how long it had taken him to ask this question.

Getting back up, Erq sauntered over to a plush chair, where he picked up a soft ball and began rolling it between his palms and fingers. Time to start at the beginning. In this case, that meant the pathetic little yeoman who'd almost gotten in their way. And who better to ask than his contact on the *Beyond*? He'd been meaning to call in anyway, to report what had happened.

Initiating the contact, he arranged a smile on his face and sat back. A geometric object spun this way and that on his display, supposedly to distract him while he waited. And waited. He was about to cancel the call when the screen suddenly blinked and revealed a shadowy figure.

"You blithering idiot!" hissed a digitally warped voice. "You double-dyed, sapbrained, good-for-nothing fool!"

"Hello yourself." Erq's smile tightened, but he kept firm control of himself. Learning the answers to his questions was far more important than enduring a few measly insults. Particularly when he wasn't absolutely sure *who* was insulting him. His least favorite part of this business arrangement was not having a clue who his contact was. The intel was always spot on, so he didn't complain too much, but that didn't mean he liked it. "Is something wrong?" Even though the figure remained a dark outline, Erq had the sudden impression of narrowed eyes and bared teeth.

"Oh, no," snapped the figure. "Everything's nebular. I'm here picking up your mess, as usual."

"What mess?" Erq made a show of examining his neatly trimmed fingernails. "I thought we handled it rather tidily."

"Well, just don't sprain your shoulder patting yourself on the back." He countered savagely, "Because she's still alive."

Erq swallowed. His grandiose plans for retirement, which had up to that point still been merrily unfurling in the background of his mind, melted away like butter on a hot pan. While there was no chance that he himself could be identified by the girl—she'd been well and truly unconscious by the time he'd seen her—if any of his crew were reported…or if the 'accident' was somehow linked to the *Reus*…

"She claims to remember nothing." The figure didn't sound happy, but that was mostly because of how hard he'd had to work to learn even that much. "And I don't believe a word of it."

"What?" Erq tensed again and became vaguely aware of moisture on his forehead. "Why not?"

"Because I have eyes and ears," retorted the figure. "You'll have to steer clear of the *Beyond* for a while. Maybe forever."

"But!" Erq stopped abruptly when the display flickered and vanished. He shot angrily to his feet, then sank slowly back into his chair. It was useless to get angry about things he couldn't control. Blast it all, though, there went his best chance at getting answers to his questions!

Or was it? He stroked his chin thoughtfully. There were other ways to find the information he wanted, starting with who the young woman was and what she was doing with a skeleton key code on her standard-issue commband.

His best guess was that she was a security plant. What else? It certainly explained what she was doing, poking around the docking bay where she'd been found. Anyway, old Montgomery had died not too long ago and someone had no doubt begun checking records. Rich folk always did that when a lot of money changed hands. If the slightest of discrepancies were discovered on the *Beyond*, an agent would be shipped over to spy things out.

But again, this was not the time to get sloppy. Especially not when it would be childishly easy for Albo to locate the answers to those questions for him.

Right, then. For now, they would stick to their schedule, delivering what they'd pilfered from the *Beyond* to one of Montgomery's other stations. Suitably repacked and labeled, of course. And from there, who knew? It would apparently be a while before another assignment came their way. A short stint as a shuttle, perhaps? The crew wouldn't like it, for any number of reasons, including having to double up on rooms, but carrying passengers would give them a legitimate reason to visit an even larger Montgomery facility deeper in known space.

Captain Erq Vyl mentally rubbed his hands together in eager anticipation of the riches the solar winds had blown into his lap.

Blissfully unaware of Vyl's plans to feather his nest without him, the self-proclaimed boss of the outfit was waiting with growing impatience for another call. As he paced his quarters, he reflected that his underlings lacked the proper respect for his position. He pulled the strings, he called the shots, and they treated him like a distant relative's birthday, unimportant and easily forgotten.

"Finally," he snarled when his commband vibrated. Opening the channel, he bit out, "You are late."

"Yes. Um. Sorry." Donovan hated apologizing. However, retirement was too close to risk jeopardizing the loss of the extra money he made via this, um, side business. So, he put up with the temperamental and often cranky shadow who relayed the orders. "It's been a long day. Something went wrong with the last…"

"I know."

Donovan, who also hated being interrupted, ground his teeth together to keep from saying anything he'd regret. "Oh. Well, I wanted to get as much information together as possible before reaching out. Thought it would save time in the end." His irritation faded into concern as the silence stretched out between them. Just as he was beginning to think the connection had deteriorated, resulting in weirdly frozen images staring out of the display while the self-tuning program struggled to reestablish, the shadow spoke again.

"Alright. Tell me what you know. If it's more than I already know, all is forgiven."

Forgiven?! Donovan fumed at the temerity of the man! This was a business relationship, or supposed to be. Stretching his patience to its maximum, Donovan relayed the debacle in detail.

"I see." The shadow paced to his left, then to his right. Paused when Donovan cleared his throat. "Was there something you wanted to add?"

Donovan shook his head mutely. He didn't trust himself to speak.

"Well. Fortunately for our continued arrangement, there were tiny bits of useful information scattered throughout your ramblings. Unfortunately, it will be some time before the next shipment can be picked up." Confident though he was that he'd successfully scrambled the signal, as well as routing it through various communication buoys around the galaxy, the shadowy figure still always took care to speak vaguely. "When things cool down, I'll be in touch."

The display before Donovan shut down abruptly, but for once, he didn't care. No, he had something far more important on his mind. Accessing the folder of display images, he opened the shot he'd captured just now. Zoomed in on the porthole and frowned. The enlargement blurred things so badly that he could hardly tell one tiny star from another.

He'd waited too long for some clue as to where his shadowy contact was located to give up that easily, though. A quick search of his programs resulted in two options for clarifying images. Rather than wasting time researching which was better than the other, Donovan dumped the image into both programs, adjusted the settings to maximum, and rose with a pleased smile.

Once the image was clear enough to view space as seen through his contact's porthole, he'd feed it into a navigation chart. It would take days, perhaps longer, but finally he would have something on the aggravating man who treated him so contemptuously.

Chapter 14

For the next few days, each time Ava ventured out of her quarters—for work or to spend time with Jean and Solène—she had the nagging feeling that she wasn't alone. After decades of hiring the most discreet security operatives available, being followed was second nature. She'd been more aware of its absence during her recent travels than anything else.

To have it resume now, abruptly and without her direct request, was unsettling at best. Ava spent a lot of time pausing in front of stores and pretending to read wall menus while she surreptitiously watched her backtrail, all without success. It was tempting to blame her failure on the increase in foot traffic. A small fleet of scientific vessels had docked earlier for final refueling and repairs before heading out, so there *were* more people on the station than usual.

But she found no satisfaction in the excuse and kept trying. She was just turning away from one such attempt when she bumped into someone coming from the other direction.

"Oh! I'm so sorry." Ava nearly choked on her apologetic laugh when she recognized the other woman. Officer...Johnson! Yes, they'd come in on the same shuttle. As pieces continued to click into place in her head, Ava suddenly felt like a complete fool for overlooking the fact that a 'tail' could walk past her and wait as well as tag along behind her.

"Forget it." Eyebrows drew together over kind green eyes. "Hey, don't I know you?"

"Me?" Ava forced herself to relax, act natural. They hadn't interacted since arriving, so she pretended to be uncertain. "I don't… Mmm, wait. Yes! We came in on the same shuttle."

"That's it." Though still physically reminiscent of a compact earthmoving machine, Johnson had a decidedly feminine voice and smile. "Wow, can you believe we've already been here two whole weeks?"

"Seems like I just synced up my commband." Ava played along, listening for a message. It had to be something important to bring her escort out from the periphery.

"Right? I have to say, though, that Chief Taylor is the best boss I've had in a while. *Really* good at his job."

"That's," Ava's stomach twisted at the direct mention of the security chief, "wonderful."

"Yeah. I'm going to enjoy the rest of my time here, I think." She scanned the crowd behind and around Ava expectantly, as if she was casually waiting for someone. Her hand came up and she waved. "Gotta go. Nice to see you again."

"I… You, too." Ava struggled to keep her perplexity from showing on her face.

Remembering that she was supposed to be joining Jean and Solène for supper at Masie's, Ava turned in that direction. No matter how hard she thought about her short conversation with Johnson, though, all she came away with was the length of time they'd been on the *Beyond* and that Chief Taylor was a good boss. Good enough to trust with Ava's true identity? Of course, he'd know that in another week when she—oh.

Oh!! Was that it? Was Johnson suggesting that she arrive 'early,' and catch everyone by surprise? Hmm, it wasn't a bad tactic. Except that she still had more research to do.

Leaning against the wall opposite the entrance to Masie's restaurant, Ava looked around for Jean or Solène, then settled in to think. So far everything pointed to the source of the supply problem being right there on the station. Now that she was assigned to the command level again, Donovan having graciously agreed to overlook her 'distracting' hair, she'd managed to poke around a bit, but not nearly enough.

Naturally, it would be a lot easier to find the evidence she needed if she wasn't having to sneak searches in between the tasks of her regular job. A sardonic smile twisted her lips as she reminded herself that the culprits were doing their best to hide the evidence, too. She shouldn't expect it to be easy. Anyway, there was one obvious solution. She was going to have to do some concentrated snooping. Maybe even use her commband access to break into Donovan's quarters, though she hated the idea.

She gasped when she realized someone was standing right in front of her.

"Hello?" Jean tried a second time to snap Ava out of her reverie. "Ah, there you are." He smiled as her eyes widened and lifted to meet his.

"Jean! I, wow." She lowered the hand that had leaped to her heart. "How long have you been standing there?" Good grief, maybe she *did* need a keeper.

"Only a few seconds." He tapped her on the nose. "Though I did wave at you as we exited the pivotlift."

Ava half-heartedly fought the blush rising in her cheeks. She didn't mind if Jean saw it. They'd already lost enough time without her playing hard to get. It was everyone else in the general vicinity area she wasn't ready to share with yet. Although, she probably should discuss it with Jean before she decided whether or not to reveal her identity to Taylor. He'd known the security chief a lot longer than she had.

"Shall we?" Jean offered her his arm as he straightened away before he gave in to the urge to kiss her.

"We shall." Tucking her hand into the crook of his arm, Ava took a mental snapshot of the moment. He'd changed out of his uniform into a cerulean blue shirt that drew her attention to his gorgeous blue eyes. From there it seemed only natural to appreciate the symmetry of his face, enhanced as it was by the slight crookedness of his nose, which had been broken more than once while he was in the military.

"Daddy?" Solène tugged on Jean's sleeve. "Daddy, Masie says we better come while there are still seats for us."

Jean tore his gaze away from Ava's mesmerizing eyes to find Solène frowning up at him.

"Are you okay, Daddy? You look funny."

Taking pity on him, Ava stepped in with a smile. "He's probably just hungry." The fire in his eyes when she went to wink at him made her heart pound. "H-how about you, Solène? What do you like to eat here?" With an effort, she regained control of her voice.

Solène somehow ended up walking between them, a small hand in each of theirs as she did her best to tell Ava about everything she'd ever eaten at Masie's in the short time it took them to cross the corridor. She continued to expound on the subject until the meal was half gone, then stopped herself with a contented sigh. "I guess this is my favorite."

Masie's face lit up as she looked around from where she was resetting a table. "You get the best tonight. First time in a while, we get the whole order!"

"The whole order?" Intrigued, she cocked her head to one side and asked, "What do you mean?"

"All of everything I order." Masie threw up her hands. "Mostly we get just this or that, or maybe some of what you order the time before."

"Ugh, that's awful." Ava wrinkled her nose, then shook her head for good measure. Inwardly, her mind was racing. There hadn't been a full delivery for months. Why the sudden change? Who was pulling the strings?

Jean must've sensed something was up, because he jumped in with a question about Masie's xintxa, and Solène almost bubbled over with joy when Masie invited her to come play with the animal after they'd finished eating. He didn't miss the knowing wink Masie gave him as she further offered to take Solène right away, so he and Ava wouldn't have to hurry the rest of their meal.

"I suppose that would be alright." Jean nodded his thanks to Masie, who excused herself to instruct her staff, then returned and took Solène off to play.

"She's a good woman." Ava smiled and returned Solène's wave before she and Masie turned the corner. "I hate that this is happening to her. I have to fix it, Jean."

"Yes, she is. I hate it, too. And let me know how I can help." He grinned cheekily as he addressed her statements in order. Gently, he smoothed Ava's hair back from her face. "I can't wait for you to resume your natural color."

She set her fork down with a sigh. It would be

so easy to get lost in his eyes, his touch. If only she had the time. "There's something I need to talk to you about." Her gaze flicked around the restaurant. Sparsely occupied though it was, she added, "Privately."

His appetite gone, Jean folded his napkin and got to his feet. Catching her hand as she slid out of the booth, he led her to the nearest pivotlift and selected a destination. Disappointed as he was at having his attempt at being romantic thwarted, he enjoyed the way she stayed tucked in close to him during the ride to the garden level, where they got off with a few other couples.

"Oh, my," she breathed. The breeze that cooled her face smelled of fruits, flowers, and damp soil and drew her further into the wonderland. When had she last spent any time planetside? Her forehead wrinkled as she admired a patch of Jinve dayflowers, then shook her head in disbelief. She couldn't remember.

Above her, the domed ceiling stretched up, up, and away until it was blocked from sight by trees, *actual trees*, their leaves shivering in the recycled air. A flock of tiny birds trilled as it swooped through an open space in the canopy, each bird sparkling in the artificial light like someone had thrown a bushel of Marquise-cut gems into the air.

"Wow, Dad." Ava leaned against the tree where she'd stopped and shook her head. "You outdid yourself."

"Did your dad design all this?" Jean's eyes caressed her face, his voice huskier than usual as he slipped an arm around her waist.

"The idea was his. I saw the sketches, but this is just, um…" Thoughts of schedules and obligations faded as she inched closer to him. "He kept insisting until the architects and engineers found a way to make it work." Her head tilted back as Jean leaned toward her.

"Good for him." His lips brushed her forehead.

"Jean, we…" Her hands came to rest against his chest, her fingers curling in the loose fabric of his casual shirt, either to pull him closer or keep him at bay, she wasn't sure which.

"Someone's coming," he interrupted. "Any minute now." Tenderly, he scattered kisses across her face, deliberately avoiding her tantalizing mouth.

She laughed despite her determination to focus on why she'd actually asked to speak with him. A rush of longing surged through her when his breath tickled her cheek and she surrendered, moving to catch his lips with hers. As he kissed her back, the entire command level staff could've paraded past and they never would've noticed.

"Marry me." She blinked up at him, suddenly shy for all that she'd just proposed. Spontaneously. She didn't even have a pledge gift to offer him!

He wore a thoughtful expression on his face as he smoothed her hair where he'd rumpled it. "I want to," he admitted. Easing her closer, he sighed and rested his forehead against hers. "I couldn't kiss you like that if I didn't wish you were mine." If only his life was that simple.

Ava's heart swelled with joy until it ached, even as she gently prompted, "But?" While she could think of at least one reason why he might hesitate, she didn't want to put words in his mouth.

"We'll have to talk to Solène first." Jean offered a lopsided smile.

"We? Both of us together?" Ava kissed his cheek and snuggled closer. Maybe she was reading too much into it, but she couldn't help hoping that he was already thinking as if they were a permanent couple. "Yes. We should definitely…"

The sound of someone clearing his throat grabbed their attention. "We need to talk." Chief Taylor stood a few yards away on the path, one eyebrow raised and the other pulled in as he studied them unabashedly.

"I won't say I'm glad to see you, Chief. Your timing is rotten." Reluctantly, Ava settled her heels back on the ground and drew away from Jean. "But I need to talk to you, too. And it's probably best that Jean be present."

Instinctively guessing what she had in mind, Jean gripped her arm. "Are you sure?" He hadn't changed his mind about her needing a security detail, he was just surprised at the apparent abruptness of her decision.

"I wasn't," she admitted, focusing on Jean while she temporarily ignored the concerned expression growing on Taylor's face. "That's part of what I wanted to talk to you about." She definitely would've preferred to have discussed things with Jean first, but she'd made other choices and would have to live with them.

"Not here." Taylor cut in, partly to remind him that he was there and in charge. "My office."

Jean, perplexed by his friend's behavior, nevertheless nodded and answered for them both. "Let's go."

Even though they were both out of uniform, Ava kept a little distance between herself and Jean during the trek to Taylor's office. Relationships counted as news on the *Beyond*, particularly when only one member of a couple held a command level rank.

Jean carefully shut the door behind them and took a seat beside Ava. He watched as Taylor and Ava just sat there, staring at each other. The urge to blurt out the truth of her identity grew stronger with each passing second, all but strangling him. He hated to see Taylor embarrass himself, yet what could he do? It wasn't his secret.

Ava waited patiently for Taylor to realize she wasn't intimidated by his silence. Then, as he straightened in his chair, she leaned forward.

"I'm going to let you go first," she told him, very nearly catching him with his mouth open. "However, as soon as it seems pertinent, I have something important to tell you."

"Is that a fact?" Taylor looked sharply at Jean, but found no answers in his friend's perfectly straight face.

"Yes." Rather than elaborating, Ava simply folded her hands in her lap and waited for Taylor to proceed.

Eyes narrowing, he did just that. "Took a while, but we got the results back on the biotraces we found in the storage closet and on your comm-band." Punching up his display, he continued, "Ruled out most of what we found as belonging to past or present members of the station crew, with these notable exceptions."

Four folders winked into view and Jean studied them a moment before remarking, "I don't recognize any of those names. Are they passengers, or perhaps guesters?"

"That's the same question we asked." Taylor nodded his approval. "And that's when it got interesting."

Ava gasped and pointed at the faces that appeared above two of the folders. "Them! They're the ones from the docking bay!" Her fists clenched automatically and her heart rate spiked, forcing her to focus on her breathing to calm herself down.

"Correct." Taylor called up more information and a row of ship names began slowly filling in beneath the faces. "Imagine my surprise when I learned that they've been on this station more than once a month for close to a year now." As the last of the ship names solidified, he muttered, "The ship has almost as many aliases as the men do."

Jean whistled softly as he realized what he was seeing. "They're changing the ship's name and repainting the designation numbers, trying to hide its identity."

"A workable theory," Taylor approved. "One that we were able to verify by checking the station security logs." Half a dozen images eclipsed the folders on the display, showing a medium-build cargo vessel. "See that? Back on the aft fin?" He shook his head in genuine disbelief. "They go to all that trouble to hide in plain sight only to get lazy about cosmetic damage."

"I'm sure they never expected us to look this closely." Under control again, Ava reached out and selected the image with the largest portion of ship in it, giving it the screen to itself. "I've seen this… this kind of ship before somewhere."

"She's a Pernix class Destroyer, decommissioned. Trim little craft and, properly refitted, capable of carrying a respectable amount of either passengers or cargo."

Jean snorted. "She's all that and more. I've seen those in action, dropping supplies and reinforcements in a battle zone. They can handle atmosphere as well as open space and gives as good a beating as they take." He rubbed his injured knee without realizing it.

Ava felt a lump of ice begin to form in the pit of her stomach. "What if she's been *im*properly refitted?" She stared at the display as she continued, "What if her guns are fully functional?"

Taylor scowled. "As distracting as speculation can be," he returned to the biotrace results, "in the real world, we deal in facts. And the fact that you should be worried about is that both of these men handled your commband." Opening the last two folders, he pointed at the faces displayed. "Who are you, Yeoman, and how do you know two of the most wanted men in the quadrant?"

Jean shook his head. "She doesn't *know* either of those redhands."

"Enough!" Ava held up both hands, palms forward. Ignoring the disapproving downturn of Taylor's lips, Ava got to her feet and walked over to the retinal scanner by the evidence locker. "Computer, identify," she ordered. Positioning herself in front of it, she closed her right eye, allowing it to scan only her left. Ordinarily, that would've prompted an error, but commbands weren't the only things she'd had tailored to her needs.

"Identifying." The computer's toneless voice did nothing to alleviate the tension in the room. "Sigrid Ava Montgomery."

Chapter 15

"*What?!*" Taylor shot to his feet.

Ava turned to face him. "I'm sorry, Chief. This isn't the way I wanted to tell you."

His face darkened. "Oh, so you did plan to tell me. That's mighty big of you." Fisting his hands, he braced them on his hips. "Do you have the faintest idea of the security risk that you represent?"

"Uh, Chief." Unable to hold still, Ava bounced lightly on her toes and avoided looking at Jean. "I doubt you can improve on the lecture I've already gotten."

Taylor huffed a little, but let it go. "Alright. Let's have the rest of it." He folded his arms across his chest. "What changed your mind about telling me who you really are?"

"For one thing, you come highly recommended." She smiled at Jean, though she was thinking about Johnson, too. "For another, something is wrong. I don't know the details, just that I received a warning of sorts earlier today."

Taylor stiffened. "You were threatened?"

"No, the opposite." Folding her arms across her chest, Ava leaned back against the wall. "I don't know exactly what's going on, only that it's important for me to tell you the truth of who I am. Which implies to me that I'm in danger somehow." Her heart sank to her toes as she looked at Jean. "I'd almost forgotten this aspect of my life. Perhaps I'm a bad bargain after all."

Jean's mouth tightened. "I didn't forget. Not for a nanosecond." How could he? Rising, he held up a hand to forestall Taylor, who looked like he was going to change the subject. "That's why we need to talk to Solène first. It's one thing for me to decide everything we could have together is worth the risk to myself. More than worth it, if I'm being honest." Now he extended his hand to Ava, smiling when she came to him. "We'll explain things to her together, in a way that she'll understand, and then she can decide for herself."

Ava nodded slowly. "That sounds perfect." Looking down at their intertwined hands, she murmured, "I hope she chooses us."

Elation filled Jean when he heard Ava speak of the three of them as a single unit. As a family. Was his dream finally going to become reality?

For his part, Taylor stifled a groan as they began holding a private conversation right in the middle of an important meeting. He was more than a little tempted to leave. Walk around his desk and right out the door. Maybe even slam it behind him. Glumly, he allowed as he didn't have a lot of experience with besotted folk, but it sure seemed like nothing short of blowing up the station would distract them. Unfortunately, he wasn't prepared to go that far.

"Ouch!" Ava suddenly jerked away from Jean and scowled down at her commband. "Alright, alright!"

Confused, Jean stepped back and watched as she answered a hail.

"Boss? Hey, is that you?" A small, round-faced woman peered at them from the display.

"Yes, Phyl, it's me." Ava stifled a sigh.

"Oh, and you're not alone." Phyl leaned closer to her camera. "Hello, everyone. My name is Phylis, you can call me Phyl for short."

Ava knew she might as well get the introductions over with. "Phyl, this is Security Chief Taylor and," she paused fractionally, "Lieutenant Commander

Kearns. Fellas, meet my personal assistant, Phyl."

"So pleased to meet you." Phyl waved at them.

"Delighted, of course." Jean hadn't taken officer's etiquette lessons for nothing.

"Now." Ava folded her arms across her chest. "What's so important you had to shock me?" The commband alert system had four settings: flashing green; orange; red; or for extreme emergencies, a small electric pulse.

"Ah, yes. Something bad, Boss. Look." The display changed to show a map of sorts.

"Is that...?" Jean broke off to look at Ava, who shrugged.

"The galaxy in terms of Montgomery holdings? Yeah."

He raised an eyebrow and deadpanned, "Maybe you're not such a bad bargain after all." He pretended to be hurt when her elbow connected with his gut, but he'd been prepared for a much harder hit.

"Uh, Boss?" Phyl's voice interrupted. "Hate to break up the party, but see those red dots?"

"Five red dots, check." Ava reluctantly refocused on the map.

"You mean five unauthorized accesses."

The breath left Ava's lungs with a woosh, leaving her feeling lightheaded. "Unauthorized?" Shaking her head, she forced herself to inhale. "Is that confirmed?"

"Triple-checked. Didn't set off any alarms, didn't even add it to a report."

"Didn't report them? Then how did we find out they happened?" Ava leaned back against Jean's hard chest, needing something to ground her.

"The computer flagged them as a logical improbability." Phyl chuckled uncertainly. "Something about how you couldn't be in all those places." They ran a low-level AI on their systems, mostly to test their security and help them stay a step ahead of the cyphers.

"*I* couldn't?" Ava vaguely registered Jean's hands on her waist, guiding her over to a chair. She sat with a thud. "Phyl, who does it say opened those doors?"

"That's what I'm trying to tell you." The display reverted to an image of Phyl wringing her hands. "It says *you* did."

Taylor's commband vibrated and Ava's eyes zeroed in on it.

"That's it." She blinked, her thoughts leaping in a dozen directions at once. "The biotraces." The redhands who'd nearly killed her had also taken her commband. Was it possible?

"What?" Phyl's voice was edged with concern. "That's what?"

"Taylor, those last two biotraces. Are either of those men cyphers?"

"Cyphers?" Taylor grimaced. "Yeah, Albo Yetz."

"Spectacular." Ava dropped her head into her hands. "One of the most wanted cyphers in the galaxy had access to my commband."

"Uh." Phyl drew the sound out. "Would someone care to fill me in?"

"Phyl, kill my unrestricted access program. Now." Anger coursed through Ava, threatening to burn her alive. This was all her own fault. If she'd used an ounce of caution in the docking bay, they never would've gotten their hands on her or her commband. But no, she had 'training' and was going to do things herself.

The display shifted with her as Phyl swung

around to a different station, where she worked for several seconds. "Done." She turned back to face them. "Okay. Tell me why I just did that. And please. Start at the beginning."

Ava gave her the short version, insisted that she was just fine, and asked for the Montgomery map display.

"You think they'll try again?" Taylor eyed the map with considerable concern. How were they supposed to protect themselves from an enemy that could waltz right through the front door?

"I know I can't take the chance that they won't." Jumping to her feet, Ava began pacing, examining the map from different angles.

"I kinda hope they do." Phyl snickered. "With the access shut off, we just alert security to pick them up when they come back."

"Did they take anything?" Jean hoped they had.

"Not so far as we can tell."

Not the answer he'd been hoping for. If they'd taken something, they might've left some evidence as to their identities. "Please ask the computer to display the distances between the red dots."

"Any particular order?" Phyl's hand hovered over the digital keyboard.

"In the order that they were accessed, first to last."

"What are you thinking?" Taylor asked, moving to stand beside him.

"Can you also show us the exact access dates?" Jean didn't have to wait long before the information appeared in addition to the distances. "Well, that's not good." Looking through the map at Ava, Jean explained, "It feels to me like this was a trial run."

"Just because they didn't take anything?" Phyl's voice betrayed her skepticism. "They might've gotten interrupted or…"

"Five times? Across a three-day time span and at different facilities several thousand light years apart?" Jean wasn't trying to be rude, but he needed to be sure they listened. "Trust me, this was all prep work."

"How many ships do you think were involved?" Ava had worked it out in her own head, calculating the maximum speed of travel in the available time between attempts versus the distances between the sites. Checking with Jean would show if they were on the same page.

"At least three." Jean pointed at the first two access attempts. "These are the closest to the *Beyond* and happened soon after our run-in with them— whomever they are. Could be they were just the next scheduled stops."

"Assuming you're right," Taylor interjected thoughtfully, "the original ship could've reached one more site, but not the other two, not in the time frame we're dealing with."

"Exactly." Jean blew out a breath. "And here's the best part." All eyes focused on him, reminding him of the briefing sessions he used to give. "We have no idea how many ships they'll come back with."

"Or how many targets they'll raid." Ava felt sick to her stomach. "Or which ones."

"Doesn't matter, does it?" Phyl now sounded cautiously hopeful, like she expected someone to shoot holes full of this theory, too. "I killed the program. Ava, you'll be lucky if your commband can unlock your own quarters."

"We killed the original program," Ava corrected

dully. "In the hands of a skilled cypher, it's as good as a treasure map."

"You're right," Taylor agreed sourly. "If this guy's earned his rap sheet, he can rework that program to get around any digital security measures you might add."

"We'd have to design a completely new program to keep them out." Ava rubbed her stomach absent-mindedly. The meal she'd enjoyed so thoroughly was now twisting in her gut.

"I'll get development on it." Phyl moved to the other station and began typing rapidly.

"That's a good idea." Jean shrugged a little at Ava's questioning look. "They'll never get it done in time to prevent an immediate, orchestrated attack, but the program will have to be replaced anyway."

"Right." Ava went to the synthesizer and ordered a glass of cold water. Maybe sipping it would ease her stomach.

"In the meantime, there are other things you can do." A cunning smile lit Taylor's face. "It'd slow them down quite a bit if you threw biometrics into the mix."

"Good thinking." Jean squinted into his memories. "Scanners used to be all over the place."

"Part of the reason biometrics went out of general use was that they can be defeated most of the time if you have the right tools," Ava objected. "And by now most of our facilities," she winced at the thought of what her dad would say if he was alive to see what she'd done, "have been retrofitted for the standard commbands."

"Then change it back." Jean spoke firmly.

"We'd never be able to keep that from leaking out," protested Phyl, who'd finished submitting the order for the new commband security program.

"We don't want to." Taylor defended the idea stoutly. "They're looking for an easy win, expecting to be able to walk in, pick up what they want, and saunter out. A change like this means security teams are on high alert. Add that to needing specialized tools and expertise to defeat a secondary access system and I guarantee they'll think twice about it."

"Some might even pull out." Jean crossed the room to stand by Ava, who leaned against him when he slipped an arm around her shoulders.

"It'll be a mix of scanners," she said quietly. "Some of the older facilities kept their fingerprint scanners until the commbands rolled out."

"Even better." Jean was glad to hear her say that, it showed she was getting her fight back. She'd gone so pale earlier that he'd been worried.

"Phyl, please get that started. Then send out a company-wide notification that we're planning random security drills." She smiled up at Jean when he gave her an approving squeeze.

"On it." Phyl's chair swiveled away.

"The bad news is that they still might be willing to risk it if the prize is big enough." Taylor frowned at the map, wishing he had more information.

"That's true." Ava blew out a breath and tapped a private communication to Phyl into her commband. "Anything else, Phyl?"

"You want more?" Phyl teased, then sobered. "It's all for now. I've got everything started. Should I put together a list of the probable high-priority targets?"

"Yes, thank you, and send it to me as soon as

you can. As far as the retrofitting goes, it's green-lit all the way. No overtime limits, just get those scanners back up."

"Greenlit, got it." Phyl waved once, then vanished.

"There's one more thing," the words stuck in Ava's throat, "we need to talk about." Gulping the last of the cold water, she dropped the glass in the reclaimer, gaining some much-needed distance from Jean—and instantly missing his warmth.

"What's that?" Taylor thought they'd handled the life-sized disaster pretty well.

"Me." Inhaling shakily, Ava pushed past her fear of how Jean would handle what she had to say. "I'm always a potential target. That goes with my position. However. Now that we're facing a coordinated attack, I have a special request to make of you." She shot Jean a look, then faced Taylor. "In the unlikely event that they come for me, it is imperative that I not be taken alive."

"What?!" Jean spun her to face him and had no idea how close he came to wearing what was left of her supper. "Are you insane? Prisoners can be rescued, you know."

"I know. But not all of them are." She wrapped her arms around herself and willed her roiling midsection to be still. "And sometimes, it's too late."

He shook his head vehemently. "It's never too late if you're alive."

"Jean. Please, listen. This isn't about *me*. It's about… It…" She took a deep breath. "Whoever owns me, owns the corporation. While that probably sounds ridiculously obvious, it makes a difference when you realize that the laws are different in every planetary system. Most of the time it comes down to a fundamental difference in what the society believes is most important, be that money, health, education, or something else." She licked her lips, wishing for another glass of water. "Nobody talks about it much, but there are still a few places in the galaxy where it's legal for one person to own another. If I was ever taken to such a place, if their law declared me to be someone's property, that someone would become the legal owner of Montgomery Galactic. And if I die *after* they take ownership of…me, then my will is null and void. I can't let that happen."

"You could still be rescued." Jean stalked toward her. "I'd move the twelve stars of Terean to bring you back. And, if we're together," his hands settled gently on her waist, "maybe you wouldn't mind so much not owning a corporation anymore." He refused to believe that being wealthy meant more to her than their future did, even when she began to shake her head.

"I'm sorry, Jean," she whispered. "I should've told you this before I proposed. I realize that now. Forgive me, I…wasn't thinking in terms of worst-case scenarios at the time."

"And the worst scenario you can think of is not being rich?" Jean's voice rang with disbelief, filling the small office.

"No! That has nothing to do with it!" Exasperated, Ava tugged free of Jean's grasp and walked a few feet away to gather her thoughts. "Billions of people are employed by my corporation. And tens of billions of people depend on them for support. That is a lot of lives to have even a peripheral responsibility for."

Eyes blazing, she whipped around to face them both. "The new owner—Shall we call them that?

Yes, let's call them that—wouldn't give two Ilyian tusspots for the well-being of the employees. Wages would go down, for starters. Corners would be cut, safety rules ignored, *people would get hurt!* Until finally they'd sell what they hadn't completely destroyed for the best price they could get." She calmed a little as she finished, "I can't let that happen just to prolong my own life. I won't let it happen."

Jean walked around the room once while he tried to process what she'd said. He didn't disagree with what she'd said. How could he? If anything, now that he understood her perspective, he loved her even more. Except he couldn't stop himself from looking for an alternative. From blurting, "I can't believe that galactic law would ever allow something like this!" If he was being honest, it was his desperation speaking, for as a soldier he'd seen enough injustice to last multiple lifetimes.

"It already has." Ava looked to Taylor, wondering if he'd be familiar with the case she had in mind.

"She's right, Jean." Taylor recoiled as his friend whirled in his direction. "It's not my fault! I wasn't even born yet. Flames and fire, my grandaddy hadn't even been born yet."

Ava intervened. "The point is, a precedent has been set. Yes, things have changed a lot in the last few hundred years, but galactic peace is still something of a novelty." She bit her lip and dropped that line of thought. Jean knew more about how fragile peace was than either she or Taylor did. "If anything, I'm afraid that lawmakers are walking a much finer line now than before."

"You've got a point." Taylor jerked a thumb toward Jean. "But so does he. Rescuing you would definitely be my preferred course of action."

"Mine, too. But here, on the *Beyond*, that isn't

a valid option. We're less than a day's travel from the Puer system." She held up both hands to stop either man from protesting. Her voice dropped to barely above a whisper. "Sending someone there to rescue me would only add names to the list of victims."

Wrapping her arms around herself, she faced Jean. Her throat tightened until she could barely force the words out. "We should probably wait to talk to Solène."

Jean gave her a short, stiff nod, spun on his heel, and left the office.

"Speaking of rotten timing." Taylor's lips twisted in what he hoped would pass for a smile. "I know you're wrung out, but I need to make arrangements for you to have proper security."

"I'm probably safer the way things are. I have a bodyguard on station and adding to that would only draw unwanted attention." Ava replied automatically, her thoughts and heart having walked out the door with Jean.

"A bodyguard?" Taylor's forehead creased. "Anyone I know?"

"Hmm?" Confused, Ava replayed his words in her head. "Oh. Yes, she works for you. Speaks very highly of you, in fact." Realizing it wouldn't take him long to deduce the truth, Ava decided to save him the trouble. "Officer Johnson."

"I know her." Taylor nodded slowly. "You're safe with her alright. Except that she can't be around all the time." He raised his eyebrows at Ava when she started to speak. "I get it. You don't want armed guards dogging your steps. Believe it or not, neither do I."

Tired and worried as she was, Ava forced herself to be patient a little longer. "So, you're suggesting something discreet?" She hadn't meant to sound so skeptical, but how much experience could Taylor have with providing the kind of security he seemed to be offering?

"More or less." Getting up, he walked around to behind his desk. "Refitting the scanners gives me an obvious excuse to ramp up the security presence on station. I can also juggle the sleeping quarters enough to assign someone nearby, someone who just happens to be the nosey-neighbor type and on a different shift."

"You can do that *discreetly*?" She hated to echo anyone, even herself, but it was a critical point.

"I'll do that and more." He clasped his hands behind his back. "If you can figure out what else I'm doing, I'll tone it down. Otherwise, I'll do what I feel is best."

A genuine smile tugged at her lips as she nodded. "Fair enough."

Chapter 16

Ava paced slowly up and down the length of her quarters. She was supposed to be formulating a plan for researching the missing supplies without the aid of her passcode, but thoughts of Jean kept forcing their way to the front of her mind.

He hadn't spoken to her for two days, not since their visit to Taylor's office. Not since—Ava rubbed away the cold tear trickling down her cheek—she'd explained the second worst thing about inheriting a business empire. The *worst* part, of course, was losing her father.

And now she'd lost Jean, too. Another tear rolled off her lashes, surprising her. How many times could she cry herself dry before it became a permanent condition? She huffed a bitter laugh. Pity she hadn't kept track of her weeping bouts and recovery times over the last several months. It might all be medically significant someday.

Her alarm shook her loose from her bleak thoughts, and she crossed the room to shut it off. As she prepared for the day, she mentally reviewed the scant progress she'd made toward anything resembling a plan. At Taylor's suggestion, they'd put out a Security Chief level alert for Pernix class Destroyers in general; and in particular, the one with the distinctive marking. He'd also insisted that she stay well away from the docking bays. She'd still go if she thought the situation warranted it, but for now she was content to let him handle that aspect of the investigation.

Dragging herself to the cafeteria, Ava stood in line for dry toast, some synth fruit she didn't even recognize, and a small glass of chocolate milk. Determined nibbling got most of it down without upsetting her stomach too much, a true victory of her head over her heart.

She didn't dare hope Jean would return to her this time, not now that he knew her darkest secret. Nevertheless, the same relentless logic that dictated that decision drove her forward. She would no more surrender to grief than she would bow to evil laws.

Steeling herself, Ava scrounged up a smile as she stepped off the pivotlift and onto the command level. Making friends wasn't a plan, exactly. Yet it was proving highly effective. She'd eliminated nearly everyone here from her list of suspects. The vast majority of the command level crew didn't have access to corporate level reports, let alone the restaurant complaints.

Not all the restaurateurs were as complacent as Masie, or as prematurely defeated as Ava's friend with the dessert café. Today, Ava's plan was to access and download their original complaints—along with any relevant station logs. While it was unlikely that whoever had tampered with the files had failed to delete such incriminating evidence, it was her best option at the moment. It helped that she only had a handful of names to look for.

"You coming?" asked one of the other girls at the end of shift.

"Almost." Ava grinned sheepishly. "I forgot what you showed me earlier, and now I'm stuck in the refresh cycle."

"Ouch." With a sympathetic wince and a wave from the girl, Ava was left alone to deal with it.

She'd already dug as far as the files just above the ones she wanted, so in the few precious seconds between her shift leaving and someone from the new shift offering to tend the cycle for her until it ended, Ava pressed the last few buttons to start the download. Then, eyes flicking around the room, she deliberately triggered the refresh cycle.

"Hey, Massuk." The shift supervisor stepped up to her desk. Spying the twisting, dancing hourglass on her screen, he allowed himself a small chuckle. "Looks like you're here for a while." A firm believer in letting those that wouldn't learn from instruction learn from their mistakes instead, he smiled blandly and didn't offer to rescue her.

"Yes, sir." Ava relaxed as he turned his back and walked away, no doubt to remind his shift not to make the same 'mistake' she just had. Her relief faded like mist under twin suns when Jean entered the room. She trusted him not to hamper her investigation, but there was a lot they still had to resolve after their last conversation.

Before she could duck her head, their gazes locked. Her foolish heart pounded against her rib cage as if it was struggling to reach him, with or without the rest of her. Then he looked away.

Jean made the rounds of the room, checking with the supervisor and chatting briefly with some of the others. Then slowly, inexorably, his feet moved him toward where Ava still sat. Her shift was well over. He'd paid careful attention to that detail so he could avoid her while he thought things over. They were running out of time, though. Terina Massuk was due to change into Ava Montgomery any day now.

"Everything alright, Yeoman?" Jean's throat tightened as he looked down at her. She'd always been good at hiding her emotions, yet today he could tell that she was struggling, too.

"Almost done, sir." Ava didn't bother giving him the excuse she'd handed the others.

Something about the way her gaze continued to rove about the room spoke of more than avoiding looking at him. Suspicions aroused, Jean shifted so he could see her screen better. His hand darted out, and he toggled between the two programs she had open.

Startled, Ava bit her tongue to keep from yelling at him and hastily switched the programs back.

Leaning closer, Jean pointed at the screen and said quietly. "You should probably leave this to Taylor. He has a couple of cyphers on his team, good ones."

She took a deep breath and got a nose full of Jean's scent. In college, he'd stuck to plain soap and water, a habit from the military. Today he wore something she couldn't identify—and she'd been subjected to any number of men's colognes over the years—but it made her lightheaded and weak-kneed at the same time.

"I, um." She eased away from him. It was pure torture to have to wonder what he'd eventually decide about their relationship. "I'll probably have to. Leave this to him. I-if this doesn't work."

"Stubborn." Jean growled the word so softly it was barely audible. "Be careful. Something's got Donovan jumpy."

"How jumpy?" She swiveled sharply to face him and nearly bumped noses. The heat rose in her cheeks, and she all but missed hearing his answer.

"Scared of his shadow." Jean tried to swallow, but his mouth was suddenly as dry as Derthsa, the planet of sand. He straightened away from her before he weakened and kissed her right there on the command level. "Come over tonight."

"Tonight?" She gripped the chair arm that he

couldn't see until her fingers ached. "Why?"

It was a fair question. He just didn't want to answer it here, where anyone might overhear, so he shook his head.

"Solène?" Ava barely breathed the name. If he said yes, that they were going to talk to Solène about becoming a family, she might just kiss him despite having an audience. Her heart sank when he shook his head again. He opened his mouth to say something, but she cut him off. "My place."

Groaning inside, Jean cast about for a solution. They had to talk and to do that, they had to meet privately. Preferably in neutral territory.

"The Asteroid Conference Room," he countered. There was a colony ship aboard right now, so he chose the least popular conference room he could think of. As its name suggested, the room looked out over the asteroid field. Apparently ignorant of the critical role the field played in the existence of the *Beyond*, most groups considered the view boring and chose any of the nine other rooms that were available.

Ava was about to remind him she'd given up her passcode, when she realized that Jean's rank allowed him access to every public space on the station. The irony of it all irked her, so she frowned and settled for nodding.

"All done?" The supervisor eyed them with an interest well beyond solicitously checking on Ava.

"Oh." Ava checked and shut down both screens as quickly as possible. "Yes, sir."

"Next time, Yeoman," Jean slipped smoothly into officer role, "just remember not to approve the end-of-shift refresh before you've finished saving your log."

"Yes, sir." Torn between the urge to wipe the

smug expression off the supervisor's face and the almost uncontrollable desire to kiss it off Jean's, Ava got to her feet. "Thank you. Sir."

She didn't look back as she made her way to the pivotlift, but when the doors closed behind her, Ava closed her eyes and slumped against the wall. She could handle condescending board members, unwanted romantic advances, and even the voracious correspondents who had pursued her for the first four weeks after her father's death. It was this aching loneliness that was going to drive her mad.

Anxiety stalked her as she prowled the corridors, all thoughts of food and rest banished by the question of what to do about Jean and Solène. Even reviewing the information she'd just risked downloading seemed inconsequential when compared with the agony of possibly losing them. That knowledge took hold and flourished in her like a tree being fed a growth serum, gaining height and breadth with each passing hour. Soon there was no room left to go around it or over it, let alone under it. She refused to go through it, which left Ava facing a simple truth.

Squaring her shoulders, she marched to the nearest pivotlift and headed for the conference level. Even knowing that she was going to be early, her feet itched to keep pace with her racing heart. She'd made a very important decision and couldn't wait to tell... *Ouch!*

Ava seized her left wrist with her right hand, confused by the amount of pain the commband was causing. It was over as suddenly as it began and she leaned against the nearest wall in relief. As her adrenaline spike leveled out, she noticed other sounds. Were they voices? Yes, of course. This entire level was either conference rooms or observation lounges.

Flexing tingling fingers, she moved toward the voices and soon found herself in front of the Ezarri room. Murals of grain-filled fields covered one-third of the curved wall, then transitioned to a large body of placid water, and finally, the last third depicted trees heavy with various kinds of fruit. Oddly enough, the table in the center of the room was a sort of hollow triangle, with chairs around the outside and two small gaps that allowed the staff to access and serve guests from inside instead of coping with elbows, heads, and chair legs on the outside.

At the moment, the staff members were preoccupied with rubbing their commband arms and exchanging grimaces.

"What was it, d'you think?" asked a burly fellow. The style and coloring of his clothing marked him as a guest, probably a colonist. Whether he'd arrived early or stayed late at the meeting, he was one of only two such people in the room.

"It's those blasted contraptions!" snapped the beautiful woman beside him, tossing her teal-green hair. "I don't trust the things. Oh!" Looking suddenly lost and a little frightened, she gripped his arm with both hands. "I wish we didn't have to rely on contraptions to get to our new home!"

"Hey. You." One of the staff members beckoned for Ava to come over. "Did your commband just zap you, too?"

Dazed, Ava nodded and entered the room. "They're not supposed to do that. I mean…" Before she could explain about the emergency safety override, someone else cut her off.

"And yet here we all stand." Encouraged by the angry muttering around her, the speaker fairly ripped her commband off.

"You shouldn't do that," Ava protested. "They'll probably send out an update in a minute. And you'll need it to access crew quarters, and…"

"Too bad." Stuffing the device into her sash, she snorted. "I'll put it back on *after* the techs give it a look and not before."

Others in the group followed suit, then began talking over each other as they speculated about what had happened.

"Are you alright, dear?" The beautiful woman's voice was filled with concern, but her eyes showed only discomfort.

Ava forced a smile and nodded. "Fine, thanks." Remembering what she'd overheard earlier, she added, "This has never happened before. Not exactly."

The man and woman exchanged worried glances, but made no reply.

"Swell." Ava fingered her commband as she hurried back to the pivotlift. Her heart-to-heart with Jean was going to have to wait while she figured out how many others got zapped at essentially the same time.

Not to mention *why* it happened. It made no sense! Direct communications didn't skip straight to the emergency shock setting. Unless they'd all gotten critical calls at exactly the same moment, she was as mystified as everyone else. Of course, if there was a station-wide emergency, it would've triggered the sirens and lights, accompanied by the dispersal of station crew with safety gear.

Had Taylor gotten shocked? Had Jean? She flinched at the thought of poor little Solène and all the other children and people aboard currently wearing commbands.

Hearing the pivotlift doors open, Ava turned to board it and ran straight into someone.

"Oof." Jean gripped her shoulders, his eyes lighting up. "There you are! Are you alright?"

"I'm," her eyes zeroed in on the welt on his left wrist, which was bare except for the security suit circlet, "fine. But are you?"

Jean allowed her to take his hand in hers, smiling at the way her fingers grazed the area around the red mark, her touch as soft as butterflies. "It looks worse than it is."

Ava felt her cheeks pink at his husky tone and refused to look up at him before she'd released his wrist and turned away. The pivotlift doors had closed, so she reached for the button again, but he captured her hand.

"I was still on the command level when it happened." Trading her right hand for the left, he gently undid the clasp on her commband and removed it. Seeing the discoloration made his stomach twist. Stifling the ridiculous urge to 'kiss it better'—and fighting the intense desire to forget everyone and everything to go check on his daughter—he instead rubbed his thumb across the faint ridge on Ava's skin at the edge of the indentation where the commband usually lay and asked, "Do you know what's going on?"

"I'm only sure of one thing." Taking her hand and her commband back, she held up the device. "These were put through every conceivable scenario, and quite a few ridiculous 'what ifs,' before we rolled them out. And the odds of even two commbands *accidentally* sending out an emergency pulse at the same time are nonexistent."

Jean's expression hardened. Retrieving his commband from his sash, he activated the display—

except it didn't work.

Paling, Ava tried her commband. "Nothing." She hadn't realized they'd stopped working altogether. Her heart sank as she realized that it further confirmed her theory that this wasn't an accident. Which meant someone was doing this deliberately. Questions screamed through her mind, including but not limited to who, why, and *how*.

"They're dead." Scowling, Jean grabbed her hand. "This way."

"Where are we going?" She jogged beside him willingly enough, but she definitely wanted to know what the plan was.

"First we have to activate the backup alarm. Somehow." Jean stopped at a hidden input panel and stared at the barely visible line that marked its location on the wall. Ordinarily, he would've used a commband scan to open it. Now, and not for the first time, he mentally berated a system of life that made carrying a useful hand tool or two seem like a waste of time.

"The suit!" Ava lifted his forearm and shook it so that the suit circlet wobbled. "Use the suit!"

"I forgot about that." Grinning, Jean stepped back and activated it for the first time in days. Metal claws sprouted at the tips of his gloved fingers, and he dug them under the edge of the panel, then ripped it open.

"Here, let me." Ava jumped forward when he had trouble retracting the claws. Entering her personal security code on the panel, she threw the lever for the alarm.

Instantly, lights up and down the corridor started to flash while a calm voice began issuing a string of announcements and instructions.

"Leave that." Jean shut off the suit and pulled

her away from the mangled panel that she was trying to close.

"Now what?" She frowned as she realized they were heading away from the pivotlift.

"Now we get you somewhere safe." Thankfully, the service tubes were spaced evenly throughout the station. Jean pried this door open as well and shoved her inside. Changing his mind, he stepped in after her, took her in his arms, and kissed her thoroughly.

"Jean," she whispered his name, then tried to sound a little less dazed as she protested, "I can help!"

"Help Taylor. He'll keep you safe." He gripped her shoulders, seconds away from trying to shake sense into her. "We don't know what's going on, remember?"

The desperation in his voice hit Ava like a solar flare, blinding her for an instant. Then she had his face in her hands and was nodding. "I'm going, Jak. I'm going to Taylor. Be careful."

Tearing herself away, she stepped onto the ladder that ran between levels, offering easy access for complex repairs and a safe way to maneuver in the event the pivotlifts were compromised. Resolutely, she began her descent one step at a time. Only three levels to go.

Chapter 17

When she reached the security level, Ava paused to shake out her arms and legs a bit. Next time she got bored with her exercise routine, she'd have to do ten minutes on a ladder. For now, though, she tested her commband once more—still broken—before opening the door and exiting into the main corridor.

"Freeze!"

Ava complied, hands going out to her sides while her heart rate spiked.

"Well," sneered a gravelly voice that came closer with each word, "somebody's done this before." Strong fingers clamped around her uninjured wrist and swung her up against the wall, then briskly patted her down.

"Anything?" This voice was distinctly feminine.

"Nah, just another busted commband. Don't none of these toy soldiers carry weapons?"

"She ain't a soldier, dummy. She's a uniformed flunky." A third voice chimed in, chuckling at its owner's cleverness. "Only security officers carry weapons around here."

Ava tried not to flinch as the commband was yanked from her waist sash. She had indeed gone through something similar to this, during her training courses. It didn't make it any more comfortable, per se, but at least she had a rough idea of how to stay out of trouble until it was time for her to cause it herself.

"Turn around," the feminine voice ordered.

Ava moved slowly, careful to keep her hands away from her body. What she saw made her swallow hard and decide she was glad she hadn't tried anything spontaneous, like fighting back.

Paella kept her weapon trained on the new prisoner, disappointed at the lack of resistance. What she liked best about the Uike 4 was that she didn't even have to aim it, just point in the general direction and watch her target shatter. While the effect of the Uike 4 on human tissue wasn't well-documented, she kept carrying it in the hopes that she'd get to use it someday.

Ava was in no hurry to volunteer as a test subject, however.

"You sure she ain't security?" Ava's commband dangled from one hand of the man who spoke, a surprisingly paunchy man with a hooked nose so pronounced it looked like a beak.

"Nah, the uniform's wrong." The other man answered, tugging on the bottom of a vest that, underneath the stains and clumsily applied patches, looked like it might once have belonged in the wardrobe of a rich and debonair man.

Somewhere in the way back of Ava's mind, it occurred to her to wonder why in an age of reclaimers and synthesizers, they were so poorly dressed. Was it a weird sort of vanity? A way of setting themselves even further apart from their victims? Each of them sported a high-end civilian comm unit on their shoulder, which made her realize they must be responsible for the broken commbands. It gave them an incredible strategic advantage on such a huge station to be able to communicate while their enemy stumbled about in confusion.

"So how come she ain't afraid?" Beak-man jerked his head toward Ava.

"Good question." The woman cocked one curvy hip and put a fist on it while she studied Ava.

"I don't like it. Kill her."

The threat fizzled instantly when the men hesitated, then exchanged uneasy glances.

"Capt'n said no killing, Paella." Vest's tone was somewhere between placating and whiny.

"I'm making an exception." She lifted the Uike toward Ava.

Ava's heart rate slowed as she faced her executioner. "Go ahead. I have no regrets." She'd even updated her will, last night while she couldn't sleep. Not that she was going to tell *them* that!

"Yeah?" The woman came a step closer. "Not even coming out that door just now?"

For some reason, the question made Ava laugh. "Okay, maybe one. But I won't be leaving any loose ends. I'm even on good terms with the man I love." *Make that two regrets.* She would've fought for more time with Jean—if she thought she stood a chance of surviving.

"Way to take all the fun out of it." A disgusted grimace twisted Paella's narrow face as she lowered the Uike. "Put her with the others."

"Huh? You said…" Beak-man's attempt at an objection got rudely interrupted by an elbow in his soft gut.

"Get moving," barked Vest, advancing on Ava hastily. He wasn't stupid enough to put himself between her and the Uike until he absolutely had to, and even then, he kept one eye on Paella until she grinned at him saucily. Suppressing a shudder, Vest continued herding Ava along.

"In here?" Ava indicated the security office in disbelief when Vest stopped her there.

"Safest place on the whole station." Vest grinned nastily, amused at her confusion. That was the end of the discussion, for he turned her over to a man as lean as a toothpick, then went back on the prowl. Their orders were to keep that level clamped down, but not to leave it until it was time to head for the *Reus*.

Less than a minute later, Ava was in a cell with a handful of others, mostly security officers. They—and everyone she could see—sported an angry red mark on their dominant wrist. *How* had that happened?

"Welcome to the club," one of them greeted her sardonically.

Ava looked around the crowded space unhappily. "What's it take to get a private room around here?"

"Wrong club, sorry." The officer on the left bunk swung around so that his feet dangled over the side and motioned for her to take the space he'd just freed up.

Careful not to trip over anyone, she seated herself beside him. From the corner of her eye, she spotted what looked like a signal being given by the man standing in the far corner of the cell. Her guess was confirmed a moment later when the feeling in the room shifted as everyone relaxed. Really relaxed, not just sitting with slumped shoulders or their eyes closed.

"Where were you when it hit?" asked the officer beside her, his voice low.

Deducing that the guard must've moved out of earshot, Ava responded just as quietly. "Conference level. Lieutenant Kearns sent me here to find Chief Taylor." Her heart sank when the statement brought only scowls.

"They got him first off," explained the speaker after a moment. "Waltzed right into his office and shot him."

Ava licked her suddenly dry lips. "He's dead?" The question came out more croak than words.

"Maybe. The guy in charge seemed upset, said to get Taylor to the infirmary right away."

"Right." Ava nodded slowly. Thieves were pursued, but murderers were hunted. "Makes sense."

"Yeah." He arched an eyebrow hopefully. "Kearns give you any idea what they're after?"

"He didn't…" Ava broke off to whip around and grip the cell bars. It hadn't mattered before, since she wasn't the lookout, but now she strained her eyes to see through the other cells to the source of the child's voice she'd just heard. "Please, no," she whispered.

"Because I said so!" The toothpick-shaped guard came back around the curve, one hand firmly gripping the shoulder of a young girl with straight black hair.

Ava drew back from the bars, pulled her knees up to her chest, and buried her face in her arms. She couldn't let Solène see her! Acknowledging their connection would be like drawing a target on the child's forehead if the redhands figured out who Ava actually was.

"Get back." The guard's voice became threatening. "Away from them bars."

And suddenly, Ava's cell erupted in near-silent motion.

"Get his gun," someone hissed.

"I've got his arm," another voice grunted. "You get his gun!"

"Here's the keys!" On a station where most things were electric, the jail cell doors were among the few exceptions. Nobody wanted to have to wonder if they were working during an emergency.

Ava's head popped up, and she stared as the

others swiftly effected their escape. She was so stunned that she might've gone on sitting there if the man beside her hadn't grabbed her arm and dragged her along.

For as skinny as he was, the redhand was putting up a terrific fight. Five of the security officers were engaged in restraining him when Ava cleared the cell door.

"Give me that." One of the other officers snatched up the gun and conked him on the head with it. "Secure him, and I mean his mouth, too. Then toss him in the last cell."

"Solène!" Now that there were no redhands to see, Ava rushed to the little girl and wrapped her arms around her. "Are you alright?" She felt more than saw the answering nodding motion and released a sigh of relief. "Honey, what are you doing here? Why aren't you on the education level with the other children?" Drawing back as she spoke, Ava shuffled their position to one side so that the officers wouldn't trip on them as they stealthily released the other prisoners.

Solène pointed at the last cell. "There are bad guys on the station. I saw them while I was going to have lunch with Masie."

"Yes, there are bad guys onboard." Ava smoothed the hair back from Solène's face, then settled her hands back on the child's slim waist. "You would be safer at school."

"But I had to tell." Solène spoke firmly. "My commband hurt me and now it's broken, so I couldn't call Daddy or Chief Taylor. And I couldn't find any security adults, so I came here."

It took her a second, but once Ava translated 'security adult' to 'security officer,' the explanation did make a vague sort of sense. Particularly if…

"Is that what Daddy told you to do? Tell security about bad men?" she asked gently.

Concern filled Solène's gray eyes as she nodded. "Do you know where Daddy is? Is he okay?"

"I don't know exactly where he is." Ava hesitated. Jean was clearly not in the habit of lying to his daughter, so neither should she. Instinctively, however, she offered the truth as optimistically as she knew how. "But he was alright when I saw him a few minutes ago."

"Does he know about the bad guys?" Solène's gaze lingered briefly on the still-unconscious guard.

"Probably." Ava bit her lip. From what she could tell, Solène was handling this all incredibly well. "Are you worried?"

"A little." Solène's eyes met Ava's. "Are you?"

Ava's breath hitched at the question. "I…I haven't had time to think about it. But yes, I am." Extremely worried, though she didn't plan to admit it.

"You love my daddy, don't you." Despite the wording, Solène's tone made it a statement of fact.

Consternation filled Ava as she debated how to respond. In the strictest sense, Solène wasn't asking whether or not Ava would be privileged to marry Jean and become a permanent part of both of their lives. Therefore, the answer was and always would be, "I do. With all my heart."

"Listen up." A sharp voice cut through the low chatter going on around them. The security officers moved up around their senior member while the civilians who'd gotten caught in the net, medical personnel mostly, edged to the back of the group. "We've sent out a distress signal. Now we're going to sweep this level and start taking the station back." Rather than sounding like a hyped-up cheerleader, as such men so often did in the entertainments, he spoke matter-of-factly.

"How're we going to communicate?"

"We'll use these." He held up the sleek, silver comm unit they'd taken from the guard. Though he'd turned the volume down so they could talk, he had one ear on it, listening as the invaders communicated with each other. "We only have one right now, but we're on our way to get more." His quiet confidence prompted a knowing chuckle or two from his audience. "I'm going to have to ask you civilians to remain here, in the cells. That way, if anyone checks while we're gone, they'll be fooled."

"Anybody comes here gets what they're looking for," muttered an angry male voice.

"Are you going to the infirmary?" Ava asked. All eyes swung to her, most wide with surprise. "They have to have a guard or two watching Chief Taylor and the rest of the medical personnel."

"Sounds like a good first target," he agreed easily, having already reached the same conclusion.

"Then after you've taken it, you should move the civilians there. It's unexpected and easy to defend," Ava asserted. She didn't suggest they be taken off the level altogether, because it wouldn't do any good to scatter their tiny forces. "Besides, you'll need these cells for real prisoners." There was nothing wrong with a little optimism.

"I'll think about it." His eyes narrowed speculatively. Civilians weren't usually so logical.

"There's one more thing." Ava got to her feet. "You should let me send another signal. There's a Montgomery ship coming, and I know its emergency frequency." Phyl's last update on the security team she'd requested was hours old, so the ship could be almost on top of them by now. She certainly didn't want them docking unawares.

"And you know that how?" He scrutinized her like she was a raw recruit who'd reported for inspection with her shirt on backward.

"Boss?" The man who'd sat beside Ava in the cell spoke up. "I don't know who she is, but she does seem to know stuff."

"He's correct." Ava hurried to corroborate the statement. Since there was no time for debate, she added for good measure, "I'm an advance member of Sigrid Montgomery's personal entourage."

He hesitated, but only for an instant. "What's the name of her head of security?"

"Dallyn. Dallyn Phydag." Her lips quirked up in a smile. "Do you know him?"

"Nope, and I don't figure you would, either, if you weren't who you say you are." Nodding to one of the others, he instructed, "Help her send that signal."

"One more thing." She gestured at the group in general. "Lose those jackets. You stand a better chance of taking them by surprise if you're not so obviously security."

"You heard the lady." The leader stripped off his jacket, then pointed at three of the officers. "With me. Taruq and Fotz, follow in three minutes. Objective, infirmary."

There were nods all around, then the small team slipped out into the corridor, running silently on their specially crafted boots.

Feeling a tug on her sleeve, Ava looked down to find Solène frowning up at her.

"I want to go with you."

"With me?" Ava once again wished the child had stayed in the safety of the education level.

"I'll be safer with you," Solène insisted. "You know things."

Ava groaned inwardly. She didn't know half as much as she'd like to. Who was out there and why—not to mention how they'd gotten the run of the station. Guesters were restricted to the docks and a few of the lower hospitality levels. They weren't even issued commbands, so…

Her thought shuttle suddenly exploded on the platform. *Commbands.* They were the missing link! Based on what she knew had happened, she could extrapolate that every commband on the station went down at the same time. As a result, station operations—including communications and access—were banjaxed. Yet the redhands had free run of things, exactly as if they owned the place. As if…as if they had a secret passcode overriding security measures.

They had *her* secret passcode. It was the only thing that made sense!

Solène gripped her hand tightly. "I can help! I'll watch for the bad guys."

"Hey!" An officer glared at Ava. "How about that signal?"

"Right." Ava took a deep breath, trying to quell the nausea rippling through her. "Solène, stay close. Be ready to move quickly if there's trouble. Can you do that?" At Solène's nod, Ava led her around the corner and into Taylor's office, passing an officer posted at the outer door.

Relieved to find the console ready to go, Ava used every trick she knew to hide the signal from eyes on the station. Since she was already there, she sent a second signal to Phyl, innocuous except for the keyword that would bring her security chief to the *Beyond* at the speed of an astrophysical jet.

She ran to the infirmary with Solène and the others as soon as it was secured, only to have the guilt catch up with her again. If anyone was hurt today, it would be largely due to her…her… Oh, what had Jean called it? Ah, yes, how could she forget—'a sapbrained stunt.'

Solène reached up and wiped a tear off Miss Terina's cheek, then snuggled close. Daddy said that her hugs made his sad go away. She hoped it would work for Miss Terina, too. Squeezing her eyes shut tight, she hoped Daddy was safe.

On the command level, Jean crouched in the shadow of an enormous potted plant. As much as he'd ignored them before, he was now forever indebted to the interior designer who'd chosen them, for they provided excellent places to hide in otherwise bare corridors. So far, he'd successfully evaded two sweeps and was astonished that nobody had suggested shoving all of the potted plants into a single group so nobody could do exactly what he was—creeping up on their forward position.

His fingers itched to grab the weapon from the guard he could see, but for now he bided his time. He didn't know enough, and he was alone. One soldier usually meant one chance for success. One against the dozen or more enemies that he'd seen ran the odds of said success down considerably.

Not that the Security Suit didn't give him an advantage. The smooth surface of the helmet kept his face from standing out in the shadows, and stealth mode silenced his steps when he ran from cover to cover. He'd test out its defensive capacity soon enough.

First, he needed more information. "Suit, enhance comm input. Specify human voices and increase volume by ten percent." Jean continued adjusting the settings until he could hear the conversation of the enemy some twenty feet away.

"Stinking guard duty," one of them whined. "Why don't we just dose them with ondoegi and get on with it?"

"On with what?" grunted another. "Captain's with Donovan now. They'll hash things out." Sniffling, he grunted again.

Donovan, in league with the redhands? Jean's blood ran cold at that bit of news.

"Yeah, well." The whiner scuffed his foot on the carpet, which looked almost thick enough to lie down and nap on. He'd been up late the night before, drinking and swapping threadbare stories, which accounted for his foul mood. "At least then they couldn't be planning to escape."

Jean reset the comm unit and called up the enhanced vision. Sure enough, in the room behind the duo sat ten or so of Jean's comrades. Scanning the corridor in both directions, Jean tried to estimate the last time he'd seen a patrol.

Deciding he was safe for a few minutes, Jean edged out from behind the plant and crawled across the corridor. The guards could still see him, if they looked, but he'd observed that they seemed to focus their casual glances on the far edge of their visibility, to where the curvature of the corridor blocked their line of sight.

Crouching, Jean ran toward them, picking up speed until…

"Hey!" Whiny's eyes got huge as he spotted an eerie shape moving toward him. A really *big* shape, coming out of nowhere! Belatedly he tried to swing his weapon into position but took a fist to the jaw that sent him reeling into the arms of his erstwhile prisoners.

Grunt, who'd been looking in the other direction, had Jean's arm around his neck before he knew what was going on. As his vision dimmed, he reversed his gun to try a wild shot at his attacker, only to drop it when something struck his wrist, numbing his hand and fingers.

Jean dragged the unconscious man into the room and laid him beside Whiny. Retracting his helmet, he stood up and inspected his new recruits.

"Lieutenant Commander?" The squeak of surprise came from one of the yeomen, a studious little fellow.

"That's me." Jean, his adrenaline pumping, grinned at them all. "Orrie, what's your weapons rating?" He listened more to the lad's voice than the score and nodded as he handed over Grunt's weapon. "Excellent. Stand over there, by the door. Out of sight from the corridor."

"What's the plan, Boss?" Orrie sprang up from where he'd just finished using his sash to gag Grunt.

"A patrol will be by any minute." Jean addressed his answer to them all. "They come from both directions, so we need to lay a flanking maneuver."

"What about us?" One of the women spoke up, Whiny's weapon gripped in her hand like she knew how to use it.

Jean quirked an eyebrow at Orrie. They were long-time sparring partners and he doubted Hway *needed* a weapon to take someone from behind, but he wouldn't make the decision for him.

Chapter 18

"Of all the colossal arrogance!" Donovan shouted. Torn between two extremes—aggravation at finding Erq Vyl in his private quarters and acute fear of being revealed to the world for what he was—he had lost all semblance of control.

"You said that already." Vyl spun slowly in the plush desk chair, taking in the room again. "Nice place."

A couch large enough to seat four ran along one wall, without a stain or sag in sight. Artwork was scattered across the walls; dull stuff mostly, people talking, plants, that sort of thing. The carpet was deep enough that he was tempted to take off his boots and walk around on it. The urge to do so was strengthened by Erq's accurate assessment that it would freak Donovan right out of his ever-loving mind.

"Get out!" Donovan ordered pompously. "Get off my station and don't come back!"

"Sure, sure. Glad to." Vyl propped a boot up on the pristine desk, then the other. "Just as soon as you give me what I want." Things were going smoothly so far. His people had infiltrated and taken the Security level as well as the level just below this one. His crew wasn't big enough to take the station in a pitched battle, but with this skeleton keycode, it was as simple as strolling in and doing what they liked.

"Forget it." Donovan was sufficiently off-balance to end the statement with a snort. "Didn't he tell you? We're off for a while. Letting things cool down." At least, that was how Donovan chose to interpret his last conversation with their 'contact.' He'd gotten accustomed to the extra money and refused to believe his source might've dried up permanently.

"Oh, he may have mentioned it." Erq shrugged insolently. "Didn't pay much attention. He ain't pulling my strings no more."

Donovan fought the urge to lick dry lips. This business of siphoning off supplies was risky enough without making abrupt changes in leadership. "I suppose you fired him," he jeered.

"Yeah. Yeah, I did." Vyl pointed at Donovan. "And once you've given me what I want, I'll fire you, too."

"Weren't you listening? I'm closed for business." Somehow Donovan managed to sound almost calm. Shouting hadn't worked, orders were useless with such a man, and since Donovan didn't habitually carry a weapon, he made the one choice left to him—to try to regain some of his dignity. Squaring his shoulders, he strolled over to the couch and seated himself.

"Should I applaud?" Vyl brought up his hands as if planning to do just that, then pushed off the desk instead and got to his feet. "I suppose I owe you an apology." He let the thought linger in the air a moment, just long enough for Donovan to begin to savor it, then clarified, "I said what, when of course I meant who."

Donovan nearly dropped the book he'd picked up off the elegant wooden table that sat at the end of the couch. "*Who?*" When Vyl stared silently back at him, a sick certainty settled in Donovan's gut. "No." Inside, he was screaming. He would have nothing to do with slavers!

"Alright." Vyl accepted the response with an almost pleasant smile. Folding his arms across his chest, he called over his shoulder, "Albo. You got it yet?"

Donovan twitched violently when the answer came from inside his bedchamber.

"Huh?" A lanky fellow ambled out into the common area, the gear on his head and hands making him look weirdly robotic. "Oh, that thing you wanted? Sure. Took me maybe two seconds to hack the password and get in. Personnel files, the works. Ha, I even found a stash of musical recordings. Stuff *he* recorded. Dude needs a voice teacher, bad." Considering his responsibility to the conversation discharged, Albo focused once again on the insides of his goggles, which allowed him to see any display that he was linked to.

"And is she here?" With an effort, Vyl kept the irritation out of his voice. It was worth a slightly protracted conversation to see Donovan squirm. And, that bit about him being a bad singer was pretty hilarious.

"Hmm?" Albo dragged himself back to the confines of the room where he stood. Processing the question, he began tapping commands into his linked keyboard, the one no one but he could 'see.' "Sure she is. But you'll never guess who else is here."

Donovan recoiled from the display that suddenly burst into view in the middle of the room. "How did you..." Springing to his feet, he gaped at the image of a star chart. The very chart he'd taken an image of during his last conversation with the boss. All further questions and protests died on his lips as he realized that it was—a *familiar* star chart.

"What?" Vyl circled the display with puzzled interest. He identified it easily. He'd certainly made enough runs to the *Beyond* to recognize the neighborhood.

"The boss is here." Albo, puzzled by their lack of response, flipped his goggles up so he could see them better. "On the station!"

Vyl gave Albo a funny look. "I'm your boss, Albo."

"Well, yeah." Albo rolled his eyes. "I don't mean *my* boss. I mean *the* boss."

Vyl and Donovan's gazes clashed with enough force to shatter a nebgass mirror. After a brief mental tug-of-war, Donovan paled and averted his eyes.

"How did you know I was looking for him?" Donovan demanded of Albo.

Albo wanted to roll his eyes again. "I dunno, unless the filename kinda gave it away." A puff of pride prompted Albo to add, "Without me, you'd have been waiting on an answer for another week, at least! When was the last time you updated your software? I had to…"

As Albo launched into a self-aggrandizing description of his efforts, heavily couched in cypher-jargon, Vyl stepped closer to Donovan. "What were you planning to do when you figured out where he was?"

Donovan glared at him, certain that the hint of respect in Vyl's voice was subtle mockery. "That's none of your business."

"Maybe I'm making it my business." A nasty smile curled Vyl's lips. He should've known better than to think that the spineless little twerp would have a plan. "Y'know, as long as I'm already *here*."

Deflating slightly, Donovan gave an uncharacteristic shrug. "I don't know. I have a lot of ideas, but like he said." He nodded at Albo, who by now was leaning sullenly against the wall with his arms crossed. "There was no hurry."

"Wasn't is right." Vyl scratched his chin thoughtfully. "But I don't have time to get my prize and chat with him, too. Unless…" He snapped his fingers. "Perfect."

Donovan shifted his weight uncomfortably. He didn't want to ask, but the words seemed to be almost pulled from him. "What's perfect?"

"I was already prepared to bring one passenger aboard the *Reus*. So instead, we'll have two. No problem." The more Erq thought about it, the better he liked the idea. Once they were on his ship, he'd have all the time in the world to persuade 'the boss' to share his secrets about gaining access to Montgomery's shipping files. After all, the skeleton keycode would only work until a cypher on the other side changed the locks.

"Uh, Boss?" Albo coughed. "There might be, uh, one problem."

"Oh?" Vyl spun around to face him. "How so?"

"We know he's here. Or, that he *was* here when this image was taken."

"And?" Vyl pressed when Albo stopped. "The problem is?"

"We don't know *who* he is."

Donovan had an instant's satisfaction in seeing Vyl knocked off his stride.

"Well, Albo." Vyl arched an eyebrow. "Sounds to me like you'd better get to work."

"Me?"

"You." Vyl pointed two fingers at his henchman. "Run a comparison scan of that image against all the males on the *Beyond*."

"Comparison? Using what?" Albo had the gall to frown. "Even assuming he has records on file here, I have no idea how tall or broad the boss is."

"Ah, but you do know the size of a porthole, do you not?" Vyl allowed a hint of irritation to creep into his voice. He shouldn't have to be the one thinking of this stuff.

"Sure, I…" Albo dropped his goggles back into place. "I see where you're going. Gonna take a while, though."

"You have until the girl is in custody." Vyl rubbed his hands together. Blasted wretch, who knew Montgomery would be so quick to figure out their plans to raid her holdings? And so deucedly effective at thwarting said plans. Every captain he'd recruited for the strike had bailed within a few hours of learning about the sweeping changes being made to security. *Her* changes. Nobody else had the authority to change the entire system like that. Well, Vyl considered it the height of poetic justice that the woman who'd cost him his grand retirement was now going to personally secure it.

"Hey, her I know." With a flick of his fingers, Albo switched the display from the local star chart to an employee's chart.

"There you are." Vyl leaned forward, eyes greedily consuming the information before him. "Posing as a lowly yeoman from the Derli system. Ha, that's rich!" Unclipping the comm unit from his belt, he instructed, "The target is Terina Massuk. Repeat, Terina Massuk. I need her alive, people."

Replacing it on his belt, he asked Albo, "Do you have to be here to run that comparison?"

"Nah." Albo's fingers pounded his digital keyboard. "I'm linked, I can do this anywhere inside the station."

"Good. Let's go."

"You can't do thi—!" Donovan's roar of protest was silenced by a hard fist to the jaw. He staggered back as far as the wall, and slowly slid down it.

In the infirmary, one of the security officers fiddled with the comm unit that was tuned to their security teams. By now more of the redhands had been captured and their comm units confiscated, enough that two had been left behind at the infirmary: one simply as a way to contact the others; and one for eavesdropping on the enemy.

Looking around at the others standing watch near the entryway, the officer asked, "Think I should pass that along?"

"Maybe." The burly man next to him shrugged. "I don't know who or where this Yeoman Massuk is, but if they can figure it out, they'll know where to lay an ambush."

As the first officer relayed the information, the others began quietly discussing what the redhands wanted with a lone yeoman.

In the first exam room down the hall, Ava's mouth went dust dry as she wished that she didn't understand, either. It wasn't bad enough that her private passcode was being used to endanger everyone aboard this station and who knew how many others—she wouldn't know until much later how badly the other locations were hit. No, now they were coming after her, personally.

The one good thing in the whole mess was that their comm units weren't sophisticated enough to project images, allowing her to maintain her anonymity with the station staff while she tried to decide what to do.

She stroked Solène's hair as she considered. With a slave system less than a day away, her options were depressing: hide with the hope of rescue by the *Ulciscor*; ask the security officers to defend her; or sacrifice her life to protect billions of others.

How long had it been since she'd sent the signal? Comforted by Solène's warmth and hug, Ava had somehow managed to doze off a little, and now she had no idea when to expect the *Ulciscor.* Half an hour? Two hours? There was a clock situated behind the main desk, but in the small exam room where they'd taken shelter, there wasn't a timepiece in sight.

As for the second choice, the only thing worse than the consequences of being taken alive would be taking others to their death in a futile attempt to avoid it. Especially security officers, many with families, who hadn't signed on to protect her from the kind of trouble that had found her.

Twiddling the ring on her finger, Ava decided to hold the third option in reserve. She wouldn't allow herself to be taken aboard their ship alive, for certainly they would lie about her time of death and claim ownership of all her family had built. But no one would benefit from her dying prematurely, except perhaps her beneficiaries.

She roused from her thoughts enough to recognize new faces walking past the room—and one very familiar one. Locking eyes with Johnson when she looked in the room, Ava made a discreet hand signal. She received no acknowledgment, yet there wasn't a doubt in her mind that she'd find Johnson waiting in the public washroom when she got there.

"Solène?" Unable to remove the slender arms fastened about her waist Ava gently shook the girl's shoulder. She hated to wake her, but she desperately needed to talk to Johnson. "I'll be right back, okay?"

"Where are you going?" Solène tightened her

hold, not wanting to be left alone.

"Just to the washroom." Ava smiled as calmly as she could. "Do you need a turn?"

Solène hesitated, then shook her head. "No, thank you."

"I won't be long," Ava promised. Clambering to her feet, she grimaced as she stretched her stiff legs. When had she last sat on the floor for any length of time?

Johnson looked up as the door closed behind Ava. "Hey." She grinned. "Small station, huh?"

Ava barked a laugh and scanned the room to be sure they had it to themselves. "I don't have time for games. Just tell me what's in the middle." She *knew* Johnson was her bodyguard, but she wanted it said out loud between them before she said what she'd come to say.

"A sculpture by an unknown artist." Johnson's grin stayed firmly in place, her watchful eyes focused on the door behind Ava.

"Good." The answer was obscure, but deliberately so. Very few people in the galaxy knew that her father had ever tried his hand at sculpting— exactly one person knew that her mother had insisted on placing one of his pieces in the middle of her dressing table, where it still stood. "Because you're about to get the most important assignment of your life." That brought Johnson's gaze squarely to Ava's face.

"I have a mission." Johnson didn't like where this was going. Her mission came from Chief Phydag himself, a man she respected too much to disappoint. Unfortunately, they'd never discussed what to do if Ava personally countermanded him.

"Starting now, your primary mission is to protect my heir apparent, Solène Kearns. You'll find her sitting by the wall opposite…"

"I saw her when I came in." Johnson cut her off mildly.

"Excellent." Ava's heart was pounding as she clarified, "Do you accept your new mission?" Her will was in order, everything prepared for her untimely demise, just as her father had taught her. Securing protection for Solène was her main priority right now.

Johnson blew out a breath. "Dallyn's not going to like it." Still, she thought she was beginning to understand. How many times had she shadowed Ava to or from a meeting with this little girl and her handsome father?

"I know." Ava's throat tightened. There were things that needed saying, especially considering that she had a better than thirty percent chance of dying in the next few hours. "If the occasion presents itself, you might tell him that I had no idea this, um," she rubbed her sore wrist, "*any* of this was going to happen. And that he's the finest personal security chief I've ever had."

Johnson's face hardened. "It'll mean more to him coming from you."

"He'll hear it the next time I see him." Ava bit her lip. "Just…if you happen to see him first…"

Ignoring the incomplete plea, Johnson pointed at the door. "Let's get the introductions over with."

Accepting that Johnson wasn't going to agree outright, Ava stiffly led the way to where Solène sat waiting.

Solène watched closely as they approached. Miss Terina's face was pale and her mouth tight, the way one of the instructors at school got when she was upset.

"Solène." Ava squatted down by the girl she'd

begun wishing was her daughter. "Honey, listen closely. This is my friend, Officer Johnson. No matter what happens, I need you to stay with her until your dad comes for you. Okay?" Wide-eyed, the child nodded. Ava, in a near panic to keep her safe, insisted, "Promise me, Solène. Say it out loud."

"I will. I'll wait with Officer Johnson till Daddy comes." Solène threw herself at Ava, wrapping her little arms around her neck. "What's wrong?"

"There are bad guys on board," Ava reminded her gently, her own eyes squeezing shut against threatening tears. "We need you to be safe." Turning her head, she kissed Solène's cheek. "I have to talk to the officers. Wait here."

What she really needed was a little space. Pausing just outside the door to catch her breath from all the sudden changes, she heard the sudden, distinctive sound of weapons fire. Frightened faces appeared in the doorways of the rooms further down the hall, but she was the only one who moved toward the entrance to get a better idea of what was going on.

The officers gripped their own weapons and shifted uneasily. The urge to rescue their comrades was strong, but their orders were to defend the infirmary and the civilians hiding there.

"Hey!" One of them snapped at Ava when he saw her. "Get back inside. You want to get captured?"

Ava almost heard the light switch on in her brain, illuminating a metaphorical door labeled *Option Number Four!*

"I'm Terina Massuk."

"So?" The man scowled and started toward her. "It's not safe up here."

"I am," she bit out the words, "the one they're looking for."

"That name!" One of them snapped her fingers. "The one that came over the comms earlier!"

"Yes." Ava nodded. "Someone suggested that we could set up an ambush if we knew where I was. Well." She sucked in a deep breath. "Here I am."

Chapter 19

"Well, obviously we don't send *her*." The officer managed to agree while winding up for the next round of the argument. "We've gotta have somebody that looks like her is all."

Ava clenched her fists to keep from tearing her hair out while they chased the idea in circles, pitting strategies against each other and stubbornly ignoring the point, which was to save everyone else. She could've put her foot down, but that would've meant proving who she was, and frankly, there was no guarantee that they wouldn't just double down in their refusal to see reason.

Spinning on her heel, Ava stalked away. As she'd hoped, they paid her no mind, allowing her to reach the counter where the comm units sat. That was the hitch in her new plan—she couldn't tell one from the other. So, she took them both.

"This is Yeoman Terina Massuk. Who's looking for me?" She kept walking, heading for the employee entrance she knew was located somewhere deeper in the infirmary. As she passed the room where Solène and Johnson waited, Ava kept her eyes forward. There was no outcry, so she assumed they hadn't seen her.

"I am, *Terina*." The same oily voice that had called for her capture seeped out of the unit in her left hand. She tucked the other unit into her sash so she could tell them apart. "Strange, you don't sound like someone with a weapon to their head."

Ava's amusement came through clearly in her voice as she retorted, "You definitely sound like someone who only thinks he's in control of a situation." On the surface, taunting hardly seemed like the right tactic to take with a man who undoubtedly wanted to see her enslaved. Except she didn't care if he liked her. She wanted his attention, all of it and immediately.

The deep, nasty chuckling sound that came next made her skin crawl. "This is Captain Erq Vyl, of the *Reus*. It's nice to meet you, *Terina*."

Suppressing a shudder, Ava snapped, "You haven't met me yet. And you won't, unless you agree to let the rest of the station go."

She kept moving as the silence stretched out, until she reached the exit she'd been looking for. Testing it, Ava was relieved and concerned to find it unguarded. Stepping into the exterior corridor, she double-checked that it was locked from the outside, then began easing her way along the wall. The sounds of fighting had decreased significantly, and she wished she knew if her plan was working or if it was just a coincidence. Not to mention who was winning!

"I suppose I should've known you'd try to set terms," sneered the voice, startling her badly enough that she nearly threw the unit. Hastily, she turned down the volume on both of them so they wouldn't give away her position.

She opened her mouth to remind him that the station and everyone on it was her responsibility, then changed her mind. There was no point in giving him ammunition against her, not when she would willingly surrender herself in exchange for the life of even one of her employees—at least long enough for everyone to get to safety.

"I'm trying to make it easy for you," she lied. "Meet me at the docks and you might get away before the next patrol swings by." All Montgomery ships were reasonably armed, and a small percentage were tasked with random sweeps of high-risk areas like the *Beyond*. "Maybe you'll even get as far as Puer." The name of the slave system was bitter on her tongue.

It rang like the screeching of an attack alert in Jean's ears as he listened in on a captured comms unit. Those clustered around him drew back warily as he activated the suit's full helmet.

"Not today, Vyl." Tossing the unit to his buddy, Hway, Jean ordered, "Take over. I've got a promise to keep."

Racing to the nearest pivotlift, Jean pried the doors open and slipped inside, powering on the antigrav as he did so. Dropping at a controlled rate, he cleared a dozen levels in as many seconds, eyes and ears open for any incoming cars. Bypassing the dock levels usually reserved for civilian transports, he slowed to a halt at the fifth level down and forced the doors open manually so he could access the corridor.

There was no one to greet him. Not station crew, not redhands. It was a little creepy to find such emptiness on such a busy station, but he wasn't there to do a nosecount. He was there to check the dock monitors.

Programmed independently of the commbands, the monitors recorded every ship that docked on the *Beyond*. Eliminating the transport vessels and all arrivals of more than three hours ago, Jean narrowed the field to five ships. From there it took a little fancy handling to gain access to the video logs, but it was worth it—he found a Pernix class Destroyer docked on Level D9.

He was about to re-enter the pivotlift shaft when a car raced past the gap in the doors he hadn't bothered to close, bringing him sharply to a halt. Once his heart had dropped out of his mouth, he forced the gap to open a little wider and peeked into the shaft. Sure enough, the car stopped on Level D9, blocking his exit. It had to be carrying the redhands--and Ava?—and maybe going somewhere else at a split second's notice.

A primal urge to scream shuddered through him, but he applied the energy to running toward the nearest service tube instead. With the antigrav unit turned off, he dropped like a stone to the desired level and burst out into the corridor.

The first person he saw was a grungy-looking man with a weapon cradled loosely in his arms. Jean smashed his fist into his face, then plucked the weapon out of his unresisting arms and checked it over while the man crumpled to the floor.

Startled to find the weapon in tiptop condition, Jean brought it to the ready position and began making his way around to the bay where the destroyer was docked. He took out two more guards silently, but the third one got off a yell before the stun round took effect.

Abandoning stealth altogether, Jean ran forward now, catching a few more by surprise before arriving at the bay. What breath he had left seized in his lungs as his gaze zeroed in on Ava.

Privately, Ava admitted that things weren't going according to plan. She'd exited the tube halfway around the station from this bay, expecting to hide in plain sight while she negotiated with Vyl. Getting surprised a second time in less than five hours by an armed redhand cemented her decision to leave future investigations to the small army of operatives she employed. Which was actually a rather optimistic decision under the circumstances.

She felt Vyl's fingers dig into her left shoulder as someone—Jean!—lunged around the corner, startling them all. He stood alone for an instant, an intimidating figure clothed head-to-toe in the silver-colored Security Suit, even his face hidden from view by the visor. For half a heartbeat, Vyl's grip on her eased.

Instinctively, Ava ducked forward, spinning under his arm to her left. She felt him scrabble for purchase, his nails dragging along the cloth of her tunic, but she twisted free. Striking out with her near leg, she caught him once in the stomach and once in the face.

The feeling of something digging into her back brought her escape attempt to an abrupt halt. She hadn't forgotten about the redhand who'd caught her trying to sneak into an empty bay down the corridor. However, she had hoped that Jean would handle him.

A glance in his direction showed that he was swapping punches with a pair of redhands, one of whom had somehow gotten ahold of his arm and was trying to twist it around behind his back.

"Nice try."   Vyl hugged bruised ribs and swiped at his bloody nose. The sound of running feet made him grin despite the pain. "Ah, good. Those lazy louts I call a crew were about to get left behind. Help the lady aboard," he ordered. "And give her the full tour—of the brig." The 'boss' was already waiting for him in one of the smaller berths, a token gesture of kindness since Vyl still wanted something from him.

Defeated, Ava allowed herself to be marched forward into the bay.

Jean broke free just as a dozen or more station security officers came charging into view. To his horror, and despite the fact that he was standing over two of the invaders, half of them brought their weapons to bear on him. Reflex warred with a reluctance to harm them, and he found himself frozen in the middle of the corridor, a nearly perfect target.

The suit had taken a few shots during the fight, but this was hardly the time to find out if it could withstand a concentrated barrage. Not while he was in it, and especially not while he still had a chance to save Ava.

Wait! That was it! Triggering the helmet retraction, Jean faced the officers, hands out from his body. "Help her! Please!" Dressed in that suit, it was anybody's guess how many of them would recognize him as Lieutenant Commander Kearns, so he didn't bother trying to give orders.

There was a moment's hesitation, long enough for Vyl to scurry into the bay and behind the wall separating it from the bay, but the officers transferred their attention to the escaping villains.

Vyl pressed himself up against the wall, panting for breath as a couple of stun rounds buzzed past him. This couldn't be happening! He'd had an all-access pass to the station, two simple targets, and right about now he should be making a leisurely getaway. How many hundreds of more difficult, more dangerous runs had he pulled off in the past without so much as a scratch?

The sight of the Montgomery brat grinning like a kid at a carnival did nothing to improve his mood.

"I said get her aboard!" he roared, running over to where she was being held behind a stack of empty crates.

"Do it yerself!" The crewmember roared in reply. "They has a clear shot at the hatch!" He didn't like being shot at, not one little bit. Give him a fist-

and-face fight any day!

Vyl scowled and bit back a retort that would've blistered the deckplating. He could address the discipline problem later, assuming they both survived. For now… Unclipping his comm unit, he barked an order.

Ava stared up at him in disbelief. "You're insane!" The enraged howl that reverberated through the bay was her only answer. Gasping, she stuffed her fingers in her ears and curled away from the noise.

Vyl hated to lose cargo, even just a terrabeast. Relatively easy to replace compared with an heiress, though. Grabbing her arm, he towed her around a corner of the stacks. They'd be truly spilgered if the terrabeast decided to stop for a snack, but he was counting on human nature to save them. The human nature of the officers, in fact. A few shots from their stun guns would put the monster in a killing mood, and then they'd be so busy trying not to die that he'd become the loose end nobody got around to tying up.

Jean's vision blurred at the sound that grew closer by the heartbeat. *No. Not here!* Shaking his head to clear it, he looked hopelessly at the security officers with their cute little stun guns and thin cloth uniforms where battle armor should've been.

"Run!" He blurted the word without thinking further. "Get to the pivotlifts!" They stared at him as if he'd gone mad. Perhaps he had, a little, for he suddenly cued up the speaker system on the suit and shouted, "Go NOW!"

They broke and ran, leaving him to face a rampaging terrabeast on his own. Turning to face the bay door as the helmet closed comfortingly around his head, Jean reflected that he wouldn't have had it any other way.

Assessing his surroundings, he tried to formulate a plan. There were no slimepits to lure it into. No one waiting to ambush it or even distract it if he got caught in a bad spot. His hope that it might at least be full-grown was shattered when it appeared in the bay, stopping to howl its displeasure at being trapped in this horribly metallic world—it was a juvenile, small enough to escape into the corridor and wreak havoc with any of the officers foolish enough to try to be brave. And what it lacked in brute strength, it would make up for in sheer maneuverability.

Seeing only one way to delay the terrabeast and hopefully let the entire security team escape, Jean ran to the bay door, dropping in a slide that kept his head from getting bitten off by the lunging, snapping terrabeast. Pain erupted in his old injury as his knees hit the deckplating and he knew he'd never regain his feet in time to escape the way he'd planned.

On the other side of the hold Ava sprang at Vyl like a madwoman, battering him back against the wall with every punch and kick she knew, determined to get control of his weapon.

Bewildered by the ferocity of her attack Vyl retreated, arms up for protection, until his back hit the wall. Having nowhere else to go, he grunted with pain as her foot connected with his gut. Balling his left hand into a fist, he lashed out. She was everywhere at once, but he knew he hurt her every time he got in a hit.

Desperately, Jean threw himself toward a stack of empty crates, scrambling to stay ahead of the slicing, stabbing claws of the terrabeast's forepaws. At last his hand closed around the lip of one of the square crates and he swung it so that it connected with the terrabeast's snout.

As he'd hoped, the terrabeast stopped to roar its displeasure, giving him enough time to haul himself to a standing position.

Ava couldn't even hear herself scream over the terrabeast's angry cry. Cruel fingers seized her by the back of the neck, peeling her off the wall and lifting her almost off her feet. Her right arm dangled limply at her side, swaying as they moved ...moved where? Desperately, she sagged as if she'd suddenly lost consciousness.

Cursing under his breath, Vyl hit her with the butt of his gun and threw her over his shoulder. Still muttering, he hustled toward the hatch.

"Take it easy, big guy." Jean didn't believe for a second that he'd be able to soothe the animal, but any thoughts he might've been able to scrape together scattered like rags in jet wash when he heard the distinctive hiss of a sealing hatch. *Ava!*

The terrabeast hadn't been fed in a while and would've eaten nearly anything. Now, sensing that his opponent was distracted, he reached out with his teeth to snag a sample.

Jean dangled helplessly from where the terrabeast had his shoulder in its mouth and even the helmet couldn't protect his ears from the horrible screeching sounds of teeth sliding across metal as he slowly slid out of its grasp. Tumbling unceremoniously to the deckplating, he rolled out of easy reach.

From the corner of his eye, he saw someone peeking into the bay from the corridor. "Get back! Get out of here!"

"We've got a plan!"

"I've heard that before!" Jean growled in frustration. "Is dying in your plan?" A quick scan showed that the shoulder of the suit was dented but not seriously compromised, so he did the only thing he could think of. He picked up a crate and threw it at the button by the door. It was a clean miss, and as it sailed out the door, the people outside yelped and dove for cover.

"Hey! We're trying to help!"

Ignoring their shouts, Jean dodged a half-hearted strike from the confused terrabeast, who was eyeing the door with interest. Running back around its tail, which he deliberately stepped on, he made it almost halfway across the bay before the creature figured out he wasn't hiding behind the last stack of crates and came charging after him.

Activating the antigrav unit, Jean braced for the impact. When the startled terrabeast plowed into him, he was too close to the wall to avoid slamming into it, and his finger slipped on the control as he ricocheted across the bay, bringing him to the floor hard.

Flat on his back, Jean tried to move. Fear lanced through him as straining muscles failed to bring him to a sitting position. Out of breath despite the suit's synth systems, he paused long enough to wonder why it was so quiet. Had the terrabeast seen the trap and avoided running headlong into the wall? There were no screams, so maybe his trick had *worked*? But then, where were the security officers? At least one of them should be checking on him by now, if they hadn't all been eaten.

As Jean gathered his wits, he noticed a warning on the helmet display. Gravity – 400%. Relief surged through him, making him giddy. That was definitely a function he didn't see a use for! At least the suit seemed to be taking the bulk of the pressure.

"S-suit," he gasped. "Reduce gravity." The words came out as choppy sets of sounds as he struggled to breathe. He was trying to figure out what to try next when the feeling of having a small house on his chest started to ease. Checking the display, he confirmed that the gravity was slowly decreasing.

Taking as deep a breath as he could manage, he managed to say, "Suit, return gravity to normal."

Dragging himself into a seated position, Jean shook his head and flexed his fingers. A large, gray heap on the floor a few yards from him answered the question of what had happened to the terrabeast. And the closed bay door explained why there were no officers hoisting him up on their shoulders. Now that he was back at a normal gravity, that was.

Suddenly, he remembered another closed door. *The airlock!* Lurching to his feet, he hobbled toward it as quickly as he could. He had to get there before they took off. Open the lock and get onto their ship. Tripping, he fell flat on his face just as the unsecured crates started rattling around the floor in time with the rumble of engines.

Chapter 20

"Welcome to your new life." Vyl hissed in Ava's ear and shoved her into a cell.

"Captain? Station's hailing us." A voice from the comm unit on his belt interrupted his gloating.

"Put it through." Tossing the cell keys into the air, Vyl caught them and, completely oblivious to the blood that had dried around his nose and mouth, faced the display arrogantly. "Make it fast, *Beyond*. We've got an appointment to keep on Peur."

"Not going to happen, Vyl." Taylor hated how feeble he sounded, but he supposed he was doing pretty well for having just undergone a two-hour surgery. "Return our personnel."

"Or what?" Vyl eyed the pasty-faced man on the display, a niggling suspicion growing in the back of his mind that something was up. Sure, he recognized the security chief he'd personally shot to get him out of the way for a while. "Say, don't you have anybody that isn't on their deathbed who could do this?"

"What's the matter, Vyl? Are you as bad at negotiating as you are at killing people?" Taylor somehow managed the dig without stopping for breath, though the effort left him shaky.

"You're alive because I wanted you that way." Vyl shook his head in disgust. He'd never killed anyone in his entire career. Patrolmen hunted murderers with a passion that made treasure seekers look like lethargic goppybirds.

"Return our personnel and we'll return yours. Two of ours for fourteen of yours." Making the offer turned Taylor's stomach, but he was a step away from having to kill them all. Including Ava.

"Whatever meds they have you on are messing

with your brain if you think I want them back."
Vyl gave an exaggerated shrug. "Those morons
couldn't even handle simple station security. Tell
them they're fired."

Taylor looked away from the display and made
eye contact with a stiff-backed Paella. "Now do you
believe me?"

Vyl tensed. The display before him shifted to
show Taylor and—Vyl sucked in a breath—Paella!
The *Reus* was moving away from the station. He
had both prizes aboard. So why did he have a sudden premonition of impending doom?

"I believe you." Paella stared hard at the display. "And I will tell you what you want to know
about the *Reus*."

"You're going to help him?!" Vyl licked his
lips, then spat right on the deckplate when he got
a taste of his own blood. "Paella, no captain in
their right mind will take you on if you do that."

"That's alright." Paella's lips curved in a preda-
tory smile. "I was planning to retire after this one
anyhow. Remember?"

Vyl broke out in a cold sweat. Was it only last
night that they'd swapped stories of what they'd
do after this job? 'The big one,' they'd called it.
Now she was using that to mock him, and all
because he hadn't chosen her over his prizes! If
their positions were switched, he knew she'd make
the exact same decision he had. Brushing past the
question of whether or not he'd do what she was
threatening to, he jumped back into the negotia-
tion.

"I'll give you Steinberg." Oh, the shock of
finding out that 'the boss' was a glorified waiter on
the side. "For Paella." He raised his eyebrows as
if to say, 'See what I'm willing to sacrifice, just for

you?"

"You will return all our personnel." Taylor locked eyes with the man. "Or I'll blow your ship out of the sky."

"You're going to *kill* them?" Shock didn't begin to describe Vyl's reaction. "Is that supposed to make sense?" Without waiting for an answer, he hollered, "Hey! If there's anybody else listening, your boss has gone insane!"

"Check your scanners." By now, Taylor was too tired to sound anything but bored. "Our guns are already tracking you. As soon as you clear the station, you're done for."

"Clear…the station," Vyl mumbled. Snatching his comms unit, he yelled into it, "Start the main engines. Get us out of here!"

"Sir, we'll damage the station!" Safety protocols were so deeply ingrained that even the helmsman of a smuggling and pirate vessel protested such an order.

"That's the idea!" Vyl fairly screamed. "And bring our guns online! Target the ore processing center!"

Ava, who'd been listening with grim satisfaction to Taylor's call, snapped out of her resigned-to-death thoughts. "No! You could destroy the station!"

Attaching a docking bay and residential areas to a fuel station had always been a calculated risk. They'd taken every precaution, from fire suppression systems to fuel cut-off valves and automated bulkheads that would seal the station off into sections. But having someone deliberately strafe it was a different prospect entirely. Outguessing where they'd target, what ammunition they'd use, what angle they'd fire from…the list went on for yards.

While a few might survive to be taken aboard the incoming ships, too many would die.

"You'll be hunted till the end of your days," she stormed.

"Better dead tomorrow than today!" he hurled wildly back. "Besides." Some of his confidence returned when he saw how rattled they all were. "Nobody in their right mind would come hunting me in Puer." Stepping up close to the bars that separated them, he demanded, "What's it going to be? My ship or your station?"

Ava bit her lip and twisted the ring on her finger. It was time. She hadn't tried it in the bay because he'd had a crewmember with him. Now they were alone. Approaching Vyl with hunched shoulders and eyes down, she cleared her throat.

"Speak up!" Vyl's hand snaked through the bars to grab a fistful of her tunic and yank her closer.

She saw stars when her cheek bounced off one of the bars, but she stubbornly choked back the cry of pain. She got a good whiff of his foul breath as he leaned down to eye level.

"Make your choice."

"I choose you." Her good left hand wrapped itself around his wrist, allowing the barb on her ring to puncture his skin. The key he'd stuffed into his belt stayed behind in her right hand as he jerked free of her grip and stumbled back. While he ranted and howled his disbelief, she calmly unlocked the door.

A loud, electronic screech blocked out whatever she might've said next, and a new voice boomed through the hidden speakers.

"This is Captain Audax of the *Ulciscor*. Surrender or you will be forcibly taken."

Vyl blinked and shook his head, trying to force

his eyes to see only one of everything. With a snarl, he dove for Ava.

"You came after me." She faked left, sidestepped, and knocked his comm unit off his belt as she shoved him inside the cell. "You came after *my people*." She pulled the door closed firmly behind him. "You lose." Entering the office area, she tossed the key into the reclaimer as she passed it on her way to the corridor.

The *Reus* had left a lot of her crew aboard the *Beyond*, and the ship felt eerily empty. Which way to go? Her plan, such as it was, involved finding a lifesuit and escaping through the nearest airlock. From there, a quick radio call could end the stand-off.

No, wait! Steinberg! Good grief, what was he doing aboard? Scowling, Ava started off to her right. She'd been pretty dazed when Vyl dragged her aboard, and now had no idea where she was, but getting caught doing something was just the tiniest smidge better than getting caught debating what to do.

The sound of voices coming from ahead made her wish she'd relieved Vyl of his weapon as well as his comm unit. What ifs chased her like a swarm of angry bees as she tried the nearest door, found it open, and slipped inside. What if someone was in there? What if this was exactly where they were going? What if… Ah, the voices had passed her position.

Bumping her right arm as she exited the room, Ava clamped her mouth shut against the yelp that hovered behind her lips. Okay, this was ridiculous. She might be able to get herself off, but she was in no shape to try to rescue anyone else.

Once she was clear of the *Reus*, she'd radio the

Ulciscor. Captain Audax could safely cripple the *Reus* and bring Steinberg off along with everyone else.

All of which still depended on her finding a lifesuit somewhere! Moving forward again, Ava scanned the walls on both sides of the corridor. Lifesuit compartments were plainly labeled and placed so that if a ship's structural integrity was compromised, crew and guests would have easy access. Sometimes people jumped aboard a lifepod without them, but she didn't have the code to release a lifepod.

An outcry and two thuds had her ducking for cover. The silence that followed made the hairs on the back of her neck stand up like teenagers trying to see better at a concert. Unable to shake the sense that someone or something was coming— this ship had one terrabeast on it, why not two?— Ava pressed herself back as far as she could into the small gap she'd found.

Her heart stopped when a figure strode around the corner, the silver of its suit standing out against the tan walls. "Jean?"

He froze at the sound of his name and scanned ahead. A shadow moved, then suddenly Ava was in his arms!

"Ow, ow," she pushed away and gripped her shoulder, but forced herself to smile. "I am so glad to see you!"

"Did I hurt you?" Dumb question. Switching his vision to the lowest X-ray setting available, he examined her shoulder. "Nothing's broken."

"That's good." Surprised, she managed a tight laugh. "Good news. Yeah, I needed some of that." She was rambling. Blast.

'Hey." He spoke to her soothingly as his hands

settled on her waist. "You're not alone anymore."

"Not alone." Ava would've given a decade's worth of profits for a safe minute to spend in Jean's arms right then, but it didn't work that way. "We have to get…Steinberg!"

"Alright." Jean had no idea who Steinberg was. "First let's get you somewhere safe, then I'll go for him, okay?"

"I…" A twinge from her shoulder turned whatever she was going to say into a grunt, and she nodded. She was hurt and would only slow him down. "Okay."

All the hidden speakers came alive at once, pumping Captain Audax's voice through the ship. "This is your last chance to surrender."

"Come on!" Jean herded Ava down the corridor to the airlock where he'd broken in. It hadn't been easy, but he'd learned a few tricks about boarding these birds during his time in the military.

"We have to find a lifesuit."

"Here!" Jean ripped open the brightly marked compartment and scanned its contents. Of the three slots—small, medium, and large—only the large was filled.

"Oh, great." Ava was already stepping out of her shoes. "Well, at least it's not the small!"

Jean shook it out and held it for her while she climbed in. They didn't have time to wait for her to shove her hands all the way down into the gloves, so he sealed it for her, scooped her up, and ran the rest of the way to the airlock.

"*Reus*, we will commence firing in ten seconds." The voice droned on in a deliberate countdown.

Ava nearly panicked when Jean deposited her in the airlock and stepped back. "Come on!"

"I have to get Steinberg." He slapped the button that closed the inner doors. "You get clear. Fast!"

"No! Jean!" She screamed, but it was just a waste of the precious oxygen limit in her lifesuit. He was gone. And she couldn't even go after him. The airlock lever malfunctioned when she tried to throw it, jamming the inner doors. Feeling the pressure around her change as the atmosphere was sucked out of the lock, Ava turned to face the outer doors as they opened.

She was now his best chance. Shoving off as soon as there was enough room to scrape through, Ava cued up her comms system for an all-frequencies broadcast. With any luck, the station's fighter squadrons, menacingly arrayed against the *Reus*, would hear her as well.

"*Ulciscor*, this is Sigrid Ava Montgomery. Acknowledge." Only static answered her. Frantic, she began adjusting the dials manually. Would anyone even be listening while they counted down to fire? "ULCISCOR! This is Sigrid Ava Montgomery. Acknowledge."

"This is Captain Audax of *Ulciscor*. Please state your passcode for identity confirmation."

"Sunset over Candeo Falls." For the first time in years, Ava didn't smile as she thought of the exquisitely beautiful place where her father had taken her mother to propose. "Hold your fire!"

"Identity confirmed." There was a hard note to the voice as it conceded, "Holding fire."

"I am no longer on the *Reus*. Repeat, I am no longer on the *Reus*." It didn't need to be destroyed anymore, but neither was she going to stand by while it left with Jean aboard! "New target, *Reus*' engines only. Fire disabling shot upon target acquisition." Ava didn't bother trying to change her course. Her drift and the *Reus'* slowly edging away from the station on thrusters put her well in the clear.

A spiked projectile erupted from a small port on the *Ulciscor*'s side, separating into three pieces mere seconds before striking the *Reus'*. The pirate ship, which had been strangely still during the engagement, now shuddered and rolled as its engines fought to go on, but a second shot ended the argument.

Ava exhaled shakily. After everything it took to get them there, this solution seemed almost too easy. With a firm voice in command, the *Reus* could've done a lot of damage before being taken.

"Target neutralized." Captain Audax's voice once again invaded her thoughts. "State your location and we'll come pick you up."

Congratulating herself on deescalating an impossible situation—and surviving—Ava moved to test her propulsion unit before responding.

Something slammed her against the front of the lifesuit as a dozen alarms began shrieking in her ears, of which "Collision alert!" was easily the least terrifying. Sundry whistles, beeps, and a line running on repeat across the digital readout, barely visible as she slid down into the humongous lifesuit, ramped her heart rate up until a warning about that added to the chaos.

"Warning. Heart rate exceeds…"

"Initiate shoulder thrusters!" Ava was already acting, fighting for attitude control as she spun away from help. Her injured right shoulder throbbed painfully as she flattened her arms against her body to keep from sliding around in the too-large lifesuit.

"What was that?!" She almost shrieked as a slab

of metal debris the size of a blast door sliced through the space just above her head. Scrambling to manually adjust the thrusters, she slowed the shoulder burn and added a few spurts from her left shoulder and knee to stabilize her position as the station edged into view.

Leftover bits and pieces of…of something littered space around the *Beyond*. In at least one spot, a chunk of it protruded from the side of the station. Atmosphere, spilling out around the edges of whatever it was, which was acting like a plug, glowed white then blue as it reflected the fire consuming what was left of—the *Reus*.

"JAK!" Her anguished scream seemed to shatter the space-time continuum so that she was forced to watch the wreckage expand in slow motion. "Solène," she whispered, her heart aching not only with her own loss but also for the sweet little girl who was now truly orphaned.

Determination seared through Ava and she flipped aft thrusters to full. She had to know, even if it meant seeing it herself.

"Proximity warning." The lifesuit's toneless voice invaded her shock and she tried to scan the area around her. Blast it! She couldn't see much over the alerts still scrolling across the bottom of her visor. Even her head wasn't the right size for this…

"No! No, no!" She couldn't adjust course fast enough—the asteroid rammed right into her. She finally saw it as she bounced off. Lucky for her it was smallish for an asteroid, roughly the size of her personal hovercraft. Dazed, she tried to reach up and wipe away the blood from where her face had connected sharply with something solid. Choked back a laugh when she realized she was smacking her gloved hand uselessly against the visor.

Just then the thrusters sputtered out, draining all the humor from the situation. Despite her slightly addled condition, it wasn't hard to deduce that the power pack on her back had taken the brunt of the collision with the asteroid. She could never reach it to fix it. Not only that, but she hadn't answered the *Ulciscor*'s request for her position. Without that information, they would have to start at what was left of the *Reus* and work outward.

Icy fear spread through Avs as she watched the growing distance between herself and any possible source of help. She was just one more piece of space flotsam now, in an area littered with the stuff. The *Ulciscor* would come looking for her, sooner or later. But how soon was soon? And could she survive until later? The lifesuit was already cooling off, the air growing stale.

Twisting about in the lifesuit, she managed to turn it enough that she could see a glimmer of the *Beyond*. Grief-stricken for the second time in six months, she frowned as she examined her emotions. The pain was staggering, yes, but she didn't honestly believe her sorrow would exceed Solène's.

A stern resolve formed in Ava then, crowding out the fear. She would be there for Jean's little girl every step of the way. Step one: survive.

Knowing there was literally nothing she could do to ensure her own survival at this point made her skin crawl. To pass the time, she focused narrowed eyes on the *Beyond* and the *Ulciscor*. It was hard to be sure, but she thought the faint blur of activity near the hole in the station was probably bots getting to work on repairs. Larger, manned pods from the station were picking through the debris now, partly to nudge it toward a central spot for cleanup and partly to locate any survivors or remains.

Most interesting of all to her were the six sleek rescuepods no doubt launched from the *Ulciscor*, probably within seconds of the initial explosion. She only noticed them now because she was looking for them. Each one operated six melon-sized search drones specifically designed to cut through the incidental radiation and noise to detect life signs such as body heat.

Squinting, Ava thought she could make out the drone closest to her. She was sure of it when another drone moved up beside it. Perhaps to verify findings? It seemed too good to be true. And yet, how long had she actually been hanging out there amidst the stars? Probably longer than she'd realized. She reminded herself, too, that this system was the best available, designed specifically for search and recover situations.

Confusion superseded her rising confidence when something even smaller than the drones began arrowing toward her. What was that silver blob? Ugh, not another piece of the *Reus*, she hoped. Mm, no, it wasn't lazily wobbling along, it was coming at speed. A rogue repair bot? She dismissed the idea as ridiculous; they were specifically programmed to stay in close proximity to the hull.

The closer it got, the more familiar it seemed, though she still couldn't put a name to it.

A name to it? Her heart began to race, triggering another alert from the system.

No, it couldn't be! Jak was aboard the *Reus* when it exploded, searching for Steinberg. Okay, the Security Suit might've withstood the blast, even an initial exposure to space...but this? And, out amongst the chaos and the uncharted stars, he'd still managed to find her. She didn't even fight the happy tears that sprang to her eyes.

"Lock in on my beacon, *Ulciscor*. Two for retrieval." Jean closed in on Ava's position with the utmost care. He'd pushed the Suit to its limits, and it looked like hers had taken a beating as well.

"Locking on, Commander. Rescuepods incoming." Thank goodness he'd finally managed to get through to them! Of course, it had taken Taylor's intervention to convince them he wasn't a pirate masquerading as a station officer.

He almost chuckled. Frustrating as gaining their cooperation had been, it was nothing at all compared to moving the twelve stars of Terean, as he'd promised he would to bring Avs back safely.

Though it was difficult to make eye contact through Ava's misty visor, Jean managed. He ached to wash the blood from her forehead and dry her tears but had to be satisfied with a reassuring smile. Knowing her comms were offline and that they didn't have much time, he kept his message simple. "I love you."

Chapter 21

A month later, Ava held very still, refusing to wince as Solène ran a comb through her hair, recently restored to its naturally pale blond color. The last of the wreckage outside the station was finally cleaned up, Donovan was serving an eight-year sentence of unpaid societal service on his homeworld, and Jean had agreed to marry her!

And he happened to have a little girl who was—*ouch!*—ecstatic to be part of the wedding preparations.

"Smooth strokes." Phyl, who'd been overjoyed at the invitation to join the wedding party, coached Solène gently. "Start at the top and run the comb all the way down to the bottom before you lift it. Ah, excellent." Impressed by Ava's patience with the girl's clumsy attempts to help, Phyl nevertheless decided to intervene. Perhaps it was old-fashioned, but she believed a bride should cry only tears of joy on her wedding day.

Two attendants jumped forward at Phyl's signal and she smiled down at Solène. "Would you like to watch while they give her a fancy hairdo?"

Eyes wide, Solène nodded vigorously and climbed up on a tall chair by the mirror so she could see. For the last two weeks, she'd been in her idea of little girl heaven, surrounded by soft and silky fabrics, flowers and ribbons, and taste-testing all sorts of scrumptious treats for the party after the ceremony. Best of all was getting to spend time with Ava. She had a way of stopping to listen to Solène that made her glad Ava was going to be her mother. Except…

Ava, who had just begun to relax under the ministrations of incredibly skilled hair professionals, noticed when Solène's forehead began to pucker. She still had a *lot* to learn about her and how to be a mother, but so far this was proving a guaranteed indicator that Solène was thinking about something important.

As soon as her hair was done and Ava had complimented the stylists, she politely shooed them all out so that it was just her and Solène.

"But your wedding!" Predictably, Phyl was the last one to acquiesce. One of the perks of being Ava's personal assistant was that they'd become quite good friends, too. "You can't be late for your own wedding!"

"If anyone will ever understand why I was a few minutes late," Ava laughed, "it will be Jean."

Phyl shook her head, shrugged, and finally retreated, closing the door softly behind her.

Ava's dressing gown made a soft swishing sound as she seated herself on the couch. "Come here, Pumpkin." Noting that Solène's smile only took the edge off the child's thoughtful expression, Ava decided there must be something especially serious on her mind. Wrapping an arm around her shoulders, Ava tucked Solène in beside her and sighed. "We've been awfully busy lately, haven't we?"

Solène nodded and rested her head against Ava's chest. There was nothing in the galaxy like her daddy's strong arms, but she liked that Ava's hugs were softer, snugglier. "Are you tired?"

Ava stroked Solène's hair and chuckled softly. "I think we all are, after observing Trafodaeth."

Orpan custom dictated that a man and a woman should spend the night before their wedding talking. Or at least, in each other's company. Older family members would join them at random, to tell stories, to listen, or sometimes to referee as fatigue dulled their wits and sharpened their tongues. The last hour before sunrise was dedicated to dressing for the ceremony, assuming they still liked each other enough to get married!

Since neither Ava nor Jean had older family members anymore, friends like Phyl, Masie, Chief Taylor, and Agent Deuyn Johnson dropped by instead. Even Edgin Tollwith, the *Beyond*'s new captain, a canny older fellow with twinkling eyes and a cracking sense of humor, had come by with his wife to wish them well and impart slivers of advice tucked inside hilarious anecdotes from their early married days.

Upon being reminded, Solène yawned so hard that her jaw popped. "Thanks for letting me stay up with you." She'd fallen asleep for an hour in the middle but woken to laughter and stayed up the rest of the time.

Sensing a pause at the end of the sentence, Ava waited as long as she dared, then squeezed her shoulders lightly. "It wouldn't have been right to do it without you, Pumpkin." Solène's answering sigh snagged Ava's attention like it was made of rare spinsilk. "Is there anything you want to talk about?"

Solène bit her lip. "Can I ask you a question?"

"Of course you can." Ava's heart rate ticked up a bit.

"Any question?" Solène clarified, reluctant to bring up what was bothering her. Nevertheless, she couldn't shake the feeling that it would be better to talk about it before the wedding than after. Every time she'd worked up the courage to bring it up last night, someone new came by and the suppressed question would dig itself a little deeper into its hole.

"I, um." Ava forced herself to breathe evenly. This was it. Their first big discussion. "Yes. Any question."

"How come you call me Pumpkin?" Solène leaned her head back against Ava's shoulder and looked up at her.

"Oh, I…" Relief and surprise collided, leaving Ava temporarily speechless. "I suppose it's because that's what my parents used to call me. It comes from their ancestral homeworld, I think."

"Hmm." Solène fiddled with Ava's fingers without realizing that she was doing it. "What did you call them?"

All the air rushed out of Ava's lungs. Nestling her cheek against Solène's soft black hair, she inhaled slowly, savoring the moment. "I called them Mommy and Daddy when I was your age. As I got older, I started calling them Mom and Dad."

"Hmm." Solène dropped her gaze. She'd never met her mother, but she didn't like what most of the kids at school called their second mothers. It was either too formal or too casual, and sometimes downright mean.

"You know, I just realized. I never asked if was okay with you for me to call you Pumpkin." Ava laid a little groundwork.

Solène gave her a shy smile. "Yes, it's okay. I like it."

"I'm glad." She glanced at the clock, more worried about Phyl's nerves than Jean's. "Do you have a nickname you'd like to call me?"

"I…" A big, fat tear rolled down Solène's cheek and landed with a plop on her dressing gown. "I don't know. Maybe?"

Ava chuckled. "I think it would be super special if you did."

"Yeah?" Solène perked up even as she sniffled. "Could I think about it for a while?" She had already been thinking about it, but somehow the idea of having permission made her feel lighter all over, like the times she got to play in the zero-gravity gym.

"Absolutely."

"And." Solène swallowed hard. "Is it okay if I don't call you Mommy?"

"Solène, I trust you to find the very best nickname for me." Shifting so that they could look at each other directly, Ava promised, "And it is perfectly fine if it isn't mommy."

Solène threw her arms as far around Ava as she could with the couch in the way and hugged her tightly. "I love you."

"I love you, too." Dropping a kiss on top of her head, Ava jumped up without letting go of her and turned in a fast circle to that Solène's feet came up off the floor. Only after she'd started giggling did Ava slow to a stop. "Now, run tell Phyl to get back in here. We don't want to keep Daddy waiting!" Her stomach flipped deliciously, and she blushed. They'd talked about it and they both wanted more children.

Halfway across the station, Jean stood, critically studying the arch he'd built of imported parpai wood. On Orpan, he would've hunted the forests for a stand of new parpai trees, then cut them back and woven them together to form a living arch. The ceremony would've taken place when the parpai flowers opened at sunrise, filling the air with their heady perfume.

"I heard that." Taylor, off-duty for the day while he acted as aide to the groom, came over and punched him lightly on the shoulder. "Since when do you sigh like you've just lost your best friend?"

"I'm sorry, I know I shouldn't be sad." Looking out over the room that was barely recognizable as a docking bay, Jean had to admit, "This is all so incredible."

Ava had hired an interior designer to program the setting. The central projector that hung from the ceiling displayed a forest scene from Orpan, so real that Jean could almost hear the tuetue birds singing in the treetops. A handful of comfortable chairs had synthesized in place and stood ready to accommodate the few guests they'd agreed on and the airlock was temporarily hidden by the arch's veil.

It was a far cry from signing a wedding contract in one of the conference rooms. Jean's lips twitched as he remembered persuading Ava to have this ceremony instead. He understood her impatience but couldn't help hoping that most of their disagreements would be as much fun to resolve as this one had been.

"It's about as perfect as you can get without going all the way home," agreed Taylor. Then, to keep Jean talking, he asked, "Are you sure you know what you're getting yourself into? I mean, it's gonna be rough being married to the most powerful woman in the galaxy, finally getting to be a pilot, going to fancy parties…"

Jean burst out laughing and returned Taylor's earlier punch. "You only think you're kidding. The hardest part for both of us will be making time to be married." He'd even worried at first about taking the job from her current pilot and had been relieved to learn that she was excited to have a shot at running the newest Montgomery shipyard.

"Yeah." Taylor nodded thoughtfully. "Well, at

least you know it."

"What do you mean?" Jean patted the arch one last time and followed Taylor toward the door.

"Nothing much." Taylor took a blindingly white dress jacket from a rack and helped Jean into it. "I've just seen too many marriages crack under the pressure. Jobs, kids, obligations of one sort or another." Grabbing his own jacket, he shrugged into it before reaching out to straighten the lines on Jean's jacket. Having a chestful of medals did weird things to how clothes hung.

"Fair point." Jean agreed sadly as his fingers flew up the first row of buttons that angled out from the center and up his left side. Typical military thinking; everything was designed for efficiency, except the dress uniforms.

"Like I said," Taylor tugged the last button of his own second row through the hole, "you already know. You've got a plan!" He was sorry he'd even brought it up. This was supposed to be a joyous celebration.

"It's never about the plan." Jean had seen plenty of plans fall apart right when they were most needed: broken equipment; bad intel; even the weather had fouled his unit up more times than he could count. Somehow, they'd had always pulled it together for the ultimate win—getting as many out alive as possible.

A cheerful voice pulled him from his somber memories.

"Ready or not." As she entered the docking bay, Deuyn Johnson looked up from her brand new, guaranteed-to-not-shock-her commband, and grinned. "Here they come." Chief Security Offi-cer for the day, she clapped her hands, sending the support staff scurrying through one more 'final check' of everything and bringing her temporary staff to attention on either side of the corridor.

The new station captain, Captain Tollwith, resplendent in his uniform, entered with his lovely wife on one arm. Depositing her safely on a chair in the first row, he kissed her hand and took up his position in front of the arch. "Ready, lad?"

Unable to speak around the lump in his throat, Jean nodded. Grinning, Taylor moved up to stand at his side as the groom's aide.

Jean smiled at the guests as they began filing in, even at the ones he didn't know.

One young man, however, instantly raised Jean's hackles with the way he swaggered in and helped himself to an aisle seat in the front row— the same aisle Ava would come walking down in a few minutes. He gave Jean a skeptical look, then slouched rudely back as if to say he was already bored with the whole thing.

Jean clenched his jaw but shook his head at Taylor's hopefully quirked eyebrow. This was one of Ava's guests. In fact, she'd insisted on inviting this…this business acquaintance. Something about how actually witnessing the wedding might make a difference in his behavior.

Deuyn Johnson adjusted her uniform and approached the man with a polished smile. "Excuse me, sir. This row is for family only." After talking about this guy with Ava, Deuyn wasn't at all surprised to find that he was exactly the kind of an idiot who'd need help with basic manners.

"Oh, um." He cleared his throat, confused as to how to proceed. Ordinarily, he'd have flashed a killer smile and expected to get his way. He had a funny feeling that this woman wouldn't be the least bit swayed by his considerable charms. "Where should I, ah…?"

"The third row has some available seats." While anybody who got invited to a wedding was an honored guest, at a small gathering such as this, the third row was the unofficial dividing line between close friends and 'just friends.' Deuyn didn't want to embarrass him any more than that; unless he gave her cause, of course. Luckily for him, he popped to his feet and hustled away.

Things went smoothly after that, if a trifle slowly. Jean's cheeks were starting to hurt from all the smiling when he saw Masie and Solène enter.

Jean tugged at his cuffs, not nervous so much as impatient. He'd waited a very long time for this. Waiting any longer roused the part of him that would've been perfectly happy to sign a wedding contract and have done with the formalities. Space dust, he'd signed plenty of other things in the process of being added as Ava's equal partner in all that was legally hers. He still wasn't sure why he'd gone along with that, other than it seemed to please her.

A familiar sound snagged his attention, and he looked up automatically. Beside him, Taylor did the same and they both stared at the three-dimensional tuetue birds that now darted between the branches displayed above their heads. Their chirps and squawks had never sounded so beautiful.

"Did you know?" Taylor lost his words and just pointed in awe.

Jean shook his head. He hadn't had a clue that the designer added more detail after he'd approved the display. Ava. Ah, yes, she must've done it, as a surprise for him.

Without realizing it, his head began to turn toward the arch. A sudden consciousness of the scent of parpai flowers emanating from it hit him like a cargotruck full of memories. His aunt's wedding. His oldest cousin's.

His jaw dropped when he saw exquisite parpai flower projections, so detailed that they looked real, appear on the arch and begin to unfurl as the light around it began to change colors and grow brighter, simulating an Orpan sunrise.

Taylor nudged his arm and nodded toward the aisle.

Jean straightened and looked around in time to see Ava take her first step toward him. Birdsong and the rustle of spinsilk were the only accompaniment to her graceful movements as she crossed the room to stand before him.

"Do you like it?" Ava asked, nodding to the flowers and birds.

"It's everything I ever dreamed it would be." Lifting their joined hands, he kissed hers gently, then guided her into position opposite him.

"Today, you stand at the threshold of a new life." Captain Tollwith spoke the words of the ceremony with quiet dignity, undiminished by posturing or flowery prose designed to make himself the center of attention. And when he stepped back to grant them access to pass through the arch, his kind eyes sparkled with unshed tears.

Jean and Ava walked forward together, parting the veil to reveal the open airlock, which led to the main cabin of Ava's private spaceship. Trays and stacks and piles of goodies waited atop the tables lining one wall while comfy chairs and couches were strategically arranged to create smaller groups out of the wedding party's whole. It was grander and more lavish than any wedding celebration he'd ever been to, and he appreciated the little touches Ava had added to make the large space seem cozy somehow.

"We would be pleased if you would join us in our new home." Jean tied one side of the veil back as he spoke, then moved to do the same with the other side.

Ava was already greeting their guests and making them welcome. Occasionally, she beckoned him over to introduce him to someone he hadn't met yet, but it wasn't long before everyone began to wish them well and politely excuse themselves. The group grew smaller and smaller until it was just Ava, Jean, Masie, Phyl, and a half-asleep Solène.

"Thank you so much for coming." Ava hugged Masie kissed her cheek. She was grateful that Masie had accepted her true identity so good-naturedly.

"Would I miss this, do you think?" Masie laughed as if she hadn't heard such a good joke in ages, then scooped up Solène and patted the child's back. "Come, little one. Time for bed, I think."

"Here, let me show you the way." Phyl, who considered helping with Solène to be part of her expanded duties, joined them with a smile. She and Masie were already fast friends, and they all chatted quietly as Phyl walked them down to the guest quarters.

"It's a good thing we're going straight to the shipyard." Ava fought back a yawn.

"Oh?" Jean slid his jacket off and set it aside so he could retrieve the medals later.

"Mhmm." Ava gestured toward her private sleeping chambers. "They're already working on modifying a popular family model for us." This time the yawn won and her eyes squeezed shut despite her best efforts.

Jean couldn't help grinning. "Come on, sleepy-head. Let's get you to bed," he scooped her up, "before you fall asleep on your feet." Testing their combined weight on his 'bad' knee, he grinned and stepped out confidently. The second-best thing to come out of the catastrophe with the *Reus* was the new synthesized joint the surgeons had implanted.

"I love you, Jak." Ava's fingers curled around a loose fold in his shirt and she nestled closer. "I always have."

"I love you, too, Sam." Jean eased the door to their chamber open and backed through, careful not to catch her legs on the door as it swung closed behind them. "And I always will."

Thank you for reading **<u>Uncharted</u>** *<u>Stars</u>*! I hope
you enjoyed it!

I'm not sure how many of you have had the
pleasure of reading a review of your own work.
Personally, I check for new reviews often and
love reading them.

Reviews can be left at Goodreads, Bookbub,
or the store of your choice and
are always greatly appreciated.

Visit me at
leacarterwrites.wixsite.com/flinch-free-fiction

More titles by Lea Carter

<u>*Contemporary Romance*</u>
"Gifts of the Heart"
Four single Latter-day Saint women find love in the tiny, fictional town of Cadmia.
A Country Mile
In Due Season
Food For Thought
Home Free

<u>Fantasy</u>
"Silver Sagas"
The ongoing adventures of the royal fairy families.
Silver Princess
Silver Majesty
Silver Verity
Troubled Skies
Dress Blues
The Seeker's Storm
Heartwood
Wedgewood
Fission
Fusion

"Coddiwomple"
Three high-flying adventures in the fictional world of Jattori.
Dragon Sparks
Dragon Fugue
Dragon Thunder
Found in Translation - also set on Jattori.

www.ingramcontent.com/pod-product-compliance
Lightning Source LLC
Chambersburg PA
CBHW011222190726
48287CB00008B/2712